UNTIL DEATH TAPS YOU ON THE SHOULDER

ETGOMA

Riverfolk Books

For You

Belarus
Poland
russia
Chernihiv
Chornobyl
Sumy
Kharkiv
Zapahorb
Syeverodonets'k
Irpint
KYIV
Lviv
Vinnytsa
UKRAINE
Dnipro
Zaporizhzhya
Mariupol'
Slovakia
Hungary
Mo...
Chornoguy
Booguy
Romania
Moldova
Odesa
Chornobaivka
Kherson
Sea of Azov
Krym
russia
Snake Island
Black Sea
occupied by ruzis
liberated in 2022

1

MARA

I'm neither dead nor alive. And no one but the dead can see me.

I like it this way. The less you contact the living, the better. People are boring. They do a helluva lot of ~~cool, important~~ stupid things, then talk about it on their Facebook like they've done something mega epic. Sometimes, they don't even do anything, just talk on their Facebook. Boring! Here, deep in the Carpathian woods, it's never like that. Woods listen. Woods understand. Woods live by what they do, rather than chatting and posting selfies.

And when someone dies, they don't talk about it on the Internet. They come to my woods.

•

It's winter. Cold creeps under my padded hoodie as I walk, ducking under the clawlike twigs of dozing firs. A heavy bundle of brushwood pulls my arms down. Aidan hops ahead, his tail up and crooked into a fluffy question mark. His little black paws barely touch the thick carpet of winter leaves. We're almost there. Huttuh, my magic home with chicken legs, lurks behind the sleepy trees. I recite the password:

Huttuh Bohattah, for all good,
stand with your face to my face
and your back to the wood.

A tremor runs through the hut. Huttuh opens her windows first, then drowsily hoists up her clumsy trunk before stretching out her long bird's legs with curved talons. She shuffles around, halts with her door facing us, and drops a set of steps down to our feet. It's the only way to get into my house. There's no need to carry keys or to suffer shrieking alarms. When you're *Baba Yaga* and live between worlds, nothing mortal ever bothers you.

"We need to make the beacons before dark." I throw the brushwood on the floor at the chimney and take a penknife from my pocket.

Aidan jumps into his favourite armchair and curls into an ink-black furball against the embroidered cushion.

You do the beacons. I'm just a cat.

I roll my eyes and set about grating the bark from the pole. Then I fit a human skull on top of it and look into its empty eye sockets. "Don't sulk, mate. Tonight, you'll help your brothers and sisters find their way back home. Isn't dying the most marvelous moment after being born?"

Are you talking to skulls again? Aidan lifts his muzzle and stares at me with his sleepy green eyes. *He's like a hundred years dead.*

"So what? The dead are charming companions," I snap and take the next stick from the floor.

The thing is, they are my *only* companions. I'm The Slit keeper, the one who sees the deceased through the gates of death. It's a noble and super responsible job that only experienced *Yagas* can handle. I was proud as hell when Mother Death appointed me.

•

The fire in the chimney crackles and splutters, reflecting gold off Aidan's glossy fur. The oven heat catches my forehead as I turn the pancake toasted side up while sucking lemonade through a straw. When really bored, I sneak a bottle from the town shop. It doesn't matter if Huttuh says soft drinks soften my stomach—I don't care, they're yummy!

I notice the ringing silence of the twilight, and my western window glitters with the colours of the dying day.

"It's starting." I leave the half-eaten pancake on the plate, grab the beacons, and stomp outside.

Aidan skips before me and leaks out like a dollop of jelly before I fully open the door. The forest has changed. It stands still, alert, and crisp, burning silently under the shimmering rays of the setting sun, perfectly deserted.

I breathe in fresh and fragrant evening air and press beacons into the ground. One by one, they form a chain fence around my house. The moment the final skull locks the circle, The Slit opens: Huttuh flickers and pulses in a growing beat… faster and faster, then… silently… explodes into a giant dragon eye, splitting the world in two.

My beacons light up with a soft candle glow. The skulls' empty eye sockets stare in all directions, luring the dead. I turn to the forest and spot the first volunteers, wandering between the trees. They look like a bunch of giant butterflies with ragged wings, fluttering around, searching the light. As if pulled by some invisible power, the butterflies sail towards my burning skulls and gradually shape back into their lost human forms. The Slit gives them this chance to remember themselves and bid their final goodbyes.

My heart pumps burning excitement down through my veins. The beacon I hold in my hand shakes so much that the skull's teeth chatter as if it's laughing at me. I root to the ground, sweating like a troll under my suddenly hot hoodie, and focus anywhere but on the dead's glittering eyes. Eyes give me the creeps. There is always something sad, lost, or angry about them. I've never seen any of them dying super blissful.

An elderly woman paces gingerly towards me, reaching out her hand with rough, crooked fingers that clasp mine. She is plump but stiff under her polka-dotted vintage dress, with long, grey hair pulled back into a tight bun. "Vasia? Vasia, is that you?" she asks, peering at me. "Oh, Vasia, it's been so long…"

"Yes, Love, we've finally met." I smile back at her.

The dead always see someone else in me—their deceased grans, old friends, or holy angels. Sometimes, I am just their dead pet they loved to the moon and back. It's fine with me, cos it immediately lets

me into their past. And it's not like listening to their tangled, foggy memories over black-and-white photo albums, but actually *living* through their lifetimes in just a split second. Tonight, in a flash, I turn into a girl named Love.

I grow up through sobbing tantrums over Mom slapping my neck for not eating her borscht and the intoxicating joys of going fishing with my brothers. The gripping wish for a Barbie doll turns into a no less gripping desire to dye my hair blonde or rip that extra flesh off my imperfect sides. I see a streetlight blink into my window. The foamy surf washes over my feet. I smell nail polish and hear my pals laugh over some silly cartoon. I lose my balance on my too-big brother's bike: the skies spin like in a turbo-speed blender, and the asphalt grazes my knee with killing pain that I'll feel only in a long, long second… The pictures of my life flip like the pages of my favourite fashion magazines. Memories flash through my mind in an endless carousel before the entire world swirls around just one person, Vasia.

The agony of loving and hating this guy is overwhelming. But it dulls eventually and tangles into millions of other little loves and hates. I find myself drowned in a boring routine with a few flashes of delight, but also despair about having my kids. Getting lost in them, then found again, older, fatter, and alone. Then I no longer understand where I'm heading. Time runs so fast behind the hard work, talks, eternal bus trips, chores, and gossip. I'm only happy when I drink because it halts this time race for a moment. If only Vasia didn't dump me, didn't die. Life used to be so fun when he was around...

I walk Love to the gates, and her eyes open wide, mirroring the shine of The Slit. They glisten with tears of fear and relief. I release her hand and watch her dissolve into the light.

If you stick there a tad longer, this swarm will start calling me *Vasia,* Aidan meows. He hops from one foggy person to another, milling about the burning skulls.

"Yeah, sorry." I rush to a gloomy teenager in all black with long, greasy hair stuck to the back of his neck. "Hello, Artur."

He hides his bleeding wrists behind his back as he glares at me incredulously. "Mom? You... You didn't die?"

Oh, boy, I was born dead, and yet I live thousands of lives without getting out of my wood. Isn't it the best-ever job in the world?

·

I let out a sigh of contentment and fall into the armchair by the fire. "Nothing is better than a fulfilled mission. A cup of cocoa, Huttuh, and I'll sleep like a happy piggy."

The floorboards beside my armchair swell, rise, and turn into an elegant table covered with a lace doily. A cup of fragrant, steamy cocoa pops out of it and lands neatly on top without shedding a single drop.

Aidan pads through the door before Huttuh shuts it tight and bolts it.

And coffee for me, please, he purrs, swishing his tail wearily.

Another table pulls up from the floor next to his seat like a magic bean tree. Aidan springs up, then—poof!—turns into a smiley guy with impish hazel eyes under black bushy eyebrows. A curly blast of fluffy hair just over his shoulders gives him an air of a dandelion, rock version. He wears a red tartan shirt this time, which looks like a warning sign: he's in one of his dangerous romantic moods.

"The woman called Love who lost her love before she lost her life," Aidan mumbles, taking his guitar from the corner and placing his springy person in front of me. "How sad."

"It's not sad, it's stupid," I grumble, picking dirt from under my fingernail. "People grasp at all sorts of garbage ideas throughout their lives, and all for what? They'll just die in the end."

Aidan plucks his guitar strings instead of answering and plays that old Italian song about love that drives me mad, "Ti Amo." He sings it to me, smiling, but the lyrics are different.

You are evil,

Your life is not living.

You talk to the dead

Instead of a friend

Young Devil.

Cos trust your old pal,

You'll cut them to bleed

And throw in The Split

To have a new skull.

"Ha. Ha." I slap my hip. "I may be evil, but I'm not a fool. Why would I bother wasting my time on the living and all their bullocks when I've got so many friends every night?"

"You can just as well watch some film and say you befriended so many actors," Aidan says, with his eyes set on the twanging strings.

"Yes. So? I'm happy with my actors. You know how it goes: when your life is good, try to make it perfect and ruin it all." I grab a book from the pile on the floor and cross my legs, holding my cocoa in the other hand to indicate the talk is over.

Aidan fingers the guitar strings and lets them dance in a melancholy, graceful melody. "I wish I had a friend for longer than one night," he sighs.

I peek over my book. "*I* am your friend, ain't I?"

"Yes, but…" Aidan stops playing and glances at me. His expressive eyes shine with a mischievous gleam. "I want a proper friend, a warm, smiling human. You are dead, cold and fat like a boulder."

"What!" I scowl and hurl my book at him.

In a moment, he turns into a cat and darts off, howling. The guitar drops from the armchair with a melodramatic bang, and my tome of *Greek Legends and Myths* hits the cushion.

The rest of the night, I'm messing around with a mop and broom, trying to rescue Aidan from under the sofa where he thrust his furry body in and got dead stuck. "Who's fat now, eh?" I chide.

Meow!

2

AGNIESZKA

24 February 2022

Woke up from a thunderous BOOM behind my window. I thought I dreamt it, but it BOOMED again, and the glass rang. Streetlights were on, and it was a stark night outside. Still, Daddy went potting around in the kitchen, and Mommy was talking on the phone. I cocooned myself in blankets and didn't see her coming into my room.

"Nesha, poppet, wake up. It started. Russians are bombing us."

I peeped out through a gap in my blanket cocoon. "They are?"

"Yes!"

Hideousity.

"So I may not go to school today?"

Mommy, in her pink bathrobe and slippers with fluffy balls, paced around my room, nervously picking up clothes from my drawers at random. "What school! We are leaving. We must run."

•

25 February 2022

We didn't leave anywhere and ran nowhere except around our flat and the nearest pharmacies and ATMs with mega snaking queues.

I watched the president on Telegram announcing that we're at war with Putin and his stinking Russia. He told us to keep calm even though he was clearly worried like hell himself because he didn't wear his tie, and in an hour, on his next briefing, he didn't even wear his shirt but some dirty green sweater.

Daddy is on duty in the hospital. He gives us one thousand and one calls and tells us what to do, and they are different things every time. Drives Mommy bonkers. We heard the jets crossing the sky right over our house like angry metal dinosaurs, deafening and fearful. Mommy said this would be the death of us all. She says it every time we hear *any* sound, even our neighbour from upstairs, Pan Borov, cavorting on his squeaky mattress at ten p.m. sharp, war or no war.

My city is anxious like lungs holding breath. Something smokes heavily in the distance, and Central Square is suddenly desolated. Empty coffee cups roll by on the frozen asphalt, and lonely black vans hurry to and fro to the background music of the air-raid siren. It's not real, it's a waking dream, Armageddon I'm living through.

Met Kangi and Nick from my class, heading to school with packs of blankets and chairs for the bomb shelter. We don't say "Hi!" to greet each other anymore. We say "Glory to Ukraine, death to the enemies, freedom or death." I felt like weeping when they saluted me but no, I must stay strong. Let the Russians cry.

At home, I scooped Tofu in my arms and buried myself in Instagram to relax with funny cat reels. But everyone posted burnt houses, bloodied toys, crushed planes, and the ugly president's counsellor saying that Russians dropped a hundred bombs on us so they had a hundred fewer now. So yay? And then all about the brave guards from Snake Island sending the Russian warship to go and squeak their rusty mattresses all they like!

•

26 February 2022

A complete stranger from France wrote to me on Tumblr, saying she was praying for me. Some Finns and Latvians started a verbal fight with Russians under my selfie in a sunflower field, and I don't even know about what because it was all in English they don't teach us at school.

They have time for this. For silly posts and comments, and disputes, all this shitting about on the net while sitting in their cosy chairs. I don't have a minute. I feel like I'm either paralysed while time rushes past me, or I run with it, trying to catch up. All I do, I do quickly, as if in a panic, even when there are no BOOMS or sirens. I move in fast dashes, taking tiny pauses to catch my breath, like a diver underwater. Some of us can't even allow the pauses.

I get so many letters I feel like the hub of the universe. Even my ~~boyfriend~~ pen pal Ben, who dumped me last summer, suddenly popped up and asked if I needed money to relocate. I don't know how to tell him, "I don't need money to relocate, I need a bag." Because all shops but groceries are closed, Internet delivery is cut, and I haven't got a suitcase big enough to fit in my life. Only an old unicorn-shaped valise I took to the seaside when I was but an egg.

Actually, I must feel exalted and totally *blissfuloso* because *he wrote at last*. Ben, Benjamin, Bennie Boo. Good old Ben who is so Americanly American and is probably my Only One, even if he broke my little princess heart. My mind keeps telling me about plenty of fish in the ocean, yet I still want this bastard, not some other… dolphin. Now he's writing me letters like novels, but I can't feel a damn thing. What do I need a boyfriend for? To die together from one bullet? *How bloody romantic.*

It's Saturday, and we're supposed to clean our house. Instead, we cleared the nearby supermarkets. Carmina and I met up and raced all about the neighbourhood, looking for myriads of things for my epic escape. No chance to squeeze into the pharmacy or withdraw cash from Mommy's debit card. If there are no mile-long lines, it's one hundred and fifty percent empty. Well, today, we did find an ATM with just five people attached to it and stood there for like an eternity. I nearly froze to death before the ancient lady in front wobbled off and declared it was disabled. Carmina guffawed her hoarse ha-ha, and everyone rushed loose like beads from a broken chain. Ow, *mierda!* We waddled back to the supermarket on icy legs like frozen fish sticks.

I've never seen Varus this bare and yet crowded. People brush stuff off the shelves like it's a zombie apocalypse, and tomorrow never comes. We couldn't even find salt or boring digestives; all the disposable bags ran out, too, so we carried stuff in our hands and pockets. The alcohol department was completely shut down. There were sheets of A4 paper sellotaped to the empty, dusty shelves, reading "Dear customers, we are at war. Let's celebrate after we win. Glory to Ukraine!"

I froze there, feeling beads of sweat rolling down inside my bra, and started to cry. Didn't want to, but my face burnt so hot, it was like the only way to cool down.

"What's up?" Carmina plucked at my sleeve.

"It's just…" I sobbed louder, then took the felt pen I always carry with me and added "glory to heroes" with a smiling heart. "It says we'll win, but others say Ukraine will fall in four days."

"Pfft, my ass we'll fall. We're Cossacks! Cossacks never fall. Come, we need to find water."

We grabbed the last two bottles, crackers, and some energy bars for our emergency grab bag (without a bag) and rushed towards the cash desks when the siren howled. I crushed against a plump lady

in cashmere when she dropped her cart and ran. The security guards yelled something over our heads, but nobody heard what exactly, because all the little kids around raised a chorus of banshees, and I knew it was going to be the death of us all.

•

27 February 2022

Still alive (maybe). In my dream tonight, I was at school, the peaceful school, having a test in physics. The explosions behind the windows were just fireworks. There were no worries at all because even if I failed, nobody would throw me down to the underground with a pack of waffles, a blanket, and an urge to save the phone battery for emergencies. The war was just a dream in my dream. The worst nightmare is waking up from normal life into a bloody nightmare.

Today they bombed the Economy College. We saw police, firemen, and volunteers dragging people from under the rubble. They looked like broken dolls, covered in white dust. Everything smelled of burnt coffee and smoke. Some women sat on the pavement with their faces covered in blood. They just sat there with a total void in their eyes and said they were fine. *Fine,* my God!

Daddy is finally home, but he has to leave soon because it's a complete circus in the hospital. He's only here to get us out of this hell of a hell. I saw the car queues at the petrol stations. I guess our turn will come only next Christmas after Russia has blown nukes, and there will be no need to run to Poland because we will all live on Mars by then. Besides, it turned out our external passports are out of date, so Mars and Ukraine are basically the only places we can go now.

"It doesn't matter, you can cross the border with the internal passport," Daddy repeated a hundred times already, and Mommy said *"NO"* a hundred times back while tucking her greasy curls.

"I won't go anywhere. If I go, it will be for good. It's a one-way ticket. I'll never return!"

"Of course, you'll return." Daddy sighed wearily. "When it's safe to return…"

"Safe to return to Russia? I beg your pardon!"

"It's not gonna be Russia. We'll prevail, I'm sure of it." Dad pressed his hands down firmly.

"Even if a miracle happens and we win, why would I return to my ruined life after living abroad?" Mommy slapped the table, and my plate of fried eggs jumped. I hurried to stuff myself with the rest of my meal and made off.

I don't want to go. This is just so *terriblemente* unfair. What will become of my dolls? My dresses? My handmade soaps? Embroidery? I saw the photos of what they do to our houses and heard the stories. All those stories of looting the carpets, chairs, pieces of lino, coffee makers, and cutlery. Russian wives neighing in the video calls, telling them to grab all the tees and sneakers. Tees! Sneakers! Some stinky son of a toad in Russian khaki killed an entire family for tees and sneakers? They trashed everything they couldn't take along, even doors, pissed on the walls, and crapped on the sofa.

They crapped on the sofa, my God.

We call them orcs like those beasts from *The Lord of the Rings* who spread over Middle Earth like a rotting disease. Because people wouldn't do this to people. Even animals wouldn't do this to people. Actually, I don't think orcs would do this either. Russians are one of a kind!

I tucked myself into the corner of my bed and scrolled the hashtag #StandwithUkraine on Twitter to restore my balance. Our flag is everywhere, all around the world, and even the Eiffel Tower is blue and yellow! Millions, millions pray for Ukraine, and I cry like a dolt because I don't believe in God but so believe in their prayers. Oceans of people flood the capitals and demand to stop this war, while our farmers steal Russian tanks and stop war columns with their bare hands. My president sleeps in the office and asks the West for ammunition, not a ride.

Wow!

Actually, that was cool. Next time Ben offers me money, I'll ask him to send me a gun.

Ohhh, Ben... Thought about dying un-boyfriend-ed. Would I feel better if I had one? We'd sit here together, hand in hand, saying things like "Love will save the world. Let's kiss the war away." Our lips will meet in a gentle touch and then... a bomb will hit my window and send us tumbling in the air like two peas into the Milky Way. The last thing Ben will see of me will be my round butt in floral panties. Good grief! No. No-no-no. NO!

Tofu joined me, plopped his big jelly bum on my feet, and demanded belly pats. He'll snap me if I don't, so I stroked his spotted fur and gave him a biscuit. Just one (there is no cat food in the supermarkets).

"Okay, enough, I've got more important things to do." I returned to my news feed, but Tofu climbed onto my lap and sat on my phone, meowing. Some things even war can't change.

Parents are still arguing.

And I'm still hungry, would kill for a candy. Three energy bars in the shoebox under my wardrobe lurk temptingly, but I must stay strong and keep them in case of emergency.

Two and a tad in the morning, woke up from a jet droning past and ate one. This *is* an emergency.

•

28 February 2022

We really need to tidy up the house. It's so effing dirty: there is not a single clean cup or fork. Bug-out bags and things for the army, refugees, shelters, and emergencies lie about everywhere, and nobody knows what to do about them except for Tofu, who nests in the midst of it all. Mommy says there is no point in tidying up when a missile can fly into our house and blow it all back into the mess. I think about it every time I sit in the bathtub. What is the point in washing myself if I can die tomorrow? But then, if I die, at least I'll die clean and pretty.

Our windows are pasted with Scotch tape like a parcel to the future and curtained with thick black fabric. We keep them this way by day, too, not bothering with light masking when the curfew starts. Great-Gran Iulita bought this fabric for her funerals, and now it's like living in her coffin.

My gosh. Is this really all I was living my fourteen years for? When I was a silly little bean, I expected to fall into one wonder world or another, because it happened all the time to girls from my books. I still think that mirrors are magic doors and Atlantis lives somewhere underwater, in cities just like ours. It was such a drama not to get a letter from Hogwarts on my eleventh birthday! Dreams never gave me smiling cats. Nobody offered me red or blue pills. No wind was strong enough to take me to enchanted Oz, and no ring I wore made me invisible. But then, those were just books and films, and I wanted real magic. Something tremendous and romantic, something truly *marvelouso!* Ben believes in UFOs and skinwalkers. He says Native Americans can turn into actual wolves. But what does it matter now? I'll just die from a bullet, that's it. Some Russian pig will kill me for a bottle of vodka.

The air sirens went crazy today, switching on and off like Christmas tree lights. Our airport got bombed to the ground. I heard the BOOM, sitting in the hallway with Mommy and Tofu, the only safe spot in our flat, and chatted with Carma on Telegram. She said the third siren in a row caught her ma in the loo, and she yelled from there "Bloody bastards, let me shit in peace at least!"

•

1 March 2022

Almost all of my schoolmates left and posted pics from the Polish border that looked like an anthill on Doomsday. I feel the creeps all over my skin at the mere thought of crossing the border. I've never been abroad and never wanted to. It's like falling into a winter pond to live forever cold, wet, and hungry. It must be some sort of karmic phobia left from my previous life. Snow maiden turned into a puddle when she jumped over a bonfire. And I will get sucked into the cosmos when I jump off Ukraine.

Carmina's ma, Pani Feya Burana, told Mommy the next time

Russian cannibals hit us, off she goes to Lviv. They hit right while they talked (and bombed our central square!) and she said God loves the Trinity. If they hit again, off she goes to Lviv. Next time they hit us, she'll probably say God loves millennia. Carmina is not going anywhere; she says it's her city, and she'll defend it with her bare hands if she has to. She came over after breakfast, and we watched YouTube master classes on how to cook Bandera smoothies, which are like Molotovs but with Ukrainian spirit. Then we gathered wine and beer bottles and rags and went to school to help adults make bombs and camouflage nets. *Triple fabuloso.*

Mommy thinks it's for stress release, but the men in khaki don't agree. They said our nets are vitally important. They mask our soldiers and tanks better than any super-neat manufactured ones because the pattern of those repeats itself, and drones can easily spot it. What we do is lame, and how it should be! Imperfection saves lives. Hundreds of hands in hundreds of places weave the blanket of safety to cover us from the evil eyes and fire rains.

I enjoyed the company of the old ladies I barely knew, even if they were all a bit batty. But they called me Pani Neshka and it felt really good. They said, in the Soviet times, there were no Misters or Missises. Everyone was just comrades to each other, which sounded like a bash at the head and not comradely at all. Then we were just "Hey, girl! Yes, you in the sky-blue dress" haha, wacky. Now we're finally back to calling men *pans* and women *panis* like in the old times, which means lords and ladies. So there, I'm a lady. No matter whether married or not, a Ukrainian woman is always a lady. YAY!

They also sang *Long Live, Free Ukraine!* over and over and shared stories like those about our president receiving standing ovations in the EU hall, while the entire UNO delegation left the Russian minister to talk to his treacherous, ugly self. He'd lie anyway. They always lie. How to tell if Russians lie? They open their mouths.

•

2 March 2022

Didn't know I'd ever write this but… I miss school and chores. I'd rather do physics, sweat down to my panties at PE, and wash dishes for the rest of my life than sit about waiting for a bomb to trash me into atoms. Whatever I start: drawing or embroidering, or crafting soaps, or pots, all drops from my hands, and I think, what is the point? Ukraine is falling.

I don't read any books, don't watch films, don't listen to music.

Nothing makes sense. Only news channels matter, and I got addicted to scrolling Telegram strings. I scroll through the news all the time, like a scrolling machine. Mommy thinks I play *Candy Crush* to relax, but I can't even play *Candy Crush*; I scroll, scroll, and scroll the journalists' reports to finally find a post about the Kremlin being bombed to the ground and Putin beheaded.

Carmina and I swore to the almighty Cossacks never to speak Russian again. I've never thought about it before, but now it's crystal clear that the Russian language, which is common here, is a tool of war. First, they forbade our mother tongue, banned it from schools, TV, and bookshelves, mocked and bullied all who kept it dear to their hearts, and then, because we know their *mierda* language, they called us *mierda* brothers, slaves of Kyiv, and came here with their guns and tanks to "save us" from talking any language at all. Logic and R-ass-ians are two parallel lines.

But how cunning! Because if you speak only Russian, you can only listen to what they say, and they only say "Ukrainians suck!" So, no, we will only speak our true language. Ever. I'm writing my diary in Ukrainian too, so if orcs find it, they won't understand a thing. Though I very much doubt they can read at all. They fire at the vans signed KIDS in their *mierda* Russian like they're totally demented. All they know is how to crash things and go home drunk and proud.

We finally withdrew some cash. It was only fifty-two people before us, and everyone talked Russian. Carmina asked me one million random questions, deliberately loud like a concert horn, and everyone looked back at us like we had dropped right from the heavens.

Orcs bombed the hospitals and train stations today. Mariupol' is in dire agony. I saw photos of dying pregnant *panis*, wrapped in bloodied blankets. The cannibals swore the women in blankets were just actresses because they looked too pretty, and they weren't even as pretty as me!

I think now, crossing the border is not that big a deal...

BOOMed again. Daddy called and yelled to pack suitcases RIGHT NOW. Mommy called Carma's ma, but she said this was her house, her castle, and her tomb. The Buranas stay. So, we stayed, too. I went so completely deranged with fright that I grabbed a dust-er and Cinderella-ed the entire flat, then hoovered the carpets and went deranged even more because the sound of it wailed like the blasted air drones.

I texted Carmina at three a.m., after ages of spinning like a bobbin on the old mattress on the corridor floor, listening to Daddy's fitful snoring. The picture of a missile flying into the window stuck in my head like a parasite. Didn't know if she'd answer, but right away, I saw the pulsing dots of her typing back. She sent me a song about our drones blasting stinking Russian tanks into piles of scrap metal. It bit into me like Tofu into his catnip toy. Hummed it till dawn. Felt better.

3
CARMINA

SLAVA UKRAÏNI!

From: Carmina Burana   02 March 2022, 18:51

To: Severin Saint   Zapahorb

Ha!

You didn't expect me, did you, Pa? You asked me not to call or text you while you're busy battling, but you said nothing about writing you emails. So here I am. Just wanted to tell ya (again) that I really, really love the dancing videos you sent me. Such fun! I actually attached some heroic Viking music to them and uploaded them on Instagram (don't go berserk) and got like five hundred hearts overnight! Everyone loves you, Pa, doing that monkey dance with the FGM-148 Javelin and swinging your leg on the trophy z-tank. But know, I love you the most, so quick, kill the Moscow multiheaded hydra and come home.

Svitlan is def coming back from London with his *BRILLIANT IDEA* to join the army. He calls us twice a day in total hysterics and says screw his college and super bright, successful future, he's going back to fight beside you, for me and Ma, and our country. His first training practice is the true battles on Telegram video calls when Ma shoots her fav grenade gun of arguments like "I gave birth to you, so I decide" which is really hard to parry especially when you are one walking, pulsing heart like Svitia.

"I'm nineteen, Ma. This is my duty. Pa says okay, so I'm buying a ticket."

"You're *not* buying a ticket. You've already got a ticket, a *white ticket*. Devil may care, but your father, obviously, does not," Ma said in her usual sardonic drawl. "With your poor sight and allergies, you are not going anywhere."

"Doesn't matter, they accept everyone now." Svitlan sniffled and scratched his scalp. He scratched it all during the half-hour call, so I guess he won't be needing any head shaving once he gets to the army cos by that time, he'll be bald all over.

"Listen to your mamma." Ma picked a cig from her crumpled pack. "Stay put and study hard. We have big hopes for you, son, so be a goodie, eat veggies, drink tea, and play tennis, like the true English."

"How can I eat and play anything when you're there?" Svitlan rubbed tears from his eyes.

"Oh, baby, don't worry, we're *fiiiine*, it's really *nothing*," she said as she smoked casually. Then something somewhere clapped, banged, and clattered. Ma jumped, shedding ashes on the carpet. "DAMN, what was that?!"

"What was that?" Svitlan leaned into the camera.

"What's the news, quick? What do they say?" Still smoking, Ma grabbed the remote control and turned on the twenty-four-seven news marathon. I ran to the bathroom and cried out from there that it was just the washing machine on the spin cycle. Everyone breathed out, and Ma threatened to kill that washer by hurling it at the Russians. Since they love stealing our washers and dragging them back to the godforsaken armpit of a village with no plumbing or sewage or even plain asphalt ever in its history.

Anyway, Pa, for the record, I want to join the army, too, and I don't care what Ma says. I already know all about not being a proper girl and blah blah whatever! I'm not a girl. I'm a warrior like you. With one exception: I won't marry. True warriors never betray their guns, and especially never for MEN! Who, by the way, started all this mess, and, frankly speaking, ninety-nine percent OF ALL WARS IN HISTORY.

I walked near the local draft board today, and it was like Ragnarök on holy fire. There were so many *gopniks* in black, it felt like the Queen of the Damned raised the entire hell population. No chance to get the gun and bulletproof vest just yet, but… I already see myself capsuled in khakis, firing a Zbroyar-Z10 in the shambles of my bombed school. I'd keep zombies at bay while my battle siblings regroup and swear commands on the radio set.

There'll be a total swarm of enemies armed to overthrow Zeus himself, so we'll retreat to hold a better vantage point. Then… *Bang!* A random bullet will slash my neck, and I'll topple onto the dusty concrete. Naturally, Chief will grip my vest to drag me off the window, but I'll say, "No, brother, I'm done, save our motherland…" So I'll press the grenade to my chest and add, coughing, "Glory to Ukraine." He'll kiss me on the helmet, like Aragorn kissed dying Boromir in *Lord of the Rings*, and say, "Glory to heroes."

I'll wait till they leave safely and the zombies come closer, and closer still, and count my breaths, as the hot blood leaves my withering veins. Hardly seeing, rather sensing them climbing into the window, I'll yell "DEATH TO THE ENEMIES!!!"

Then blow a grenade in my hands.

Poof! Fifty zombies down, and a tank. Maybe a helicopter :) And a ship. They say ships are the pride and glory of Putin's black heart, plus cost a total fortune. Then Ma will get fifteen million hryvnias, a medal, and a free country in a few months. Of course, she'll be up-

set at first and really ballistic, but then, she'll be proud of me, cos…
Isn't it the only right way to die for a soldier? I wouldn't like to die
otherwise once I take a gun in my hands.

•

Most of my mates left Zapahorb, but you raised me as a warrior, and
warriors make a difference. They don't flee. They look their enemy in
the eye and know who they are. Remember Liza? The swanky gal from
my school? She says Russians are not our enemies, but hapless victims
of the Moscow regime. It's all Putin and his vicious puppets, she says,
and I say, of course, those are just innocent Russian soldiers who just
kill, trash our homes, rape all they see, and leave only ruins behind as a
symbol of their great culture. Just innocent Russian mothers just bless
their innocent sons for the invasion of another country; just innocent
Russian children just make swastikas in their school ceremonies. Even
if they are all *forced* to be like this, isn't it their problem?

Liza is in France now, posts pics of her insect-sized doggie on the beach and types sheets of shit about pure love that stops wars. Like, a sincere smile builds a friendship, and a heart open to compassion brings peace, so let's drop our guns and hug each other like brothers. And just TALK. Yeah, so cosy to dwell on open hearts and smiles when nothing whistles and blasts in the air. Talking to Russians now is like shaking hands with a zombie that is already eating your brains.

But Liza is a cosmopolitan and a pacifist, i.e., she doesn't believe in wars, only conflicts. These Netflix-ed hipsters are so bloody *rational*, they think freedom is something they get with their plastic IDs, not something we must actually fight for. Cos any fighting apart from boxing on camera is Middle Ages for them. Like, it's the twenty-first bloody century with free Wi-Fi in cafés and money that buys anything. If there is a *conflict*, both sides are equally wrong, equally victims. So let's like be *rational* and give all the gunman wants! Is this their plan? Duh.

Blimey, I can't believe Liza is serious. She says taking sides is wrong and Nazi-like, and I say when you're already on the bombed side, what do you do? Def not sit around, blowing bubbles from chewing gum while posting pics on Instagram and saying the war is the side you don't take. IT TAKES YOU.

I mean, if some nasty cretins drop a petard in your window, you don't say, "None of my business, I'm a cosmopolitan! Off to Nice." I mean, gee, why do I even talk to her? She sounds just like the bloody Russians.

Can't even call them orcs. Agnieszka says it would insult orcs to the bones if they knew, and she's right. Orcs are warriors. I don't remember them dragging someone's forks and panties from the battlefield or raping kids. So better call Russians what they really are—Ruzi. It's their label now; they are tagged. There are no more Russians; they screwed it up. All their Tolstoy and ballet, and bears with balalaikas, all of it is burning with the Ukrainian women and kids in their blown-up houses, hospitals, and schools.

Then, maybe in twenty years, Hollywood will shoot a mega five-star blockbuster about this mess. They'll show Russians as they are: murderers and looters. I'll buy popcorn.

•

To the good news: Guess what billboards local governance put on our street? Two instruct us on how to bring down tanks and APCs with Bandera smoothies (no kidding!). And one is all sunflower fields—the colours of our flag—and the words:

SOUL AND BODY OUR ALL WE OFFER AT
FREEDOM'S CALL

No kidding, two hundred percent true (attached the photos). So absolutely epic and tremendous! I mean, not some boring Varus butter with a discount or tours to Egypt, but a mega battle cry that gets right to the guts and raises all the dead heroes from their graves to fight beside us!

Agnieszka just cried. As always. She cries even when I wear a blue sweater with yellow pants. I told her Cossacks don't cry. And she said she was a girl Cossack. Like it matters. Girl Cossacks only cry from laughter when Ruzis have a go at saying "bread" in Ukrainian and say some shit instead. But she's really that hopeless.

Holy cow, the siren! Need to run and hide in the bathroom. Call us when you can.

Slava Ukraïni!
Your Skipper

4

MARA

Something's changed. I know it even before I open The Slit. A strong eastern wind bends the treetops and runs through the forest like a comb through hair. The hollow sockets of my burning beacon's eyes blink and squint quizzically before the gust of air blows out its gleaming light. The dead don't ramble around me, but the horizon is looming with a ghostly haze.

I scoop up Aidan and scurry towards the dying sun that gilds the naked oaks and firs and sets the eastern peaks on yellow fire. He twirls in my grip and climbs on top of my shoulder, clawing into my hoodie.

Is it snowing again? he asks as we stop at the marge, where trees thin out into the downhill, and we gaze at the torrents of the dead streaming across the valley below.

"Snowing men?" I raise my eyebrows in disbelief.

A pasty mass of shapeless shadows drags by the ground, floating above the shrubs, tangled in the branches, drifting high in the wind like stray seaweed in the water. Separate snippets soar over the highest trees and remind me of old kites, lost in the woods.

Holy tail, so many in one night! What the hell happened?

"No idea, but we're going to be quite busy tonight." I slap my beacon on the top until it glows again.

Aidan jumps down from my shoulder and skips to shepherd the first volunteer, but nobody seems to notice him or gives a damn about my torch. I roam among the ragged clouds of the dead with my burning skull like the only sighted person in the land of the blind. "Excuse me? Hello? Hey… *Pani*… Do you…" For the first time in my memory, the call of The Slit falls on deaf ears.

They are weird, Mara. Aidan hops from one baggy bunch of "seaweed" to another.

"Like heck. They don't see us and don't get back into their human forms."

This one does. Well, almost. Aidan stops at one man gripping a rifle, swaying silently in the wind. He lacks the lower part of his left leg, and a few fingers are missing. I peer closer into the distance and see other disfigured bodies, not just soldiers. With blood and dirt on their clothes and tangled hair glued to their cheeks, they float past in a quiet grey soup. Their faces are twisted with pain, and their eyes are still like glass balls, reflecting nothing.

"They are dead but still alive." I blink at them, confused. "I can't get into their minds. Like they are ghosts. They stay locked and looped around some shocking… blast. Or… a crash."

What kind of crash? Like an earthquake?

"We'd surely know about an earthquake, Aidan. Just look for someone who's ready." I slap my beacon again to brighten the glow. The fire in it flutters like a candle in the wind.

In a moment, Aidan cries *There are children!* and skitters ahead, hopping over the bumps and hillocks. It pins my chest with an icy needle. Children are not supposed to die.

I slide between the dead and pace down to the empty highway. Twice, I stop to shake my beacon, then struggle through the snow-peppered shrubbery. Three small kids no older than six,

perfectly solid and aware, crouch there by the road sign, playing with my cat. If not for the blood on their muddy winter coats and a nasty scratch on the girl's face, anyone would take them for lost little travellers.

I sit beside them, pulling my hood down, wondering if they can see me.

"Hey, kiddies," I say. "You like Aidan, huh?"

"Is it your cat?" the girl asks with a soft giggle and turns to me. Her left temple is a mess.

"Yes. He's Aidan, the scout, a guide of the dead. What are you doing here all alone?"

Her face goes blank. The boys exchange pop-eyed gazes and gape around as if suddenly aware of the woods and the hazy road ahead. Then the oldest one springs to his feet.

"I was on the boat!" he exclaims in a little fairy voice. "Where am I?"

"Booguy is down there." I wave in the town's direction. "The forest behind you is Mor."

Their eyes stay vacant, so I add, "You're not from here, are you?"

"I live in Sumy," says the little one with utmost certainty. Others just give me shocked faces.

"Right…" I take the toddler by his cold fingers. "Come, I'll take you all home."

They follow me obediently, like three ducklings. Aidan skips ahead and meows to hurry us before The Slit pops shut. It's quite a long way to my hut, and the kids are so real, they stumble and trip over every rock and root. Meaning, they *think* they are solid and don't remember dying at all. The little one soon starts to snivel. And I pant from exhaustion.

Aren't we supposed to find their parents first? Aidan suggests.

"How can I find bloody anyone in that mash of the dead?" I grumble and put the flopped-down oldest back on his feet. "Here, carry this." I give the girl my beacon and start to drag both boys by the hands.

"Halloween! Yay," the girl exclaims, poking into the burning skull.

Look into their memories, Aidan offers.

"I tell ya, same as looking into a cup of jelly. They don't know they are dead."

"Who are you talking to?" the oldest boy asks, dragging his sausage feet a step behind me.

"To Aidan, of course," I say. He goggles back at me like I said something mental. "It's a magic cat," I explain. "He can talk."

"But he doesn't say anything." The girl points at Aidan with my skull torch.

Okay, if they don't hear me, they aren't dead enough, Aidan huffs. *How do we push them through The Slit then?*

"How do I know? Ask me after I've done it!" I blow a strand of forelock off my forehead.

As we approach the burning crack between the worlds, which is pulsing softly through the lace of trees, it's almost dark. I have seconds before it blows back into Huttuh. I hope this will be enough, but I forget that the magic of the afterlife light appeals to those who are ready to go. The kids catch a glimpse of The Slit and scream at the top of their lungs like three supersonic missiles, then scatter and flee, dropping the beacon on the ground.

"No! Stop! You'll get lost, you silly beings!" I stomp a few steps behind them, then halt and slap my hips angrily.

They roll in all directions, three jumpy peas turning back into clouds. Aidan has caught up with the eldest boy, pounced at him, and pinned him to the ground. Still, the boy's puffed into an egg-shaped fume and will stay like that till he recollects at least some of his little life.

"Let him go, Aidan," I cry. "It's useless. They don't remember. They're ghosts now."

The last sunray dies and sucks the glow from the beacons. The Slit slams back into a hut on chicken legs like a giant mouth clasped shut. A door opens with a welcoming squeak and drops us stairs from the wooden porch. Aidan pads up to me and sits at my feet with his whiskers down.

•

We kill the rest of the night, staring into the fire and listening to the shambolic chorus of the crows flocking behind the windows. Sometimes, when the dead can't find their way home, they turn into birds. Tonight, hundreds of them swarm around Huttuh, croaking their songs of pain and despair.

"Maybe it's not that bad?" Aidan breaks the silence for the first time. "I'm sure it happened before."

"But this is not right," I burst. "Mother Death told me that the power of The Slit gives life to everything, then takes it back, enriched. It's the breathing of the Universe: in live, out die. That's how the world goes. What happens when we breathe in and never breathe out?"

Aidan shakes his head and shrugs, his curls dangling along. "Ghost stories happen."

"This many?" I give a loud sigh. "And all rummaging in my woods now."

"Well. You like the company of the dead."

"But that's the problem!" I flick my hands. "They are not dead yet, and I've no idea how to… kill them." I stare back into the fire, kneading my lower lip between my thumb and index finger. Then it comes to me. "I'll go to town tomorrow."

"Why?" Aidan frowns, leaning back.

"To ask people."

"You mean… *living people*?" he adds carefully with a nod and raises his thick eyebrows.

I clasp my hands on my stomach. "If I must."

"They can't see you, remember?"

"Not in their faces, of course." I roll my eyes. "I'll just listen to what they say to each other, sneak into their phones and tellies, steal some book, I don't know…"

Aidan giggles. "You're gonna throw up all over that book. They are mostly about love."

"Hey. I do care about those buggers." I point at the window.

"Y'know, Mara, there is a thing called zero Celsius." Aidan starts with a mischievous smile as he taps the armchair arm with his finger. "Below that is zero Fahrenheit. Below that is absolute zero. Below that is how much you care about humans, who are…" He raises his hand and bends his fingers. "Petty, dumb, selfish…"

"Yeah, yeah, yeah." I wave at him.

"Corrupted, destructive, lazy, lustful…"

"Yes, all right!" I cry. "You'll be needing more hands to say how little of a damn I give about people, but if I don't bring them to peace in one piece, they'll haunt me till I go nuts. Then more will die and go nowhere. What if nobody goes anywhere? Shall I scoop them up and keep them all in sacks under my bed?"

"You're right." Aidan puts his hands down. "I'd love to visit Booguy, anyway." He shifts his bum in the armchair as if there is still a tail to swish. "I miss the company of the living."

"Just don't make me regret this." I turn my eyes back to the smouldering embers in the fireplace. "Last time you 'missed the company of the living,' you knocked over a postcard stand, nearly gave some granny a heart attack, and stole an ice cream cone from a kid."

"That was a 'hi' to my human mates. What? Don't I deserve an ice cream for my pretty, fluffy tail?" Aidan smirks and takes his guitar from the floor to play some rock version of Vivaldi.

5

AGNIESZKA

3 March 2022, Day 8

I feel like I'm living my seventh life already. Everything is happening so fast, even though I do nothing but eat the same fried eggs with onions we had yesterday, the day before that, and the day before that. The radio in my head never stops broadcasting news, experts' views, and war memes.

Even in my sleep.

I talk like a freaked-out politician now and know heaps of cool clever words like "escalation," "moratorium," and "excise tax on fuel," whatever that might be. *Increíble.* School never taught me as much as a week of war.

Before this, I thought politics was rubbish. All those important people in suits with their castles somewhere in France came on camera to say another random collection of clever phrases that meant nothing. Then they returned to their luxurious offices to do luxuriously nothing. But now it is different. My president wears a barmy olive jacket, saves lives, never sleeps, and talks three hundred percent human. He keeps pleading with the West to be human too and help us, and they are like, we are so deeply concerned, but don't worry, we'll ask Putin not to be a dick. They sent us tons of petrol, probably to burn that piece of memorandum or whatever promised us safety.

Mierda! Mierda!

Poo! Poo! Poo!

Cannibals captured Kherson. Marina from my pottery class, who's there now, texted that those pigs mess around in the streets, break into homes and stores and grab all they like, even toilet pans. They think it's some Ukrainian miracle, a mineral water basin because their own toilets are just dirty holes in the ground in some God-lost dump of a village.

I want to write something nice, patriotic, and uplifting to Marina but can't find words. How can words help her anyway? What will they do to her if they know she is a patriot? How she must be frightened! And I can do nothing but fright along. Such a sissy.

Carmina and I rumbled around the city, counting Ukrainian flags in the windows, on the rooftops, and on the walls like magic amulets that ward off the evil spirits. We had ten when we got to Nova Ave. and the crumbled houses behind the burnt trees. Some walls were missing, and the insides had fallen out like the guts of a killed giant. Chipped glass crunched under my boots and cold, wet winds sang in the broken corridors and crooked staircases. Everything once cosy seemed like trash, like total rubbish: the fluffy rugs, the microwave, the head of a Barbie doll, the gilded frame with no picture, the ticking clock in the shape of a cat, still pinned to the wall on the second floor. Kids, like a swarm of busy bugs, played around, digging in the dirt, dragging all the broken things as their treasures. They looked happy.

Someone wrote THERE WILL BE SPRING AND THERE WILL BE UKRAINE on a piece of the crumbled wall. And we counted the eleventh flag. I took a picture on my phone but deleted it right away because if the Russians get me, I'll die just for this.

Carmina says she's citing our national anthem in her evening meditation. I learned it too just in case I meet Putin, and the priest asks me if I have anything to say over his stinking grave.

•

4 March 2022, Day 9

Cannibals fired at the Zaporizhzhya nuclear power plant! Oh my God, oh my God. OH. MY. GOD!

AAAH!!!!!

It's six times as mighty as Chornobyl and six times worse than just a painful death. WHAT ARE WE GOING TO DO? I'm the prettiest fourteen-year-old, never-boyfriended, secret princess of Ukraine. I can't just kick it because a crowd of zombies headed by a Communism-possessed Kremlin mummy decided to blow up the Earth. And the rest of the world is in pyjamas and hasn't yet had their coffee to decide… like anything.

Okay, okay, no panic, no panic, NO PANIC! I'll pack my parents in my unicorn valise and run. I don't care if Mommy says she doesn't give a flying pig.

"I don't give a flying pig!" she cried when I insisted and again, when Daddy returned from work and said there was a free evacuation train to Lviv. We won't have to stand in line for petrol.

"No. No, and no, I won't go without you, I won't." She crossed her legs and sobbed into the collar of her pink fluffy bathrobe she hadn't parted with since the dreadful first night.

"Masha." Daddy sat next to her on the sofa and Mommy's top leg jerked up and down. "Try to understand, I can't leave now. Hospitals are running out of hands. Someone has to stay and help."

"I can stay and help." Her leg jerked faster.

"How can you help if you die or get injured?"

"How can *you* help if you die!"

Nobody wondered how *I* could help if that power plant flew into the air and everyone died, even moon people, elves and hobbits, magicians and smiling cats. Dammit, dammit, dammit. I put on my reeking-of-the-daily-terror coat and stomped to Carma's flat to go and trash my last tips on candies (or whatever was left in the shops).

All the way to Varus, she kept talking about the companies that left the Russian market and sent Zombieland back to their beloved medievalism, which was rather impressive. But not when we found out that Nestlé stayed and sponsored those missiles flying at us.

"We won't buy a single thing from them," Carmina stated as we turned to the confectionery row. "Not even with hazelnuts!" (She loves hazelnuts.)

My goodness.

There was hardly anything BUT *mierda* Nestlé sneaked into every chocolate and biscuit on the shelf. We ran out of breath searching for any single stinking candy that would not be Nestlé's and pissed off the shop assistant when we got him to find us some. After ages of trying, he suggested looking for a frying pan instead.

"It won't contain Nestlé," he said, and Carmina squinted at him.

"Are you sure? Look at your shirt's tag. Nine out of ten it's blasted Nestlé."

Ohhhhhhh, I can't even have a chocky! (Cry, cry, cry, cry.) When I told Tofu no yummies for tonight, he scratched the sofa handle, got slapped, hissed at me, and clambered up the bathroom door, waiting for someone to come in and get a new hairstyle from his claws. There is no way to tell him that Russians did this, not me. But by the time they beat their bloodied way over here, he'll be so cross and hungry, he'll eat them all together with their tanks and bombs.

Thought about writing to Ben, saying how miserable I am. So if he loves me, he'd better come now or never. Let him marry me and take me to a sunny state of Idaho or Arizona or Obama or wherever he lives, I don't know. Somewhere with natives. Even in a smoky wigwam, anything's better than with cannibals. I don't even mind if he gets fatter, grows an ugly dead caterpillar over his top lip, and wears shorts, not capes like cool anime boys. I promise-promise to be a good wife, pretty and hard-working like Demelza in *Poldark* and… Bleh, gosh, no, ten p.m., not again. Pan Borov went shagging his rusty bed! Does he even like care about anything but *this?*

Ben and I will do this, too, right? It means being married, right? It's how children happen, how family happens, how love happens. Right? Hell, I'm gonna be someone's wife.

BETTER DIE, DIE FREE, *MALDITO MIERDA SEA!*

•

5 March 2022, Day 10

Yippee! Good news at last. Mommy agreed to move out. We packed the bags. Carma gave me her old suitcase stamped with silly stickers, and I spent all day stowing clothes, soaps, gadgets, magazines, dresses, energy bars, and my embroidery kit. I could hardly clasp it shut.

Then I sat on top of it and looked at my bed, at Helga, the old teddy bear that walked the world with me since I could remember. I couldn't leave her behind. Unclasped and rearranged all anew. Done.

Then I remembered that my toothbrush and makeup bag were still in the bathroom. Unclasped, rearranged, had to put away some skirts with a bleeding heart. How about shoes? I can't walk in boots when it's finally spring in a few weeks, can I? Practically hammered them in with an English dictionary, so tight it was already, and got a scornful glare from Helga.

"What?" I huffed at her. "I can't look like a bum. What if that train takes me to Hogwarts after all?"

Okay, done. No. Oh, no, oh, no, my hair pins, bracelets, and books of Irish fairy tales! Was halfway through parting with another dress when my schoolbooks caught my eye. Goodness me, would I ever need those again? Maybe leave them for cannibals to learn the basics?

Er, no, I wouldn't leave ANYTHING for them, and definitely NOT my diaries. There were like seven notepads of super shameful secrets. I either take them with me or burn them. I looked at the blob of a suitcase and decided I'd better burn them.

Then Mommy came and asked if I packed the wool socks because it was going to be cold on the train, and I yelled I would rather die of cold than open that bag again.

•

6 March 2022, Day 11

Saw videos of rocket attacks on Chernihiv. It's surreal: a video game, a fantasy fiction. Between the burning houses, in the thick smog, human phantoms stumble upon dead bodies and fragments of dead bodies and cry like the hounds of Baskerville. Is this still the twenty-first century, or did I fall through the ground into the Faun's Labyrinth? I must get out of here.

I begged Carmina to go with us, but she's adamant about staying and "making a difference." She says somebody has to, and running away is for mommies and babies, and wall flowers, not Cossack warriors like her.

"We're fourteen!" I cried into my phone. "What difference do we make? Parents decide everything for us."

"No, they don't. They give us options and directions, but nobody decides for us."

Sirens sound like car alarms as if someone is trying to steal my country. Every night, I wake up with a shudder and think about where it may hit this time. Then it BOOMs. I don't check the news because I'm scared. Any sudden sound startles me.

When everything is quiet, I'm kinda fine but inside, I'm the violin string ready for a touch of the bow. All these endless 4D live dramas and tragedies are like a blown dam. Sleeping in the corridors, Mommy's sour face, battered posters flapping in the wind, grannies buying all the sugar from the shelves, empty streets, dubious dudes in black hoodies hunting after curfew, looking for traitors, people arguing with anyone suspicious taking pictures on the crossroads, children in the underground singing our anthem like psalms, meals with no taste, daily roll call in FAMILY chat, *How are you? They blew in the kitchen windows but we're fine, you?* It's a dream or slow dying. It's not life. Carmina is my only solid beacon. I don't want to text her every morning, knowing she can never write me back. She's the crazy one; she can do something really stupid.

Daddy took a break from his work to give us a lift to the station since public transport was paralysed. It was grey and cold outside, and the snow melted slowly into the dirt. Everything looked like one giant, stinky garbage bin. The bleak, sombre houses and boarded-up shops, monuments lined with heaps of sacks, the crumbled walls of Economy College, and the Czech hedgehogs everywhere. I wondered if I would ever see my friends again, go to my boring school, and pet my beast. Tofu didn't even care to say goodbye, ran away and stuffed himself behind my wardrobe, bastard.

When we drove off the highway, the skies went black, not with clouds, but with birds. I've never seen so many crows at the same time. It felt so tragic. As if they tried to cover our land from the bombs. Our sky turned into a battlefield that raved and howled with sirens and bombs. I wonder how the birds are now. Will they stay, will they flee, will they die?

Daddy did his best to cheer us up, but I don't think talking about sixteen hours of a stuffy ride in a squash of crying babies without any toilets or water, or even a seat, could do the trick. Mommy grumbled that she didn't give a flying pig while really meaning that she missed him already.

Is my father a warrior who makes a difference? His eyes looked older in the back view mirror, withered blue and sleepy. I noticed his cropped short hair had turned almost grey, like these streets under the whiffs of snow. I can't remember seeing him this grey before. Did it happen overnight? As a matter of fact, I barely noticed him since I had my first period and he stopped buying me dolls. It's just that he's always somewhere around, like the shadow of a tree that does really nothing, if not giving shade. But he can't just stop giving shade, can he?

We arrived at the platform long before departure time, but it was already swarming with stiff and gloomy people, glued to their bags, pet carriers, and kids as one titanic motley tide. As the train barely stopped, they crushed against its iron side like a live tsunami. Old, stout *panis* in ten layers of clothing and *pans*, fit to stay and make a

difference, yelled and pushed, elbowed their way through, propelling children up to the doors while holding them over their heads.

Mommy and I jostled in that chaotic mess like two beans in a soup, dragging bulky luggage behind. She waved her handbag left and right like a ruthless Boadicea to get us through. Still, I got a shove under my ribs. Somebody trod on my foot, then left a greasy smudge on my violet coat, and that was it. I didn't want to leave; I wanted to drop flat on my face and cry an ocean.

Then the Pani Conductor, who'd been pushing bodies into the carriage like they were post sacks, cried over the heads, "No suitcases! One backpack only! You hear? We're not taking luggage!"

The human wave broke up and scattered. Some still tried to poke their bags in, but the merciless train lady threw them down. Many dropped their things right on the platform to fit into the carriage.

Not us though. Mommy clawed into her suitcase and declared that she was not leaving without her dad's (absolutely worthless) coin collection. I said I wouldn't go without Helga, and anyway, I wanted to make a difference, not run like a coward.

We took a taxi back home, and all the way, Mommy argued with Daddy on the phone. The taxi driver was so blown away by two damsels in distress (my mother is such a drama queen) that he gave us the number of the private transporters who helped evacuate on their minibuses.

Meanwhile, Russians targeted humanitarian corridors (again), hit hundreds of civilians evacuating from Irpin, and said it was all our fault. Colossal *mierda!* I saw a pic of an entire family lying about on the asphalt, like broken toys. A suitcase stood by, probably stuffed with the same things as mine. It gave me a jolt, and I snivelled all over it like a fool. Mommy thought it was because I couldn't take Helga with me on the train, but I showed her the pic and said if I lay there instead, how would it matter?

Mommy said I shouldn't watch the news; it's too disturbing and not for kids. What should I watch then? Comedies about cats, love, and happy Christmas? Duh!

Carmina texted that she planned to join her dad in the army to personally shoot them all for that. She sent me our patriotic song "*Oi u luzi chervona kalyna*." Everyone sings it now, even foreigners, and I do too, like that old music box that rolls it over and over until someone shuts the lid.

> *Oh, in the meadow a red viburnum has bent down low,*
> *For some reason, our glorious Ukraine is in sorrow…*

Then I scrolled through videos of brave Khersonians going on a strike against the Russian armed forces, climbing their zombie tank with our flaunting flag, and snivelled again, only from pride. Ukrainian women google how to drive a tank and shoot rifles. They are so tough. They could kick Superman back to his Krypton. Like one Kyiv *pani*, while chilling on her balcony, killed the enemy drone with a jar of pickled tomatoes. So there. No bombs or lies can break my people.

6

CARMINA

FUCK U PUTIN

From: Carmina Burana   06 March 2022, 20:17
To: Severin Saint   Zapahorb

What do you mean I can't join the army? So what that I'm only fourteen? Ruzis kill even younger kids: I watch the briefs about casualties The Office gives every day. If all people were warriors and had guns, they'd give Ruzis hell instead of giving their lives.

Yes, I think about possible risks, but you told me yourself, "No drowned person has hanged themselves yet." Remember? It's not that I'm going to the war as cannon fodder. We're not Russians who don't give a peg about their soldiers, the more meat the better. Special training first (my daily kung fu with YouTube masters made me like ten percent ready already!). And then who knows, maybe some superpowers will pop up and turn me into an X-Man Krypton Avenger like *Ghost of Kyiv*, the glorious, humble aviator that shot down dozens of Ruzis' flying buckets*?* (And don't say it's a myth, I'll kick you.)

Anyway, I'll be something more modest, like say, a human-sized chameleon that takes *any shape*. As a lizard, I'll sneak into the enemy ammunition depot and put dynamite among their stock of missiles. Then Ruzis will catch me red-handed, of course (they are always dilly-dallying around their bombs, smoking cigs and playing with the gasoline), but find a Russian minister instead! He (I) will blurt, "Hey you, comrades, good job killing innocent Ukrainians, go and drink some vodka to celebrate!" They will roll off like, YAY, VODKA and won't notice their honourable minister wagging a lizard's tail, hahahah-di-haha.

And if the Russian minister himself drops by to check on the depot, which they never do, cowards, (but if drunk, who knows), I'll turn into a missile. I mean, *any shape*, right? Why not a bomb? They'd never find me, ever. La-di-dah-dadah. So there, one little innocent bomb will lie there until the coast is clear. Then I'll light the dynamite cord, creep safely out, mince quickly on my tiny lizard legs, then dart and hop and BUAHAHAHA at full lungs as the giant cotton flower of a blast will grow behind me in the air.

I will be irreplaceable in this war, Pa, promise. Far better than sitting in the bathroom, praying the bomb will fly by and waiting for someone else to hand us victory on a silver platter. What if we lose? I won't bear it. Better die than live in rotten Russia. Pan President states in almost every briefing that fighting on the "back front" is as important, but I don't believe that giving away my clothes and buying you meds and bagels makes any difference.

Okay, we do go to our school to weave the camouflage nets, but it's so girlish. Neshka goes all ecstatic about it, though. She even started embroidering *vyshyvanka* for the soldiers, the national shirt that is, cos it's *magic*. I say, only if you make it into the chain mail Frodo wore in the battle with the Nazguls. Princess Agnieszka tut-tut-ed me and cited our history teacher to prove that Cossack magic is stronger than elven cos elves were *born* cool while Cossacks *forged* their power in their own blood, sweat, and tears of fighting as long as Moscow stands. I slept through all his lessons but now, wow, I'm intrigued…

•

More news on the school front. Chicken Tural from my class took the last scraps of his courage (and the only brain cell he had) to write me a love letter. A LOVE LETTER, my ass! He said if we were bound to die, I should know he always liked me. And just because of that, he asked me to show him my tits and end his unbearable virginity. Holy cow, I nearly threw up my breakfast. Why would this piece of an idiot even think about tits when it's WAR? Lunacy! Wait. Is this what they call LOVE? Thanks, but go fuck yourself.

I only tell you this so that you won't go ballistic if you suddenly get a call from Pan Principal about me kicking some balls. Mind you, I was exceptionally polite with Tural when we met next at the masking nets factory. I said I was asexual.

He went agog and said, "What does it mean? You show me your tits and feel nothing?"

For like forty years, I calmed my inner chi and replied as patiently as I could (well, at least without hitting his face), "No, it means go sniff some other butt."

"Ha-ha," he choked, laughing, "Ha-ha-ha-ha-ha." Like I made a hilarious joke (not). He probably thought it was funny, and that he looked so damn cool and sexy, bloody Jason Momoa fresh from the ocean. Only he laughed as if someone smashed this Aquaman on the head with Thor's Hammer (which, incidentally, somebody should do).

Eventually, cool and sexy Aquaman ran out. He coughed and coughed like something got into his gills, cos it was a dust inferno in the gym with all the rags and nets. He coughed till I hit him on the back to stop him from coughing to death. Instead of being even a bit grateful, Tural said he'd throw himself from a skyscraper if I turned him down, and I did hope he would, but he just bunked off to sit with Maví and smiled sweetly at her. He'd probably sent her the same love letter I got. And they ask me why I am so feminist. Boys are STUPIDOID.

Anyway, Pa, guess what? Neshka and I invented a new way to help Ukraine win! Every time we go to buy something vital, like eggs, and we have like two-something hundred hryvnias left, I buy myself a pack of hazelnuts picked in Kherson or cheese from Sumy (if there's any left), and Agnieszka chooses one more notepad with sunflowers or a blue-and-yellow pen for her enormous stationery collection. Ma goes off her rocker every time I bring home the checks, but we still go and buy them. We imagine ourselves Aragorn and Legolas standing in front of the black sea of stinky, sneering orcs, raising our swords and bows and purchases, and running to the cash registers, yelling,

FOR THE UKRAINIAN ECONOMY!

If half the nation did the same, we wouldn't need any loans from the Western world. You'll be shocked to know some people here couldn't care less about this war. Pan Doopa from the flat next door, the one with a new pipe system every spring, drills into our wall AGAIN and would renovate his stupid bathroom even if the moon drops on our house, and nothing will survive on Earth but those freaking pipes. Agnieszka's old man from upstairs is even worse. He's a real fossil and as deaf as a post. When he doesn't bonk his wife like a mad rhino, he watches war news on telly, and three more flats watch it with him. Sometimes at two in the morning. We tried to bang on his door but, naturally, he doesn't hear (look out of the window, man, war is here!).

There is also ancient Pani Lyudmila downstairs, who never goes out since she turned eighty a few centuries ago. Can't say she even knows about the war cos when Neshka suggested visiting her to offer help, the only thing she said was, "Is it you throwing rubbish from the windows? It litters my flowerpots! I'm telling everything to Captain Saint, young girl!" And slammed her door in my face. (It's not me, Dad. Cross my heart!)

There is good news too. Remember Pani Iryna? The mad woman from the ground floor who shouts "Fuck you, bitch!" out of her kitchen window over and over throughout the night, every time she runs out of antipsychotics and her second self wants some fun? Well, she's back from the nuthouse and feeling so much better. Cos now she yells "Fuck you, Putin!" And we don't even mind it.

Oh, you asked about our safety in the streets. It's super safe, Dad. Everyone is looking for missile trackers, and they call everyone else if they find one. There are gangs in black hoodies prowling around like creeps down the spine. They are volunteers in search of anything suspicious. One stopped me and asked the time. I noticed a smartphone sticking out of his pocket so my ass he needed that. After hearing my Ukrainian, he smiled. We wished victory to each other and parted like old friends.

Then just the other day, two old crones from next door traced Nesha and me up to the blown houses on Nova Ave., like two spies on a pension. They thought we were traitors (cos we took pics of the flags) and reported everything to our mothers. Even old ladies stake out.

That's how safe it is. Haha.

I miss you, Pa. The videos of you firing the Javelin are so super cool. Will probably ask for one for myself for Xmas! Just in case Ruzis come to celebrate it together.

Just kidding (:

Better ask for a tank, hohoho.

Your under-soldier, Skipper

7

AGNIESZKA

7 March 2022, Day 12

Parents called one million and one minibus drivers who offer lifts to Lviv, and they demand as much money as it costs to fly to Venus (when it was possible to fly). Then Mommy and her workmate-beauticians moved their salon to home, and people told her that she'd better not as the roads were swarming with pirates. I can't imagine them dragging their ships by our snowy fields to loot some grannies on a bus, but anyway, I'm staying. I'll raise the Ukrainian spirit by volunteering.

We went to help clean the rubble from the boiler houses blown in the night. Bricks are so heavy when you move like six billion of them. Carmina says it's good kung fu practice, but I say, thanks, I'd rather keep my hands. Mommy donated her blood to soldiers in the vampire room of Daddy's hospital. Carmina'd kill to give hers, which is super rare, like X Neutral, but the hospital vampires don't accept teens. To cheer her up, I said it was good because if someone got her blood, they'd turn ginger red and kung fu crazy, lose their gender and go swinging bricks in a ruthless warrior way. And she said, "Cool! I'll finally have someone to talk to."

Gosh. Like she's not talking to me right now.

Though I don't quite like talking about kung fu and stuff.

A van comes to pick up donations at the local shopping mall daily. I brought them my heart-shaped handmade soaps, cookies in a tin box, and my favourite knitted scarf with tassels. They need them more than I do, and anyway, if Ukraine falls, what's the point in having pretty things in the first place?

Oh, dear. I am a never-crowned princess of a falling land. How dreadfully tragic.

Apart from a camouflage nets hub, our school has also turned into a hostel for those who lost their homes. Carma and I are now "making a difference" there. We dragged the old mattresses, pillows, and blankets from our homes, and I nearly dropped dead under that weight. My hands grew so filthy! I got soil under my fingernails like a street bum. Ohhh! *Mierda poo.* Wanted to go straight home and soak in a bathtub for five eternities, but Mommy called and said we'd run out of eggs, so we went shopping instead, with Daddy's credit card.

Wandered by the ghost labyrinth of sad, empty shelves, trying to find anything to eat but eggs. It felt like we were in a freakish reality show. Like I got into some old black-and-white films about World War II that I hate. They only pictured brave and desperate black-and-white men and women, broken by some epic tragedy that made me depressed. Because it's not pretty, it's not magic. It's just dirty and sad. Besides, they were only actors who pretended, so it was the epic tragedy of epic nothing. Now, it's different. I'm that black-and-white woman, and all they filmed about war is true. Nazis were the ghastliest evil of all possible evil the planet ever carried, and Russians are like, *oh cool, let's be Nazi, too, but blame everyone else.*

I wish I could speak to my Great-Gran Iulita. Before she died, she talked like a looped audio track about the bombing, eating wormed bread and listening to the cranky radio set in the corner. I thought she'd gone bananas, saying, "I don't wanna die, just rest in peace." Now I feel just like that. There was no peace for her cos that war was never over. Nobody will rest in peace here. Not until Ukraine does something really, really phenomenal.

Carmina showed me photos of British soldier-volunteers who came to Ukraine to fight for our freedom. There were also Americans, Mexicans, Georgians, and some from countries I don't even know what planet they're from, and South Koreans who can't even return home because of that. They all left their cosy homes and families to come all the way here to… die for us?

So triple unbelievablemente!

I started hiccupping and sobbing, and breathing super high. Carma romped all about the flat, hunting for Tofu. She said I needed to pet a cat like I was having a panic attack, but I said, I wasn't in a panic. I was just upset that I couldn't give them all my handmade soaps. ALL OF THEM.

"Did you know, our president has been given a Reagan medal?" I asked her while stroking my slightly angry cat. "It's the highest honour. It's like getting a knighthood in America."

"Meh." Carmina barely broke away from the news feed on her phone. "Cool, but they better give us planes. If I had that medal, I'd sell it for a jet."

She can be so very brutal.

•

8 March 2022, Day 13

Women's International Day. Mommy took Carma and me to a café to celebrate (because of stress, and because she's a lady, war or no war). Surprisingly, Fairy Café was open, and they even served my favourite strawberry cheesecake. But it took ages to order because everyone in the line (including us) tried to treat soldiers, and they went all shy, shy, shy and refused. Then everyone insisted, even grannies who shoved apples into their pockets and called them "children."

I wanted Mommy to buy me the pink cappuccino with a heart drawn on top from the billboard, but she said it wasn't time for that. Guess I have one more reason to wait for the victory. My heart-ey pink cappuccino, a beacon in the dark days of war. A true princess's treat. Just wait till the bloody Russians piss off, and we'll be together forever and ever.

A blue-and-yellow flag flapped in the wind over the café like a dancing angel, protecting us inside. I could see people in a crowd across the street crying and hugging each other, yelling "Glory to Ukraine!" as if we had won a world championship. A rare, timid sun slid by the backs of the ice lumps on the roads. Utility workers sat on the curbs, resting from the crazy, frantic cleaning they did every day. It felt like I knew the faces of everyone in my city, and you know what?

Those are damn pretty faces.

Russians bear the faces of anti-people. They have no idea how to treat ladies if they even have them there. Stinking rockets flew around all evening. The air siren wailed for hours and trapped Carmina in our flat. We sat on the floor, leaning against the front door, aimlessly scrolling the news feed. Saw a video of a girl playing the violin in the Kharkiv bomb shelter, so beautiful and sad that I cried. Then news about Russians shooting at children, at priests, at everything that moved. And everything that didn't move, they shot, too, like total assholes.

I grew so very cross, then so very desperate that I watched all the cringey interviews with Carpathian *molfars* fortune-telling the great flop of the Russian Empire when the Ukrainian sun will rise like a phoenix from the ashes of the gunfire. *Molfars* are sorcerers and shamans from the Ukrainian mountains, so you bet they know what they are talking about.

Old bat Molfarka Marichka was a total blast. She tossed some beans on the table, gazed at them clicking with her tongue, and said that all Russian leaders got possessed by Satan. To keep his power, Russians mummified their chiefs like evil genies in magic lamps and fed them bloody sacrifices from wars and repressions. But now, years after the USSR has gone belly up, Satan is so hungry that he needs to devour the entire country!

Meanwhile, Ukrainians and our partners are like the dwarfs, elves, and people of Middle Earth, resisting the total darkness of chaos and destruction.

Carmina went crazy about the idea—she'd kill to be Aragorn. I wanted to tell her that we're only hobbits in this war, but I'm not that suicidal, LOL. We spent a lifetime discussing who was going to be our Gandalf, but then, the lights went out. Everything sank into darkness: my flat and my thoughts. Mommy rushed to draw water into buckets while it still ran.

Another dark eternity passed. The air siren hooted and hooted, but nothing happened, and Carmina cried, "Do they carry that missile on a bicycle, or what?"

And then whizz, WHUMP! BOOOM!!! It wasn't even a noise but a tidal wave of supersonic power that rang in the windows, shuddered through my rattling teeth, and sent a cup diving from the top shelf. The cars outside broke with wailing, and all the mongrels joined in. In shock, I jumped on top of Carmina and nearly squashed her bony frame.

"Stay here," Mommy ordered, grabbed her coat, and ran out. We stayed there for as long as six seconds, then grabbed ours and followed her outside. A truly titanic crater smouldered in the backyard, just a house away from ours. The playground, benches, and flower beds, all trashed, sunk into that moon pit. There was a hole in the house's front wall. Windows were blown, bricks crumbled like in a dollhouse. I spotted a bathtub through there, and a cupboard, covered in debris and dust, and burning profusely. Just a minute ago, we hid in the corridor with stuff just like that...

It stunk like burnt plastic and made me sick, and I yearned to fall through the ground, but I couldn't move a finger. In my Hello Kitty pyjamas with bunny-head socks and slippers, I was glued to the asphalt and shivered under my coat like jumping jelly. There were people inside that house, I thought; don't look there. *Don't look.* *DON'T. LOOK.*

The fire engines and ambulances nosed into the mess of trash and human hustle, and the rescuers unfolded their ladders. Mommy pulled me back. "Go home, girls, make yourselves sweet tea. Feya and I will stay and see if anyone needs help."

Carmina took me by the hand with her thin, icy fingers. We dragged our wobbly feet back to my flat, lit some candles, and sat silently on a corner of my bed, shivering from cold or fear, or both. Nobody wanted tea. I only craved having Tofu on my lap, but he probably fell into Narnia behind the wardrobe.

"Do you think it's painful? To die from a bomb?" I asked in a feeble voice I didn't recognize.

"No." Carmina kept staring at the prancing unicorns on my wall. "If you die like a warrior."

"I don't think I'm a warrior…"

"After this war, every Ukrainian will be a warrior."

I didn't want to be a warrior. I wanted to fall into Narnia with my cat.

Squeak! Squeak! Squeak! Ugh, ten p.m., Pan Borov went jumping on his rusty mattress right above our heads, like nothing had happened, and I was just… done.

·

9 March 2022, Day 14

WE ARE LEAVING! YAY! (Dance, dance, dance.) With Carmina and co. *Wonderfulous!*

After yesterday's horror, nobody remembered why not, and Dad personally packed Mom's bags. *Dying* to run away from here so badly, I keep scurrying around my flat like a tiger in a cage, picking at things, fixing my books on the shelf, and stroking my dolls.

Mommy's face is stone-grey and rock-hard. She still doesn't give flying pigs at the breakfast table. Her curls are finally set, and Marilyn Monroe's makeup is back, but now, it's like a rubber mask. An invisible leaden cloud hovers above our heads as we eat our eggs in an absolute school-exam silence. I cast a furtive glance at Daddy. He chews slowly with his greyish brows almost kissing each other on his forehead, and I beg him one last time to come with us.

"I gave an oath, Poppet," he says solemnly. "To save people's lives."

How about my life? I wanted to cry. *They are just people, and I am your daughter!*

But I don't say anything because parents talk, not listen. And if *you* talk, they send you to your room to *think*, i.e., change your mind and agree with what they say. And I won't agree with that. Ever.

Carmina's father, Captain Saint, is on leave, and he's taking his family to the Carpathian area, a small town called Booguy, where Carma's granny lives. Pani Feya, her ma, said they could take two more people in their car with as much luggage as we could fit in, and Tofu, too.

It drove me out of my wits, trying to fish that beast from behind the wardrobe. The bastard wouldn't peep out even for a biscuit! So I shredded the last cat sausage, made a line of it out to the corridor, and hid behind the hall door. Tofu sniffed his favourite salmon and padded from piece to piece, carefully picking them with his teeth. I launched at him, like Batman, grabbed him in my arms, and rushed downstairs. Yippee! I did it, I did it, I saved my cat!

Why can't I do the same with my daddy? Those bombs turn all they touch into trash. How can one man, even a doctor, save anyone from that?

We set off right after breakfast, in a long column of other cars and buses that moved west and crawled like an earthworm on a rainy day. So boring and nauseating. I couldn't even entertain myself with Molfarka Marichka's beans telling, because Tofu was dozing on my lap and snapped at me if I moved.

Carmina bombed her dad with questions about the war and fights and all that boy stuff. He smiled his lopsided toothy smile that always gave me the creeps and told us a story about a soldier nicknamed Zeus who was the eye and nemesis of Gostomel airport none could catch. Cannibals planned to capture Kyiv through the

spot where Zeus and three other super guys of his team hid and gave coordinates to our artillery. Poor orcs could do nothing but run around yelling while their vehicles got mysteriously smashed, smashed and smashed, smashed.

His next story welled my eyes up. After the airport was saved more helicopters came, like giant bees in smoky air, stuffed with angry goblin-soldiers. Ukrainian forces had no anti-helicopter weapons back then and brought them down with just guns. Nobody believed it would work: they just fired with pure rage and pain for Kyiv, and the blasted thing fell. The whole world gasped and forgot to breathe. Four against an army! A bullet against a helicopter! Totally *marvelouso.*

He said since our army had little weaponry, we had to be super cunning and resourceful. Like when several brave soldiers garbed in orcs' clothes, walked towards the enemy tank column and whined in pure Orcish that they were poor lost Russian buddies (we speak Russian, too!). They occupied the head tank, killed the drivers, turned around, and BANG! BANG! BANG! destroyed the rest of them. There!

But my favourite was about a simple dude from the post service who PEW! PEW! PEW! brought down two enemy jets. Just a postman some week ago, now a plane assassin, my goodness. Next time I receive my post, I'll look closely at my deliverer. She might be a secret Avenger from Krypton who kills the invaders with one glare.

The route we took lay like ten ways away from any way, through some godforsaken fields of nowhere. We made only one stop at a decrepit village shop to buy water.

We said, "Good day."

And the furious Valkyrie behind the counter roared "Don't you 'good day' me! Glory to Ukraine!" and drilled holes in our heads with her bulgy eyes.

We saluted from our hats, "Glory to heroes!" and everything was suddenly right. Good days will come only after we win.

Then we got stuck every now and then at block posts where people in khaki inspected our IDs and rummaged in our luggage. I think all the glorious Ukrainian army knows Helga, and when we head back home, they'll salute her from their caps. We were lucky to have Cap Saint because they all saluted him all right and didn't mess around with the papers more than necessary. Some had stood in line since yesterday, trying to say *"palianytsia"* (orcs can't do that, they only say what their zombie TV says).

A few times, thunderous jets crossed the sky, and something smoked behind the horizon. Panic wrapped me in hot sweat every time they droned right over our heads, but Carmina whooped and hailed from out of the window and said those were Ukrainian aces. How could she tell? All warplanes look the same to me. Then another kind of panic bit at my bum. I imagined that a zombie tank would peek with its muzzle from the trees and spit our way like they say they do around Kyiv. Fire point-blank at the civilians and drive over the tops of the cars, crushing people inside.

Thanks to the Almighty Cossacks, there were just empty, gloomy meadows bordered with ragged black bushes and cloaked with clouds of frightened crows. Passing villages and towns gradually shape-shifted into something I barely recognised. I had never travelled this far west and only knew boring concrete boxes of Soviet architecture in Zapahorb. Now, I drove by old stone bridges and fancy, fairytale cottages and was amazed that Ukraine could be this… artful.

"Pa, I need to pee," Carmina voiced what I hadn't dared to say since midday. "And no, it can't wait."

"Air alert in the nearby city," Cap Saint said and tapped at his phone in the panel holder.

"Why didn't you go at the block post?" Pani Feya added, leaning from her seat.

"Cos I didn't want to then. Pa, stop the car, or I'll do it here."

"All right, there are some shrubs over there, but be quick."

"I'll go too." I quickly pushed sleepy Tofu off to Mommy and unclasped the seat belt.

This was the most shameful moment of my entire fourteen years of life. I swear to the mighty Cossacks, I'll burn this diary the moment I fill it. It wasn't too dark yet but chilly to the bones, so when Carmina and I crouched behind the cobweb-dense, flimsy bushes, I was dead certain the whole world saw our frostbitten butts. And since I bore my morning tea stoically for hours, I was like going to water that bush until the last orc kicked the bucket on this soil. Then, a bolt from the blue, whizzzzzzzzzzz BA-DOOM! behind us, like the wrath of mighty Odin, and Carmina went, "Shiver me thimbles!"

We shot out of there like two chicks set on fire, pulling up tights and jeans on the go, cursing to the heavy metal of BOOM BOOM in the background.

Oh dear-dear. Double *mierda terriblouso*. If I die here, I wish nobody knew how.

•

10 March 2022, Day 15. I'm in Booguy. Finally!

This place is weird. There is only one shabby ATB shop in the entire city! The main street is the only street. And all the rest is a chaotic cluster of old houses, desperately trying to wriggle into the picture like an extra tooth in a Hollywood smile for a toothpaste commercial. In the outskirts, it's not even a city, but a hamlet, with patches of gardens and meadows attached to lopsided medieval huts. Cows and goats prowl along the roads like lazy, overweight models on the catwalk, and stink of poo. I met a goose at the doorstep of Carma's granny's house, A GOOSE!

He tried to steal my phone, but Tofu chased him all around the car and then danced some samurai kung fu ritual with him. Until

Carmina's granny peeped out of the window and cried,

"Where are your manners, boy? These are our guests!"

The goose folded back his battle wings, lifted his head, and walked away, swaying comically with his butt. He quacked as he passed me and hopped over the threshold.

"This is Shrimp," Carmina said and whumped the heavy suitcase down from the car boot (she really does think she can outlift Hercules, Son of Zeus). "He only looks like a bird. In fact, he's a guard dog."

"Does he bite?" I pressed my phone to my chest.

"Only if you bite him first."

He bites. He gadded around the house, following me wherever I went, and pinched at my skirt. It frightens me more than all the bombs put together. So I asked Carmina to lock the door to our bedroom. Mommy went up the wall about it and said why would we lock our door, we mustn't lock our door, what if something bad happens to us and she won't be able to help?

Like what, Mother?

A cannibal crawling into the window with a grenade in his teeth? Shrimp will peck him to death before he even swings his leg over the fence.

And anyway, no cannibals will come near this lost place of atrocious oblivion. People here don't even know what air-raid sirens are for. When it hooted in a tidal wave of mega-sonic power, and I, with my blood bubbling in my veins, ran around in search of a solid two-walls-nook to hide, Pani Burana Senior just pished and said,

"For Chrissakes, child, if it hits here, we'll make a parade."

•

11 March 2022, Day 16
Pani Burana Senior is a witch. And I'm *absolutamente* sure about it.

Because:

a) she looks exactly like Professor Minerva McGonagall from *Harry Potter*, only with a spatula instead of the magic wand (she's a potter);

b) she makes crockery and scary clay dwarfs she sells into every house so they will possess the owners and turn them into her eternal slaves and ghastly ghouls;

c) her husband looks exactly like Gandalf the Grey only shaved, in a funny hat and round glasses and with a spade instead of the staff (always somewhere in the garden, burying corpses);

d) she cooked us borshch that tasted like a witch's brew (because of the beans?);

e) she does have beans in a red pouch, and she can read them like Molfarka Marichka;

f) for heaven's sake, her dog is a GOOSE!

Okay, okay, breathe, Princess, breathe and don't, DON'T think about it.

I spent most of the day locked with Carmina in her bedroom, doing homework. We are sort-of-maybe back to school like in the good old pandemic days, only now hiding from the viruses we can actually see. The Internet here is a *complete catastrophe*, so glitchy that it gave only bits and bats, and it seemed like Pani Larysa taught us rap and R&B, not algebra. Also, we only have one textbook for two because Carmina *fundamentally* refused to pack anything in Russian (and some of our manuals are still in Russian). She's gone really barmy about Ukrainian, talks nonstop like a news marathon. She even speaks Spanish with a Hutsul accent. And when she lacks words, which is often, she just invents new ones, and, surprisingly, I understand her.

Speaking Ukrainian is hard, feels like I have a second mouth inside my mouth. Most of our mates have shapeshifted too, and sound hilarious in the open chat. Cos Ukrainian is so marvy and totally *grandioso*. It sounds elven. But not when Mommy tries it on like a new perfume and talks like an alien breathing oxygen for the first time. Or when Valeriya, our class star, uses "What?" as a comma in every sentence, and it's a total blast, as if we're listening to the old radio leaping between the waves. *Sho-sho-sho... sho-sho...*

Kangi joined us from the back seat of his car somewhere on the road: his face jumped in the camera between the bulky boxes. Ape Román is in Germany, so is his gorilla gang, and Maví is doing schoolwork from a lousy bomb shelter back in Zapahorb. Nobody heard what she was mumbling because the siren there wailed like crazy, and we all begged her to evacuate. She said, "If we do, we'll probably crash somewhere on the way, like that unfortunate bus with Ukrainian refugees in Italy. It's doomed. We'll die anyway."

Then we argued about doom, if death was something set in the stars, and nobody cared for cotangents and sinuses because they were all set in the stars before we were even born and will be there after we all die, and it's just so very sad.

So Pani Larysa stopped rapping math and lectured us about "psychological health" instead, whatever that was, and Liza the Cosmopolitan (from Nice) advised us to see this war as an exciting adventure. Carmina said, "What, like when you are on your way to school but suddenly get run over by a tank? Yay, my life is a jolly carnival!"

Liza shut up and went off to her sunny French Riviera and yappy little squirt dog, *kurwa*. (Carma says it's Ukrainian for "peacock with a chicken butt," but I did suspect it has something to do with female dogs and the Russian warship's destination when her gran spat *Putin's kurwa!* at Pan Potato, aka the president of Belarus and Putin's partner in crimes.)

Oh, I miss, miss, miss school so much! I miss wearing something fancy to show off, making a trillion selfies to pick just one for the avatar. And then go and comment something somewhere, maybe even Román's stupid memes, doesn't matter, just to see my new pic in a little circle attached to my messages, hate it eventually, and go make one trillion more. Why do I have to sit in this dump armpit of a village, like a castaway in my own country, wearing a shapeless knitted sack of a sweater, hunt for chocolate like a magic beast of Neverland, and fear the bomb will drop right on my head before I finish lining my second eyelid?

Ben may end up being the only boy I ever charmed. Life is not fair.

Better go and talk to Carma's gran (what's her name anyway?) Maybe she'll teach me new Ukrainian words.

•

Her name is Bozhena (and her husband is Bohdan), but she asked me to call her Granny because she's old like Dimetrodon. It's a dinosaur, she said, and she would know, must have kept one as her guard dog when the planet was still flat like a pancake. I don't think I learnt something new, though; she kept wandering in her "good old days," and I have no idea who the glorious Adriano Celentano is and why he sounds like a pizzeria and, frankly, I don't care unless he comes and kicks all the cannibals off my land. And no-no-no, life *wasn't* better before Instagram and smartphones! Things were <u>sloooow</u> like Russian brains trying to solve five times seven and NOT get a chimpanzee with nukes as an answer. The Buranas have a phone like a box (called TELEPHONE) with a wheel that you SPIN. It takes absolute ages to crawl back, and if it's a zero you need to dial, you can just DIE waiting.

Pan Burana is even more ancient. He says he's only seventy, but seventy what? Million? His first selfie is on a cave wall in France.

When he joined us for the evening news, it went totally *ballisti-camus*. We all sat in front of the TV, in total peace and quiet, watching President Zelenskyy asking us to break the truth to Russians, kinda shake them from that sick Soviet hypnosis. Pan Burana blurted "This boy is so naïve" and then for no apparent reason, he started making smacking and slurping sounds with his lips and gums like he was a dog lapping from his bowl. For like ten years before Bozhena rolled the newspaper and whacked him on the nose.

My. God.

I want to go home…

8

MARA

"Is this the Booguy I remember, or did we accidentally step into a Turkish bazaar?" Aidan asks as we walk along the hectic, narrow street of our small mountain town.

Clock square, church, library, and a cluster of shops along the main street turn into a clotty human hive. People hustle everywhere, mostly *panis* with babies or youngsters. Wrapped in long, puffy coats and endless scarves, long-haired and bare-headed, they batter the cobbled pavement with their heavy-heeled boots and look more like Netflix phantoms rather than real women. Children romp all about, crying and demanding things and, basically, playing nasty gremlins. With angry cars that beep from every lane, the mix grows absolutely infernal.

One little gremlin racing his kickscooter through the crowd gives me a shove. I dodge aside, pushing Aidan on the shoulder. "Hey!"

Then a plump little *pani* follows shortly after and drops "Beg your pardon" in Russian.

I stare back at her as she pulls the little rider and his vehicle aside, telling him how dangerous it is to play in the busy street and blah blah blah.

"Did she just talk to us?" I turn to Aidan.

"In Russian?" Aidan raises an eyebrow.

"Right! I need a lemonade." I turn on my heels and stomp across the street to the local grocery.

"Slava Ukraini!" Pani Orynko the cashier, whose mother I recently saw through The Slit, lifts her round, rosy face to us, but I ignore her and dive between the stacks.

There is a crowd of people in the shop, right? Right! She could be speaking to anyone. I take the bottle from the shelf and notice two little girls (like a tangle of kittens) skipping up, pushing each other. One grabs an apple juice. The other wants a lemonade like mine, but it stands two shelves beyond her reach. In vain, she hops and stretches out, then gazes up at me with huge brown eyes, like two burning coals. Slowly, I take a bottle with my two fingers and place it in her doll-sized hands. She beams and runs screaming to her mother, "Can children drink this? Can they drink this, Mommy?

Is it for children, Mommy? I want to drink this!"

I don't want to drink anything anymore. All I want is to get invisible again. On my escape route, I bump into Aidan, who is talking to some guys. "So, you're from Kharkiv? Cool. Eastern Ukraine, huh? Why do you speak Russian then?" I grab him by his leather jacket and pull him to the cash desk.

"Hey! I found friends…"

"Shush! We need to get the hell outta here." I drag him to Orynko, leave a fifty-hryvnias banknote on her desk like I always do, and rush to the door. Aidan is right behind me.

"Wait, *Pani*! The girl in black! Your change!" Orynko cries to my back.

I let go of the door handle, and the bell dings as the door closes. Keeping her smiling face in focus, I pace back to Orynko and take the change from her warm, soft fingers without breaking my gaze. "Do you really… see me?" I tilt my head and squint.

Her smile fades for a moment before she bursts into a loud giggle. "Why, yes! Where are you from?"

"What do you mean? I live here."

"Oh, I'm sorry. I don't remember seeing you before."

"I don't remember you seeing me before either," I grumble, sliding the change and the lemonade into my big hoodie pocket.

"We have so many guests now. New settlers come every day. Few stay though," she twitters on, ignoring my grumble. "This dreadful tragedy brought the Ukrainian family together. East and west met at last."

I have no idea what she is talking about.

"Aidan and I found it rather shocking." I point back with my thumb. Orynko stares behind me with a question frozen on her face. There is nobody around but a black cat, sniffing the dried fish packs on the ground shelves. "I mean my *cat* Aidan and…"

I don't finish my sentence because of an utterly thunderous howl that hoots, growing in strength all at once from everywhere. Deep, inhuman, it hits my ears like the wail of all the hounds of hell. And as it happens with hounds sometimes—one wails, others join—all the kids in the shop add their harrowing cries. Women hoist them up and rush to the cashier, asking if there are any bomb shelters.

Orynko is perfectly calm, however. "Oh, don't mind that, dears. There's nothing to hit here."

I pick up Aidan from the floor and pop out of the shop like a champagne cork. The noise is even louder in the street. Deafening! It needles under my skin and freezes the blood inside my veins. All the magic beings in the town flee, scattering around into the woods, down the lake, up the mountains… A black cloud of startled crows—the undead—rises from the hazy crowns of Mor.

I race back to my forest, dropping Aidan on the go, and he skips beside me, casting a long, human shadow on the cobbled lane. We cross the road and nearly hit a van that halts with a screech, and the driver pokes out to call me Harley, queen of the suicide squad, and… many other things. Like I care. I won't stop until the trees of Mor envelop me in their soothing silence, and the scarred bark of their ancient trunks leaves scratches on my palms.

"Holy lemonade and cutlets, what the heck was that?" I pant and slow my pace, gripping at the bottle inside my pocket, then look behind my back.

Who cares? That was sensational. I liked talking to people… Aidan smacks with his tongue.

"Duh, what's there to like? Just talking. I could get into their heads and see all the answers."

That's cheating. When with people, you need to play people. Aidan huffs, lifting his tail with the tip dangling in the air. *Don't you know that all the world's a stage?*

"All the world is a bunch of idiots." I'm not giving up.

All the world is a bunch of idiots on a stage. Neither is my cat.

"Well, I'll enjoy the show from my balcony, thank you."

As we catch a glimpse of Huttuh behind the trees, the smell of the living makes me freeze to the spot. Aidan huddles to the ground, straining his ears. In a moment, a tall, slim girl in a rainbow-striped sweater, shabby jeans, and puffy jerkin walks around from behind my house. She wears a fluffy headpiece on top of her carrot-red curly hair, and her face is so heavily freckled that I almost take her for a forest spirit.

"No doors or windows from my side!" she cries in a funny Eastern accent.

"No doors here either," replies a softer voice, and another girl walks around the other side of Huttuh. Small, blonde, shapely, in a lilac beret, with a matching calf-length vintage coat and tiny laced-up boots. With her silky, porcelain complexion, big blue eyes, and burning, rosy cheeks, she reminds me of an old collectible doll, only not that creepy.

"Oi! Why are you sniffing around there, you two?" I call, walking closer.

Startled, they turn to me. I can't say I scared them to death like any death witch properly should because the doll looks ridiculously relieved to see me and the forest spirit never breaks her smile, as if it's forever carved on her lips.

"A living soul at last," says Doll and clasps her hands in front of her like the model in those oil portraits in museums.

"I wouldn't jump to conclusions." I toss back my so-big-deal fore-lock.

"Is this your house?" Forest Spirit pipes in, pointing at my hut.

"No, a magic trap for the nosy parkers, what else! Of course, it's my house. What are you doing here?" I cross my arms on my chest.

"We are lost." Doll steps away from Huttuh, carefully placing her feet to avoid stones and twigs on the ground. "We walked into a park zone, but it turned out to be a real jungle! My name is Agnieszka, by the way. But you can call me Nesha or Neshka." She reaches out her miniature hand with glossy pink nails, and I stare down at it suspiciously. Then she spots my cat and cries, "Ah, look, a kitty!"

"Don't!" I yip, but she's already scooped Aidan in her hands and cuddled him like he's a stuffed toy.

Meeeow! Help!

"It's Aidan, it's dangerous to touch him!" I put some power into my voice.

She rubs her nose on his ears, pressing him with his back to her chest. "Why is that? Is he a bad boy?"

Aidan purrs. *Aw, that's actually nice…*

I scratch my forehead with a sigh and say, "No, but he brings bad luck."

"I don't believe in that." The other girl strides up to stroke Aidan's little nose. "I'm Carmina. We've recently arrived from Zapahorb. So… you live here? In a barn without windows?"

"It's not a barn," I grumble. "What's wrong with your Zapahorb? Why are you all here?"

Carmina raises her eyes at me, startled, green, and shiny. "You don't know? There is a war in Ukraine."

I stare back at them, processing the news. My face is a stone mask of a dumfounded statue as my heart gongs the seconds away, and memories kaleidoscope in my mind, shaping a new mandala of the world. *Disfigured bodies. Still, empty eyes. The kids…*

Oh, right… My cat meows. *That explains so many untimely deaths.*

My silence electrifies the air between us. Agnieszka shuffles from foot to foot awkwardly. "You don't look shocked," she says, and she's right. Why would I? War is also part of life.

I squint at her. "I've seen wars through the eyes of old men. That was… *informative.*"

They blink, and Neshka drops my cat down. Aidan lands softly on all fours, shakes his body like a turbo drive, and sits down to lick his rumpled coat on the sides.

"Blimey!" Carmina exclaims. "How can you be this… heartless about such things? Don't you like, feel sorry or anything?"

I turn to her, sensing the heat emanating from her chest. "How can feeling sorry help people who died in the war?" I ask them, linking my hands behind my back, and they have no answer to that. So I continue, "There are two types of human emotions. One is the real feeling, which is the mere fact about the world you perceive, and the other is a sentiment you build up on top to create a halo of drama around it, for the effect. It requires a lot of your time and energy and is completely inefficient, if not impressive. I don't go for that trap." I catch their frowns. "Human compassion has nothing to do with weeping and aching together. It's merely feeling the same. So yes, I have a heart, I just use it in a much more functional way."

Aidan turns his head away with an almost human eye roll. *Good grief, Mara, that was the weirdest way to say "Hi, nice to meet you."*

"Shut up," I snap and the girls step back from me simultaneously. "No, not you. Aidan."

Carmina bursts into a thunderous ha-ha that throws a bunch of birds off the trees above our heads and slaps me on the upper arm. "Holy cow, you sound like the Avina hologram, I mean the AI in the Mass Effect video game. What did you say about emotions again? I need to write that down and tell my teachers that I have a heart for study, I just don't give a damn about it!"

Agnieszka giggles with soft soundless shakes of her shoulders, covering her mouth with her little palms. Even Aidan sways his tail with enjoyment. I can't get what's so funny in what I've said, so I peek into their minds. I'm still in the dark, but their laughter is so candid and contagious, that I catch myself chuckling along.

Then an idea strikes me. What if these two human specimens can help me with the undead? If the ghosts are people who can't let go of something, then only the living can know how to loosen this grip. Meaning… I need them on my side. How do people befriend other people?

They say something nice about them, ask silly questions about their day, and offer a cuppa. Aidan comes to my rescue.

"Right… um," I shove my fists in my hoodie pocket, clasp the lemonade bottle and sway on my feet up to my toes and down on my heels. "How do you like my Mor? I mean er… woods."

"It's horrible." Agnieszka hugs herself, and I stop smiling. "Like in a bad dream."

"Is it?" I blink at her.

"Can you get us out of here?" Carmina asks. "We're freezing. I can't even feel my legs. The paths here are so tricky: you take one, and it brings you three more that lead nowhere."

"Yeah, sure, why not?" Mor has *no* paths, only energy lines that you grasp and follow. You can't navigate by the ghost forest, thinking like a human. "Actually, before leaving, you could pop in my hut for a cup of hot chocolate if you like." I shrug to shake off the heavy feeling of a monster luring the innocent travellers into its den. This does sound a bit like a trap, so I add a little chuckle, and it now goes like, "Welcome to the house made of bread, cake, and sugar, girls, I promise not to eat ya, he-he." How do people sound nice and civil? I can only sound *diplomatic*, and everyone knows it means lying bloody well.

"Really?" Carmina beams like I wasn't that suspicious creep in the forest with a black cat, inviting them into a barn with no windows or doors. For a moment, I wonder if she was a cunning witcher in her previous life.

Agnieszka pipes in, "Ah! I'd *die* for a hot chocolate right now."
And I think, *you better not say this aloud.* Not here anyway.

9

AGNIESZKA

12 March 2022, Day 17

Dreamed about dogs that wailed like air-raid sirens, chasing Daddy riding a black horse. I yelled through my sleep "Daddy, no-o-o!" and woke up, moaning "o-o-o," with a jerk and thumping heart at the sound of the explosion. It was just Pan Burana, chopping wood in the backyard. Silly me. War is far away. But is it? I pondered about our houses not being designed to withstand the rocket attacks. I should tell future architects to build underground huts. From now on, I will never keep any jugs on open shelves.

Still get flooded by messages from all over the cosmos, even got one from Bangladesh! (Is this a country or a magic spell? *Expecto Patronum* Bangladesh! Wooo!) Russian Zombies write me too, mostly donkey poo, even though I've never crossed their way in their stinking Stupidburg. A boy from North Italy with a cute kitty as his avatar pic sends me funny cat GIFs signed *Stand Strong, Ukraine*, and I cry a little every time. We don't talk much because I don't speak the pizza language, and he speaks mine like half his brain is missing.

Besides, I don't really know what to say. Sometimes, my head is buzzing with so much going on around me it's like I stuck it into a beehive. Sometimes, I feel frozen and would rather lie in a crystal casket for a hundred years, waiting for this war to roll off my stage (I don't even care about the first kiss; I'd sell it for the victory).

It's really so very sad. People find the guts to send me, a stranger, their good wishes and tell stories about their grannies escaping wars just like this, and all I have to write back through Google Translate is "I'm scared."

It's not the kind of fear I felt before the exams, or when Mommy caught me using her lipstick, or when I heard a stray dog following me in the empty street. It's big, so big, like the evil queen's apple piece that's stuck in my throat and doesn't let me breathe. A fear that springs inside with every BOOM behind the windows. Fear of leaving home even for a second, but then the food runs out or the bin starts to stink, and we have to. We go outside and fear stumbling upon a body or seeing a dog carrying something in its mouth, shaped like a human limb.

Fear of your neighbour going to buy bread and never returning because Russians blasted the shop to pieces. Fear of not getting a text back from your pals and sitting all day thinking about them dying an awful death. And it's not just a figment of my imagination. It's real, always around. It wakes up before I do and pinches at my sides, sneering, "Are you asleep? How can you sleep? Don't sleep! It's a war!"

I'm not that scared *here*, though. Just bored. But when we don't get the call from Daddy, I go jelloid and think Russians locked him in the cellar and beat him for helping Ukrainians. Daddy is a quiet and sensible person who talks about quiet and sensible things in a quiet and sensible voice. He's not a fighter, he's a DOCTOR. He should be here, with us.

I thought distance mattered. But this war is never *there*, it's everywhere I go, in everything I do. Entombed in Carmina's room, like in that Disney cartoon, *Tangled*. Except I could go out if I wanted.

But I don't want to move a finger until this nightmare *mierda* ends.

But it does not, and Carma said we should entertain ourselves and exercise if we don't want to go bonkers. So today we went to "open new horizons." Carma assured me she knew the town like the back of her hand. But it turned out she'd no idea how her hands looked because we went into some park and stumbled onto a rainforest! Wandered there for ages before spotting a wooden box with a roof and a girl who lived there ALL ALONE.

"No shit!" Carmina said because, really, she seemed no older than we are. Tall, fit, sturdy, with pixie black hair gleaming like raven's feathers, and big sparkling cherries of eyes. Her skin was so pale, I almost suspected it glistened under the sun's rays like Edward Cullen's.

But anyway, she was a teen!

"Okay, I lie, I live here with my granny," she added in her low, boyish voice that didn't even sound like joking. "Baba Yaga Bony Leg, heard of her?" Very funny. Baba Yaga, Mother Death from the fairytales. Why not Jesus Christ and the Holy Spirit?

Her name is Mara (too folklore! Maybe she's Masha or something? Like my mom). She's got a foot-hoppingly cute and hands-clappingly cuddly little bun of a purr-purr meow *kawaii* kitty, and her house is an artwork of technological genius. It opens to her voice, I mean windows, doors, fireplace, everything! It even has legs like a chicken's from incredibly real silicone-like material.

I wonder if it walks. Because if it does, she could pack her house instead of packing bags. Clever, eh? If I lived in the woods like Mor, I'd buy a smart house too. Because no ordinary locks can protect us from Ruzi raids, like those who looted our Cosmopolitan Liza's posh dacha and painted it all black, including, probably, her brainless Chihuahuas.

Inside, Mara's Huttuh Bohattah (it has a name!) reminded me of the cosy pics of old cottages in Provence style I collect on Tumblr. All lace curtains, knitted carpets, shabby chic furniture, and a brick furnace. The cushions were absolutely majestic: someone put their soul into embroidering poppies, mandalas, and sunflowers. I passed my compliments to Mara's gran, and she laughed, almost spilling the cocoa she was making. It seemed the hut laughed along; the floor trembled, and the fire flared in the chimney.

"What is that?" Carmina jumped to her feet. "Are we under attack?"

"What? No. Huttuh just says thank you. It's all her doing, the cushions, the carpets, the violets in the pots. She's a caring hostess." Mara patted the furnace lovingly, and it purred back like a big grumpy cat. "Kicks me sometimes for not doing the proper cleaning. She hates dirt and disorder."

"Who built such a strange house?" I parked my bum in a seat in case it started shaking again.

"Nobody built Huttuh. She was born this way and learned to do stuff as we all do. Would you like pancakes to go with your chocolate?" She actually said that.

"You can make pancakes?" Carmina widened her eyes at the sight of her mixing flour and milk.

Mara only shrugged. "Why not?"

"My mother can only fry eggs," I said and took Aidan on my lap. "When the war broke, only rice and pasta were left in the shops. And Mommy eats none of that because it makes her fat."

"Why did this war break out?" Mara asked and then asked one trillion questions more like she was born yesterday. We discussed war, the army, and presidents like their lives depended on us.

It was actually nice talking like super grown-ups in serious, big voices with a cup of cocoa in hand and a frisky cat on my lap, biting at my pancake. We remembered Europeans calling us BRAVE for just being, well, us: simple old women who cry over their kids, wrapped in bloodied sheets, then go baking bread for soldiers in the ruined furnaces of their homes. Or warriors sitting in the cold ditches for days, raided by a tsunami of zombies. They get out with just one gun and a few bullets and BANG BANG BANG them all off. Russians thought since we had no weapons, we were easy prey, but they probably never saw *Home Alone*.

There are like forty million little Culkins at home.

I thought it only happened in comics and films; I thought legends died with Hercules and Vikings. We were no heroes until someone banged us on the head. As far back as I remember, my country was just a stinking, boring bog squeezed between posh Europe and *satanoid* Russia. And then some hard-to-remember paragraph in future history books flashed in front of my eyes. A brand-new Ukraine rises from rage and ashes. My people turn into heroes, and I'm so proud of them…

Mara showed us the shortest way back home and said the only way to get to her house was to *intend* to get to her house, but since we found it once, we could easily find it again. We should only follow the queer trees. Yes, she did say *queer trees,* lol. No, don't laugh, that's wacky, but all in a good way. I like her, even if she looks like a guy and makes me feel hollow inside when our eyes meet. But you can't be too evil when your cat is such a cutie!

We promised to come again and asked for her Instagram handle. She looked at us like we were complete loons and said she had nothing to post there.

"Can we text you then?" Carmina took her phone from the jacket.

Mara raised an eyebrow at it. "About what?"

"Just... stuff?" Carmina shook her head. "Ask you if we could hang out somewhere."

"Oh, don't worry, I'll find you when it's time to *hang out.*"

Then she ripped Aidan off my coat like a piece of sellotape, because he was obviously going to stay with me till victory, and waved at us to go because the sun was about to set, and I assumed her granny was mad at her wandering in the woods in the dark.

Ahhh, Aidan is such a marvel! (NOT like Tofu the Wild.)

We walked home in silence. Carmina kicked pebbles on the road, and I brushed black fur off my coat. The skies were beautiful, vast, deep and pinkish. The crescent hung there like a curved silver dagger and gained its glow. It was hard to remember about the war.

"Don't you think Mara is... weird?" Carmina asked with her hands in her jeans' pockets.

My thoughts exactly. "Like she's the witch from a fairy tale?"

"Her house has legs!" she exclaimed.

We pondered it, watching the ragged clouds drifting lazily across the skies, then giggled.

"Nah."

"Nah!"

·

13 March 2022, Day 18

Scots made a blue-and-yellow tartan and called it UKRAINE FOR-EVER. Actual real tartan, and all about us! I feel so very springy. I think I might explode, and everyone in Booguy will finally dig bomb shelters. I mean, Scots did it just *because*, and now people walk all about the planet, swinging Ukraine Forever (NOT Russia-something) on their hips. Extraordinarily fantastic. If I ever go to Scotland, I'll ask Mommy to buy me a kilt from that, with that lovely furry purse in front. And when anyone asks me what clan it is, I'll proudly declare: Ukrainian!

Carmina said kilt bags were only for boys. She can be spectacularly dumb at times. Tiny purses are all the rage now. Every girl should have one if she cares about style, fashion and stuff.

Okay, I Googled it. It's a purse for boys. Scots are weird.

Some Russian wrote to me on Instagram chat, saying he wanted me to die a slow and painful death because of my pic of sunflowers, a symbol of Ukraine. Saint Cossack's breath, I don't even know this guy! What is the matter with these people? (Apart from the obvious.) Felt like talking to a stinky sock who wanted to bite my foot. Yuk!

More letters from strangers praying for me. Never thought that being a celebrity could be this fabulously irritating. I don't write back because writing from this pit, with selfies in Mommy's old sweater, is just killing me. Besides, war is boring. I'm so tired of fear and suspense, daily roll calls, endless news about something blasted somewhere, and orcs taking full control of yet another village. Why don't we talk about something, like, fun? Then some guy from Australia wrote "Hi, I'm Mark. I love sport" and sent me a photo of his bulldog. I wanted to shoot him.

DON'T YOU BLOODY KNOW I AM AT WAR HERE!!!

I think I'm going mad. My nerves are so wrecked. I'll probably die on a therapist's couch, recalling all the worries I worried about when I was fourteen. I roll in bed like a sausage on a grill, and not even because of bombs. It's inside my head, not out there. I can't stop thinking about that ugly dog pic, the *gopnik* goose lurking somewhere in the house, ~~my~~ Ben probably dating someone else, Putin dreaming of drowning my country in blood, and a hut (a hut!) that embroiders cushions better than I do.

I share a bed with Carmina, which is fine; she's so thin, I can easily press her to the wall like a sheet of paper. But goodness me, she kicks like a wild horse when I start shifting my body.

"Stop wiggling!" she cried.

"I can't. It's… an existential crisis," I huffed in an adult voice like I knew what I was talking about. Truth be told, I'll be the last one to know what I'm talking about every time I talk about anything serious. "I'm having a panic attack. It's war, for Cossack's sake: to worry is to care. How can *you* sleep?"

"Look"—Carmina sat up—"remember Buddha. He cared like hell but never worried. Relax."

"I can't relax my head. It will talk and talk and talk even if I play dead," I complained.

"Of course, you can. It just needs to talk about something relaxing." Carmina reached for her phone and put on one of those yoga songs with sea and dolphins talking their cosmic language. It was mostly waves rustling, then squeak, squeak, squeak—and rustling again. Squeak! Squeak! Carmina started snoring softly into the pillow in a second, traitor. SQUEAK! SQUEAK! HE-HE-HE-HE-HE. Why do they say dolphins are clever? They talk like rusty old doors. Magnificently annoying. I would have shut up that brain panacea but was too depressed to move my hand.

Finally, I decided to watch psychos instead, predicting our victory in a week… every other week, so we wouldn't send them to hell if they gave this war, say, a fortnight. Because nobody wants it to last. Molfarka Marichka, however, doesn't give a damn about what we want. Right away, she blurted it'd take four years at least, and also, Putin is already dead. Yes. Rubber-faced Putins we see on TV are his numerous doubles. They are baked like fake van Goghs to turn him immortal.

My God. This is beyond bonkerdom.

Enough magic talk! I must grow up now and focus on real things. I better watch something educational and soothe my nerves with brain nutrition. So, I ate up my emergency snack and searched You-Tube for some war experts' opinions.

Two a.m. Right. Now I feel not just worried but also fat and stupid. I hardly understand anything that's said about politics and battle tactics. But they keep droning in their sleepy voices on and on, boo-boo-boo and boo-boo-boo. I think I'm passing out.

•

14 March 2022, Day 19

Brave women from Bilozerka walked unarmed towards the crowd of Russian cannibals and demanded they put their guns down and fight them hand-to-hand. *Women. Challenged. Soldiers.*

MAGNIFICO!

Elon Musk, the Mars man, challenged Putin to fight him instead of destroying our churches and hospitals, and fake Putin pretended like he's got no Twitter or Internet, or any black belt. He's just afraid his fake face will fall off from shame before he even puts his boxers on. Chicken.

But if they did fight till death, any result would suit me. Go to Mars, Musk, you're drunk!

Ben doesn't write. Nobody desires me but Shrimp, whose sole life purpose is to make me scream. I saw his incredibly long shadow on the grass today, and it looked like a maniac with an axe. So now I try to stay home as little as possible.

Carma and I went to Mor and tried to find Huttuh, but the paths kept taking us back to town no matter how deep into the woods we dived. So we decided to mark the trees with my felt tip pen and then head in the opposite direction. Three minutes later ALL the trees around had little pink hearts on the bark, even if we only made a few marks! That was frankly creepy. We darted back to the highway like bullets, and I swear I heard someone laughing at our backs!

In a frenzy, I thought I saw Lisovyk, the spirit of the woods, as a dark figure with deer antlers on his head rising from the ground. Honestly, in my panic, I could take even a stump for a monster! And it *could* be a stump if it didn't hop at us like a locust, and we screamed at the top of our lungs, stumbling backwards and hitting the bushes behind.

I wrapped my arms around my head, pressing my eyes tightly shut, and prepared to *mierda* die when Carmina stopped her scream abruptly and said, "Mara?"

"What did I tell you about this place? The living can't wander here without a damn good reason," Mara's levelled voice replied. Slowly, I lowered my arms and saw her in front of us.

"Actually…" Carmina swallowed. "We were looking for you. And it would have been much less dramatic if you just gave us your number."

Mara scratched her temple. "Okay. Er… Thirteen." The look on our faces made her shrug her shoulders. "What? I like thirteen. Also, zero and eight. They are magic."

I couldn't help giggling, though it rather felt like uncontrollable lung convulsions. I was still at odds with mastering my breathing. "Your phone number, silly!"

She sighed as Daddy used to sigh at my twentieth-or-so plead to buy me another doll for my collection, stuffed her fingers into the pocket of her skinnies, and pulled out an iPhone that couldn't possibly fit into there and not stick out like a third leg. "Seriously, I don't get all the fuss around these phones. But fine, let's chat and... do other stuff on the little screens."

We exchanged numbers, and she led us out of Mor to our great relief. Instead, she promised to show us the lake and, if we're lucky, the flying fish.

"We've only been here for a few days and got lost twice in these trees, basically, in a place as small as my head," Carmina complained as we walked along the shore on the town's outskirts, crunching tiny pebbles under our boots and breathing fir trees, moisture, and dung.

"You could get lost even standing still if you don't respect Lisovyk's domain," Mara replied. "Drawing on the trees, seriously? He hates that."

I snorted. "Lisovyks are fairytales, they don't exist. In pre-Internet times, people invented them to keep children away from the forests." To be honest, at the moment, I didn't believe myself saying that because that eerie laughter in the woods still rang in my ears.

Mara tilted her head to me. "Why would they lie to their children?"

"Because"—I lifted my chin—"they did it to scare them, to..." I stopped, looking for reasons.

Mara shrugged. "They might just as well tell them the scary truth."

"Fair point." Carma joined our conversation. "Truth is scary. Like Russians. Nobody knew the truth about them before they revealed their true face in this war. Did you know that they brought mobile crematoriums to our occupied territories to burn all the evidence of their crimes? There are also special forces trained to torture the captives, the butchers, just like in the Nazi times. And the gang rapes are..."

"Can we please not talk about it?" I snapped with a shocking flip of my stomach.

"Yeah, okay, sorry. But know that not talking about it doesn't make it untrue. Ah, just look at this view! Majestic…"

We came down to the lake: a massive gleaming mirror ran into a soft line of mist that blurred the horizon. The mountains, huddling behind, reminded me of the backs of sleeping giants, covered with furry blankets of pine forests. Mara hopped on top of a boulder, half drowned in the water, crouched, and squinted at the silver surface in the distance. "If you sit still, you can catch the flying fish pivoting in the air," she said.

Carmina joined her and sat there, staring at the water. I was too afraid to wet my boots, so I found a log of a dead tree, lying there like a broken monster's arm, and parked on it, stretching my aching legs and enjoying the soft sun on my cheeks. The wind in the trees swished and whiffled, making the naked branches chatter. The grey ripple on the lake came and went, and the sloshing at the rocks on the shore sounded almost like a lullaby.

I thought about what Mara said about fairytales and must have let my mind drift too far because one little wave on the horizon suddenly leaped into the air and dived underwater like a tiny dolphin. I blinked and leaned forward, staring. And the next wave did it again!

"There! I see it!" Carmina's yell snapped me out of my daze. "Blimey, they have wings!"

"Agnieszka, come look at this," Mara beckoned me with her hand. I must have looked like a cat at the sound of a drill, because she added, "Relax, it's not scary."

I skipped towards the rocks at the surf and clambered on top of the flattest one. Mara and Carma sat crouched on the boulder next to mine and peeped into the water.

"Just don't startle her," Mara warned me.

"Who?" I asked, and Carmina muttered, "Jeez, is this for real?"

When I looked into the water, my heart punched me in the ribs. A pair of big blue eyes on a pale face stared back at me from the dark depths. A tiny nose with holes and lips stretched in a perplexed down bow. A crown of fins and wing-like hands on a little body ended with a skirt-tail floating in the water. It was a fish but… with a human face!

I jerked back, but Mara held me by the hand. "It's okay, she doesn't bite. She only wants to tell us something. They come up from the deep waters just before massive disasters, to warn people about coming danger…"

"Like wars with Russia?" Carmina whispered.

"No. As far as I know, natural disasters, earthquakes, fires, and floods. I keep seeing them often nowadays. Difficult times are coming." Mara lowered her hand into the water. The strange fish blinked, tucked her nose into Mara's fingers, and turned her gleaming back at us, curving her spine like a serpent. She was almost white, and her creepy skin bore no scales. Then she waved her tail at us, not at all fishlike, as people do, spread her wings and whisked to the bottom.

We gazed at the ripple until my ankles hurt. And we retreated to the shore.

"I've never seen a fish like that," Carmina declared, dropping her bum on a tree log beside us. "What did she warn us about? We're at war already! Will there be earthquakes too?"

"Hmm. Maybe not exactly here, not exactly now," Mara suggested, leaning back on her hands and focusing on the horizon. "But more people will die soon."

I sighed and looked at the skies, shielding my eyes with a palm. The sun rolled out of the ruffled clouds, and the mood changed. Now the scenery seemed bright and cosy, filled with hope, promising something good, not more disasters and deaths. "I don't want to die,"

I blurted before I knew it. "I have so much to enjoy in life. I think if I die now, I won't be able to rest in peace."

What was I talking about? God. Alarmingly, Mara seemed to think I made sense. She leaned towards me with the look of a scholar discovering a new type of mushroom, two dead pools of drilling black eyes. "And what do you enjoy in life?" she asked firmly.

Honestly, under that stare, I wanted to sound like a paragon of maturity, a shining example of expertise, but I caught myself talking about my dolls. About their personalities, their hobbies, and their quirks, what fashion they followed and what profession they mastered. I had cosmonauts, actresses, fairies, mermaids, gods, and crazy scientists. When I got my first camera, Carmina and I filmed an amateur TV show featuring something somehow happening in their doll world, which was never as cool as it unravelled in my head, yet we enjoyed it. We even invented a special doll language, which was just the usual one but with the bits dropped out and some vowels twisted.

I came to my senses only when Carmina burst out laughing and the sound of it washed over my face with a hot wave of shame. "Come on, Nesh, are you really still into that?"

"Well, I…" I gulped some air and curled my fingers. "I just like dolls. Is that bad?"

"No, it sounds cool. Go on," Mara said softly, and the hot balloon in my chest immediately landed. I giggled and said she was the first to call it "cool" and not "childish."

"You talk about dolls then, and I'll go stretch my tendons. Kung Fu time!" Carmina jumped to her feet and went rolling cartwheels on the sand. Then she decided it was time to learn some backflips and we held her by the sides, while she kicked her legs back like a horse on a pin.

And when she made her first (not anything close to perfect)

backflip, she screamed and ran all around kicking and cartwheeling, and fell in the surf, soaking her feet.

Mara watched that with the expression of an elephant tamer, whose beasts climbed the trees and flew to the skies. "What's wrong with her?" she asked.

"Oh, nothing is wrong with Carma," I said. "It's probably the sun."

•

At night, I lay in bed for almost an eternity staring at the ceiling, unable to sleep. For the first time in weeks, the war didn't scare me as much as fish and the pink hearts on the trees I didn't paint. I must be going mad with stress. Yes, that's it. I'm slipping into fiction to protect my mind from too much drama I hate to be a part of.

Still, Mara seems nice, I feel… safe around her like she is a GPS and Carmina and I are the dots on the map. And she loved my doll stories. I wonder if she's ever played *The Sims?*

I sigh and open YouTube on my phone with war experts talking about Cossacks' drive and urbicide. Whatever it is. I don't care. I don't get a single thing they are talking about, but they say normal, solid stuff about how we'll definitely win this war, and I sleep happily.

10

CARMINA

NEW HERO

From: Carmina Burana   14 March 2022, 22:51
To: Severin Saint   Booguy

Pa,

Everybody needs a hero, and I don't mean some mutant from comics. But someone to look up to, someone who'd remind us what people can actually achieve if they work hard on their real superpowers. For Agnieszka, it's Marilyn Monroe, the epitome of style and beauty, keeping her spells decades after her death. For me, it's you, soldiers, and President Zelenskyy, people who defied death and, in cold blood and stone face, stood to defend millions against a zombie onslaught. But I guess now I must rethink that after I've met a fish with a human face who left her cosy cold abyss to come and tell this bunch of idiots called people to hold on and get ready for Doomsday.

A fish with a human face, Dad!

I mean, we actually eat her kind, find them dumbos, and don't even speak Fish-ish. And she still came to warn us. She's my hero now! And all fish are my friends.

Speaking of which, I have a new friend with a weird name (Mara) and a weird home (with legs!) and weird everything. She lives in the woods in one of those smart houses that respond to your clap or voice. And she keeps skulls on the shelves. They are plastic, of course, but still. Who keeps a string of plastic skulls in a lonely hut in the woods? Only a true goth girl from the Addams Family. And I thought they'd all died out along with bikers, disco, and emo kids.

Anyway, Mara is cool. She knows how to survive in the wild with a pancake and cocoa for breakfast but has no idea what to do with a smartphone. I installed Telegram and Discord for her and showed her how to text and call people. And she said, "If you try to teach me Facebook too, I'll cut your shadow off your feet." How cool and wicked is that, eh? I must write that down and the next time someone gets on my nerves I'll know how to freak them out, haha.

Today, we went dilly-dallying near the lake, and I wetted my feet doing cartwheels. But the weather was so anomalously warm and sunny that it didn't prevent me from going to the market to replenish my tangerine stock. Agnieszka needed to buy something for her embroidery kit, and Mara ambled along for company.

The market here (big as a sovereign country) is a magical place to find anything your heart desires! Zucchini and strawberries in March, books published before books were even invented, or that freakish dream you had at age five, with a huge discount. I wondered why Booguy was so reluctant to open new shops. Well, the chances of them finding anything to tempt the marketgoers are plummeting faster than Galileo's objects falling from the Pisa Tower. I so enjoyed jostling along the kaleidoscopic tents and stalls, listening to quirky accents and imagining myself a warrior-pilgrim in a sci-fi world, getting to a mosaic bazaar on the crossroads of unknown galaxies.

As always, I did the talking, Nesha only asked questions she was certain sounded Ukrainian enough, even if nobody heard her tiny squeak in that infernal ruckus anyway. And Mara followed us like a grim and bulky bodyguard scanning the crowd with her X-ray eyes, holding one hand on the laser gun trigger, and the other on her laser sword's hilt.

But then this weird thing happened.

We stopped at the fruit stall to buy some tangerines, and Agnieszka turned to Mara to ask her if she would like some apple jam to go with her pancakes. She shook her head, saying that Huttuh takes care of that, too. I exclaimed, "What, your house goes shopping?" And the salesman stared at us like we said something absolutely cringey, which it was, even if also absolutely true.

"Who are you talking to?" the young man asked with an awkward grin.

I stubbed my thumb behind my back. "To our friend, of course."

He glanced over our shoulders, and his eyes went a bit glassy. "Oh, er… I see."

"No, he doesn't see," Mara said, shaking her head. "This one doesn't, huh." She glanced at us and added, "He doesn't see me, so you better pretend I'm not here."

And I swear she was right. That man nearly hit the roof when Mara flicked her fingers at his face. He gaped around and did his best to adjust the mess that was his hair as if it caused all the mess in his head. Agnieszka thanked him for the tangerines, grabbed the packet, and pulled me away, mumbling that the poor man needed glasses if he wanted a fair trade.

"He doesn't need glasses," Mara said. "He needs to stop wandering through his life with his eyes stuck in his butt."

I giggled like a donkey. "I suppose he's just not accustomed to women looking like people, not dolls on their tiptoes." I think Neshka didn't like that, cos she gave me a tangerine so I would shut my mouth with it.

Luckily, I wasn't in my feminist mood. And on the way back to town we discussed films, or one particular one, that isn't even shot yet, but must be—the one about this war, Putin, and the feat of our people fighting for their lives, for the light in the darkest times, for freedom. Even if *some* Westerners call us cruel to hit terrorists back and would rather we sit still and wait till Big Boys *buy* us peace. They forgot that those who wait for someone to save them are slaves, which we are not. So we cry this message to the world by simply NOT giving in at any cost.

The idea sounds gripping, right? Though we mostly squabbled about who was gonna play Zelenskyy, cos Agnieszka wanted to see her stupid Timothée Chalamet as our President, as well as our Commander-in-Chief, our Prime Minister, and probably also Putin! ("Cos Tim is so talented!") And I tried to bang it in her head that he looks like none of them and, brutally honest, is just a cute Holly-wood toddler. Anyway, we squabbled, bitched, and bantered like two limping gladiators in the Roman Amphitheatre until Mara got fed up with Tim, films, and us both.

"Why are you quarrelling about something that doesn't exist yet?" she asked.

"Because!" Agnieszka spit, like it explained everything.

I rolled my eyes at Mara, lifting my hands to my hips. "Okay, who would *you* like to see as Zelenskyy in a film about this war?"

"Zelenskyy," she said, swinging her phone in her hands like it was a tangerine.

"No, I mean as the leading actor who could play him."

She shrugged. "He is an actor. He could play himself."

This sounded like a *BRILLIANT IDEA* that left us silent for about a million years to raise our brows and look wise and adult-like. Then Agnieszka got nervous which she always does when people around don't speak. I said it was cos she had bees in her head, so the

silence sounded too contrasting. And she said, "Which is hilarious coming from someone who cartwheeled into a lake."

Touche!

Then our princess offered to play her fav game. About BOYS.

"Okay, Mara," she snapped her head to her, lashing my arm with her curls. "If you had to choose between the prettiest boy in town and all the money I have…"

I growled. "Ugh, Nesha, this is so pants!"

"Shush, I'm not talking to you." She linked her arm with Mara's and looked up at her dreamily. "So, Mara, what would you take?"

Mara turned her eyes from the cloud of crows crossing the skies and focused on her smile. "And how much have you got?"

"Um…" Nesha gave me the packet and rummaged in her cat-faced purse. "Ouch, I've spent almost all of it. Only half a hryvnia… and a last year's chestnut."

"I'd take the money," Mara fired without thinking. "I love chestnuts."

I bent in two, laughing, and Agnieszka's face turned into a mask of a cartoon crazy scientist, post-explosion. "What's so funny?" she demanded. "Stop it. I'm talking about… true love. About *romance*. You know, like in the romantic films. There is nothing funny about it!"

"No, there's not," Mara agreed. "It's actually pretty sad."

"Oh. Don't you ever dream about true love? When like, you're half asleep and feel someone plant a gentle kiss on your cheek. It's heaven."

"Unless you're home alone," Mara added without a hint of a smile and let our conversation meet its merciful death. The rest of the way we walked in complete silence nobody felt awkward about. Haha. Honestly, Dad, Nesha is *that* hopeless. Are there any meds for the "true love" virus she gets from all those romantic comedies and stuff? I need an antidote!

Before sleep, I got a weird message from Mara.

Mara

> *Agnieszka's life's sense is playing with dolls. What is yours?*

Carmina Burana

> *I dunno. Big question. Mb freedom?*

Mara

> *From Russia?*

Carmina Burana

> *Yeah, but not only. It's bigger & live, like freedom in the process. Like first u r free from school, from parents telling u what 2 do & then from other ppl making u do stuff. From eating sugar cos then my belly aches & I h8 it haha. I think it's my aim in life, yeah. Freedom.*

Mara

> *Until one day you're free from your life, too.*

Did I tell you she's a true goth? I didn't ask her about *her* life's sense cos I was a bit afraid she'd say "cutting people's shadows off" lol. Miss you, Dad. Don't die there, ok?

Your free Skipper

11

MARA

The day is almost over, but I keep The Slit shut. Aidan pads along the path to the valley of the lost, and I follow him with all the working

beacons under my arm. I stick them around the meadow in a hap-hazard pattern. As their eyes catch a flickering fire, I climb one of the rocks and watch the evening skies slowly drain of colours. Aidan hops up and puts his fluffy bum next to mine.

The misty shredded butterflies that once were people flock to-gether around the burning skulls, like homeless beggars at street fires on frosty nights. They hover, wiggling and shimmering. Then, slowly, they grow their eyes, hands, and feet, even if just for a moment.

I stroke my cat and sigh.

"It will take them time to remember themselves and all that hap-pened."

Why can't they remember and go home? Aidan purrs, swishing his tail this way and that.

Agnieszka's talk about dolls pops into my mind like a message on my phone with a *ping!* and in a cloud of frozen words like in graphic novels. "Cos they have something important to finish first," I reply, very oracle-like, tuning into my cool, no-bullshit voice. "Some want revenge, some need to say goodbye or catch up on some deal or a trip interrupted by the war."

War sucks. Aidan plops to the side so that I can rub his belly.

"Yeah." I play with him, push his clawed paws, and scratch under his chin. Then he startles and stares at me with his gleaming eyes, like a human suddenly recalling a missed appointment.

Do you think the living can see them too? Like they see you and my human body?

"I don't think so." I hope not. "I've seen none of it in their mem-ories. I guess people only see us because they feel death is hunting them. They never see us under ordinary circumstances, even when they are depressed and want to kill themselves. Death is always something surreal or too vague, or too horrible to look at."

But death always sticks around, I've seen it. Aidan flops on his side and shakes his head. *I mean, we'll all die one day. It's just obvious that it's here, following us from the day we're born.*

"Yes. But it frightens people so much that they turn a blind eye to it. Literally. They stop seeing it, they forget it even exists till something drastic shakes them up. This is the saddest part actually. This is what I hate most about the living. They forget. And then, when reality thrusts back into their minds, they just…" I wave at the valley of the lost souls. "Go like this."

Aidan gazes at the ghosts in the gathering twilight and turns back to me. *Carmina and Agnieszka will remember. They are our friends now, right?*

"Pfff!" I jump off the rock. "The human mind is a tricky thing, kitty. It erases any memory and fits in any silly lie just to keep them from pain. Or anything as weird as us."

Nah, they seem fine. Aidan yawns.

I bite at my lower lip and say nothing. Now they are fine, I think, all agog and insightful, but give them just a month of peace, then say "Guess what, a mad horse has just slit my throat and my head fell off. Have you seen it anywhere?" and they'll be like "Oh God, eggs cost as much as a downed helicopter!" That's why wars happen. People forget all the important stuff. Carmina and Agnieszka will forget us, like an odd dream. Because it's hard to *always* remember. Because that's what people are—forgetful, lazy cowards who barely know what they even live for.

I push my fists into the pockets of my hoodie and turn my back to Aidan. The dim outlines of the trees against the washed-off inky skies are my sole focus. They stand like a fence between me and my inner bitterness. I don't want Aidan to know it. He might think I feel for the funny girls from Zapahorb, which I do, and I hate it. Because when they stop seeing me, I'll be all alone again.

12

AGNIESZKA

15 March 2022, Day 20

Every night, while brushing my teeth, I look at the transparent one-litre bottle of liquid soap that we bought on the day of our arrival here. It's my secret clock, a soap calendar that shows how long I've been away from home. Maybe the war will be over by the time we finish it?

It feels like it's over when I don't think about it. This place is so quiet. But I remind myself of the horrors back there when embroidering my magic battle *vyshyvanka*. I decided to send it to Daddy, once I finish it, to protect him from the Russian zombies. He'll need a clean shirt anyway, so why not a magic one? *Vyshyvankas* are like Scottish kilts. They carry the power of our ancestors through centuries. It doesn't matter if Daddy has Polish roots. Unlike the Nazis, Cossacks accept anyone who accepts the Cossacks' way. It's not in the blood, it's in the spirit.

Our history teacher once said that "Cossacks" translates to "free people." There!

Today, it was so unexpectedly warm outside, I opened the windows and breathed spring. It smelled not at all like in dusty Zapahorb, but strong, fresh, and fragrant. Of damp soil, raindrops, and smoke. The sun was shining, birds tweeting, dogs barking, ducks quacking, chickens um… chickening? I must ask Mara why she doesn't keep poultry. There's plenty of space in the wood.

Shrimp was out pinching baby grass in the clots of snow. Pan Burana messed about in his sort-of-a-barn. I could see his back with a wet smear down his neck, pushing on and off gracefully like he was rowing a boat, not planing planks. He's a "just do it" kind of man. When he doesn't fly the broomstick to some coven with his wife, he builds and fixes things, like people did when you couldn't order anything online, some centuries ago or whenever he was born, I don't know.

My daddy once tried to hang a picture in our living room, whacked his hand instead, and called the ambulance. Then for days, he walked around with a bandage, and everyone nodded at that and said my dad was a super dad, so manly and handy. Mommy laughed like crazy. Because there is a hole in our wall, and the picture is still collecting dust in the closet.

I spotted Tofu crawling along the garden path in a hunting lion crouch, his belly wobbling like an old woman's tit. He's so completely bonkers when in his *Call of the Wild* mood. Whenever I take him out somewhere, he treats all that moves like walking tuna sandwiches. Now, he's probably after goose pâté, so I'd better waggle a sausage at him and thus prevent another war in my country.

•

What is the matter with Shrimp? How in the name of Mighty Cossack am I supposed to deal with my wretched nervous system if this bird is after my bum every time I peek my nose out? I *saved* him from Tofu of the Wild, and he danced his menacing tai chi and gah-gah-gah, gah-gah-gah-ed instead of being grateful. If Pan Burana hadn't emerged from his shed to shoo him off, I'd probably be the next war casualty on the news.

"He's just fooling around," the old man said. "It seems he rates you."

I suppose he meant *he hates you* in the wacky local dialect. Trying to look all cool and indifferent (in my case, blushed and shaking), I stated that I was a lady, and ladies despise "fooling around" attention from boorish country bumpkins. Pan Burana gazed at me like I was a talking duck. Why do villagers always give me this annoying I-survive-the-apocalypse-and-you-die-from-a-sneeze look? It's rude.

Then he chuckled. "Well, if you want to ward him off, just say the magic words."

This got my full attention. "Magic words?" I peeped. "Like Elven? Or Latin?"

"I don't think he speaks Elven." Pan Burana unstuck his axe from the stump and started on his way back to the shed. I followed him, dying to know the spell words. "Walk towards him like you're gonna chop him up in a stew and chant *'fork and knife, fork and knife.'*" His voice came muffled from inside the shed. "The magic is in your tone: it must be intimidating, and so must your eyes."

I stood on the threshold of his dark and scary workshop, full of dark and scary shelves with bulky extraterrestrial-looking objects. I was too wary to come in and see corpses hidden around.

"Does it work?"

"Of course. Shrimp is smart. He understands all that people say." He noticed me peeking around his shed. "Come and look at what I'm working on."

"No!" I cried and darted off, sending dirt flying from my heels.

•

16 March 2022, Day 21

Tried a fork-knife spell on Shrimp when he attacked me on my morning promenade to the church with Mommy (there is nowhere else to go in the drizzling rain). He ran after me, swinging his butt left and right, hissing and stretching his head low, really scary. But I thought, I've had enough of being a sissy-ninny, I'm a princess Cossack! So I turned and walked straight at him, looking straight into his beady eyes, and yelled, *"Fork and knife, fork and knife, fork and knife!"* He quacked, turned, and fled. Haha! Gotcha!

I think Mommy cried in the church. She's pagan to the tips of her curls, was never baptized, but she cried, and I know it because her so-called waterproof mascara ran.

Was it because of Daddy? We never talk about him. She would never admit she cares even one little flying piggy about him, but I'm not stupid. Why does she think I'm all stupid and won't like understand a thing? What is the point in having kids if you are going to treat them like idiots all their lives? You might just as well get a brainless pup and get on with that.

I miss Daddy, too. I don't miss a single doll I left behind, just him being around and saying really nothing, just watching silly blockbusters together, munching salted sunflower seeds and laughing. I miss him calling me *poppet*. He always treats me like a princess, like I am special. I don't feel special here.

Folks here are really into prayers and all that, which is weird, considering how much they are into spirits, tarot, and beans-telling (and human-looking fish in the lake). Although the local priest, bald and short like a walking egg, wasn't into prayers today but into my magnetic mom. He goggled at her as if the Virgin Mary herself landed in his shabby church. And none would blame him for that, even the Almighty. But *I* will, because Daddy. And anyway, it's a sin, is it not?

So, this Humpty Dumpty smiled oilily at Mommy like a poo on

a stick and said we should give our grief to God (he didn't clarify which one, so I imagined Perun or Odin). Then he said that God will take care of it all because he is our father. I think he had no biology at school. How can one be a father to me, him, and my mommy and NOT be a perv? Besides, I already have a father and he IS taking care of us, by saving lives and keeping cannibals at bay.

Well, okay, suppose I play along, I thought and fell to my knees (which was painful, NOT at all romantic like in the Bible pics). I prayed like "Dear God, please end this war and bring Daddy to us. I promise never to eat energy bars at night, call Liza a *kurwa*, and wish Russians to rot in our soil… Okay, maybe just those who want my land so badly that it would be fair to lay them into it. Amen. Oh yes, one more thing: send me a boyfriend who'd be so much groovier than *kurwa* Liza's Tomas from France she's so proud of, so I could finally say 'Ha!' to her smug ~~snout~~ face. And please please please, let it be magic. At least once in my life. Amen and out."

Shrimp met me on the way back and I cried fork-and-knife at him again and made Mommy laugh because he leapt really comically and clambered gah-gah-ing into the house.

Carmina was doing her Shaolin kung fu in the backyard. She really does think she moves like the *sifus* in Korean fantasy TV shows. Like, you know, those girlish boys (or boyish girls?) in flourishing, flattering kimonos who turn into snakes and dragons and never ruin their perfect waterfall-like hair. But in fact, it's a silly insect prance. She's a giant mosquito hopping around the lawn, spooking the chickens and driving the neighbours' dogs insane.

Of course, I didn't tell her that (she's my best friend, after all). I just said, "Hello, oh mad one, did the circus leave and drop you on the road?"

Don't know why she went all miffy and Carminish and started chiding me like she was on a sacred warrior way, and I was so *estupido* that I couldn't take a pancake from a pan and cake (no idea what she meant but some deep survival instinct told me that it meant something phenomenal). To prove that, she made her super legendary kick in the air and whacked into the pillar supporting the shed roof. Since it was after two days of rain, the gutter came loose and showered her head with a grand splash. I thought I'd die laughing.

Then Carmina kicked again at the opposite pillar, and the water plopped from the other side of the gutter, right on my felt hat. She giggled as if someone bashed her on the head the day she was born (and incidentally, they just might have).

Oh, great balls of Saint *Mierda.* I want to go home.

But instead, we went to do our studies on Carma's laptop.

We were having a ~~rap~~ biology class with Pani Amoeba when something utterly *estoundioso* occurred. I've no idea how our bedroom door happened *magically* to be open, *but it was,* and Shrimp flew through it like a rampant locomotive, clattering along with something in his beak. He rushed straight at me and whacked it onto my lap. It was a fork! In a moment, he was back, adding a knife to it, then another fork, and another knife… There was a full cutlery set on my skirt by the time I came to my senses.

Carmina fell off her bed, head over heels, neighing. But the worst thing still: the camera was on. Our classmates, all of them, even Liza and the teacher, were glued to their screens, baffled. They said, "Is that a GOOSE out there?"

My. God. How embarrassing. How utterly *embarrassanomdo!*

What in the Saint Bandera Smoothie is going on?

I'm going to eat that goose.

13

CARMINA

IT'S NOT THAT SIMPLE

From: Carmina Burana   16 March 2022, 23:10

To: Severin Saint   Booguy

Dad,

Sit down if you're standing. Lie down if you're sitting cos guess what… I know geography!

If I had a test right now, I'd give Pan Globa a heart attack with my flying results. I checked where Eritrea and all the little pimps who support Putin are, to know my enemies' faces and all that. The map of Ukraine is always in front of my eyes, on the wall in my bedroom where I press pushpins to follow the movements of our army. I know where we have our coal and gas and other super rare trillions of dollars' worth mineral resource deposits, and the biggest nuclear stations: right where Ruzis are now getting it in the neck.

This isn't a war about people. Moscow doesn't give a dead mouse's last shit about the people they kill daily, even their own. Putin is a tyrant. He wants to rule the world—but all he'll get is his stinky ass chained to a seat in the Nuremberg trials. He'll only walk on our land when none of us breathes. And we are a legion. All their bombs aren't enough for our rage.

We had another row with Liza, in the politics class session, about Mahatma Gandhi (who is this?). He said, "I am prepared to die, but there is no cause for which I am prepared to kill." Apparently, he never talked to Ruzis.

Liza says she can persuade zombies to wake up, smell the coffee, and see FASCIST written across their faces in red, screaming letters. Well, I accepted the challenge and texted one Russian boy I met playing *The Elder Scrolls* online. It's a so damned ancient game; only forty-something weirdos play it now, so I assume that boy is not a boy anymore. Anyway, he seemed fine, and when I asked him about this war, he was so very sorry and so on. But then, Pa, attention! I

asked him "Whose is Krym?" and he took ages to type "It's not that simple."

Not that simple, my ass!

God, I hate Russians. And if Pan Mahatma is going to defend killers, I especially hate him. Gran keeps saying that burning with rage harms me more than it helps Ukraine. I should stay human, she says, or else I'll become just like *them*. Ughhh! I can't do anything about it, Pa. Imagine a choking to death allergic man, who is taken to a hospital and asked, "How did you like the peanut cake?" That would be me and Russian nuts.

Anyway, why do I have to feel sorry for those who don't feel sorry for anything or anyone? Even our main church guy said that killing to defend oneself is not a sin. So I hope I'll kill a bunch of them to defend my people and my land. We have such a beautiful land, with a helluva lot of brave people, and every other woman is a witch.

I could be a witch, too. Why not? Gran is a seventh-generation *molfarka*, and Ma does come from Planet Crazy. So there, I decided if I can't fire a gun and I wouldn't risk my life on the front line (like you said), maybe I'll join the magic troops. I gave it a good adult-like thought (like you asked), and now I regard the matter with utmost seriousness, like an absolute and total grown-up. No more fantasies about dying a hero in anime battles. I will not turn into lizards and bombs; I will hypnotize Ruzis!

Okay, this still sounds crazy, but in fact, it's a five-hundred-percent scientific phenomenon. I read all about it in one scientific newspaper. All I need is to learn the whales' language. They use the airwaves we can't hear. However, our minds react to it even against our will! Imagine me yelling through the speaker "U-u-u-uh-o-o-oh, u-u-uh-a-a-a-ah" and all enemy tanks hit the offroad trees. Zombies slug out of there, stoned and wobbly, calling for their mommies and wanting to go home. We won't waste ammunition, just scoop them up, tie them together into sheaves, and throw them back to their beloved Russia. Perfection, eh?

So, can I go to the army? Can I go, Pa? Please, take me to the front. I'm SOOO BORED here. I'm wasting my sleeping superpowers on pulling Nesha's cat off the local dogs (he eats dogs), chopping veggies for Gran's brews, and solving stupid trigonometry equations that will so help me in my life (not).

Oh, by the way, do you know that Svitlan is coming home? He has another *BRILLIANT IDEA* to save Ukraine. Grandpa and Grandma are volunteering at Chornoguy train station, helping refugees who arrive there daily, squashed in trains like tunas at a tin can party. They say they are always short of hands, plus the local animal shelter is in dire need of kind souls. Svitlan's a trainee vet; it's the same as being an animal angel. Only our pagan Ma is not that religious. She went even more dragon than she normally is, called three hundred friends to blame your stubborn genes, then smoked two fags in a row and ordered a max-degree protection vest and a mega helmet. For a vet. In this countryside appendix. But whatever, my brother is a hero.

More good news! No more Dostoyevsky's brain sick about Russians' deep and enigmatic (not) souls or Tolstoy's endless rigmarole about brave and honest (not) Russian soldiers. Schools are going to burn all Russian classics out of the curricula. Holy cow, we raise a revolution against it every year. But a WAR had to start before the teachers finally stopped banging it in our brains.

In a bookshop today: not one single little Russian tome, yay! Also, all the world's history books expired, and all the motivational literature sounds pathetic. I read the title of "How Not to Die Among Toxic People" as "How Not to Die" and remember the day when I went to the hospital with Ma to donate blood. The mortuary was just across the road, and there were so many dead people in white sacks that they lay right on the asphalt in uneven rows. It smelled awful, but not of death. Of Russia.

There's really nothing to do in this crowded place. We mostly hang around the woods with Mara, but today we raided the kids' playground, loitering on the swings, feeling happy cos it's so rare to have a swing all to yourself.

We'd just shared two bananas between the three of us when some super groovy-like lad in a leather-like jacket walked by, saw us chomping on bananas, and said my hair looked cute. Meh. (Probably cos his own was shaved off on one side like there was some kind of an accident.) Then he showered all could-I-add-you-on-Facebook shit-talk at me and smiled like he gave me a million dollars. I wanted to bang him on his half-shaved head, but not cos he humiliated me as a woman with his poxy "cute," but cos he said it in bloody Russian. Yet I can't just bang men on the heads, can I? Not in front of Princess, anyway. So I just told him to bugger off.

But boys never do what they are told to cos, man, they think we are like those bandit slot machines that say "go home, you lost!" only to keep them close and play on. And yes, they do think that every single breath we take we take for someone to call our hair fucking cute!

So he laughed and said he liked it when the cats showed their claws like Wolverine, which they never do except in stupid cartoons. I suppose he had other bearded compliments in his ammunition belt, but then Mara started to sway her swing, taking speed, and the guy nearly shit his pants, gaping at her.

"Wha... what the f...?" He stumbled back. "D'you see that? The swing..."

"This is our friend, Mara," I said. "How do you find her hair?"

He darted off like all the hounds of Hades were after him. I giggled and turned to Mara to give her a high-five. Agnieszka went crimson. Patches of red spread across her face in a burning rash, and she choked on her banana cos a) eating bananas was lousy and unladylike, even in this lousy and unladylike village, b) that dude looked like a superstar, and c) he didn't call *her* hair cute.

"My goodness, I'm an ugly frog. Nobody notices me anymore," she said, watching him go.

Mara disagreed. "I think he noticed you all right, he didn't notice *me*."

And I added, "Pfff! Who needs some buffoon noticing you? He spoke Russian!"

"That's not the point!" Agnieszka cried and chucked the banana peel at the trash bin.

Mara stopped her swing. "What is the point?"

"The point is… Nobody says that I am pretty. Ben did. But he's busy and also in America."

I expected Mara to ask her about Ben, but she nodded like she knew all about him, with her lips pressed together and eyes down. God, I wish I was this calm when talking about stupidoids. I told Nesha she was a stunning beauty, but she started to blubber and said she felt lonely without someone LOVING her. I said I loved her superduper much.

And she cried, "No. It's different!"

"Yes, it is! I won't bonk you to then dump you, so I'm far better than a boyfriend," I replied, and she cried even louder. Shiver me timbers. I'm off.

Bless Mara who jumped to her feet exclaiming "Ay, no! I forgot to feed my dinosaur!" and made her stop her silliness on the spot, cos more than boys loving her, Neshka loved loving cats. So we went to Huttuh to cuddle Aidan, who, as it turned out, ate only what he caught in the woods all by himself and on his own. For that, I swung my arm around Mara's neck before leaving.

"What are you doing?" she asked in her no-bullshit voice, a robot testing new emotions.

"Nothing. You are a good friend." And she looked at me like there was an earthquake that didn't move a single pebble, or a hailstorm without a single drop, or just me telling the truth.

She stuffed her fists into her pockets and leaned her shoulder at the doorjamb. "Thanks."

By the way, the videos of your entire squad dancing to *Good evening, we're from Ukraine* are a bomb. I nearly split my pants from laughing. Agnieszka forgot all about the buffoon in the leather jacket or even Aidan the cat and chortled with a funny sound like a choking piggy. SO FUN! We jumped around like jelly balls till Ma started banging on the wall cos her telly was jumping along with us. Holy cow! I think you can kill a Ruzi with just one swing of your hips, Dad.

Just don't forget to swing it back home :) I promise, next time you have a three-day leave, Ma won't ask you to fix the kitchen tap and all that. I will personally ask Grandad to fix all taps in this decrepit house with my super mind power. After all, I need to work on my whales' language.

Believe in Ukraine. Good night, Pa. Tomorrow, we'll wake up one day closer to victory.

Your witch, Skipper

14

AGNIESZKA

17 March 2022, Day 22

There is no point in asking God anything because he never listens, never replies, and does nothing. Because there is no god called God, and he has no face, no heart, and no power. Because the war is still on, and bloody Russians have bombed a theatre in Mariupol' with six hundred people hiding in there. Risking their lives, people wrote "KIDS" in huge letters on the asphalt all around it so that even a blind cosmonaut in a spaceship on the other side of the galaxy could read it, and they STILL BOMBED IT! Maybe *especially* because of the "KIDS" written there. Because they are absolute and total stinky rotten socks.

If there *is* a God, he must be Russian.

I'm going to pray to Buddha from now on. Does he understand Ukrainian? I'll try my lame English and even lamer Spanish just in case, all the way better than killing my knees in the church for nothing. Nothing!

And I thought horror movies were scary. I scroll through pictures of corpses lying in puddles of blood with their hands tied behind their backs, children in pieces all smudged by censorship, and blasted soldiers with their guts out. All these blood-chilling stories of not making it through, ever-growing names and numbers of the missing in action, burning candles on the graves, crying faces with their hands over their mouths; empty eyes, dirt, disorder, broken furniture, and shit on sofas; news from abroad where our refugees got harassed by the fanatics of Russian Peace. The slow dying of Mariupol', Marina from Herson who no longer reads my texts, all *you ok?* in a family chat, unseen… I want to yell and smash things. But I sit still and do my homework.

Where is Ben? Why didn't he write me seven pages of teary compassion and promise UFOs would come and save me from this black abysm? Moron.

I want to text Mara, but she'll probably say those are just silly sentiments. And war is also part of life. Dying is part of life. So, there, everything is *fine*. Fine, *caramba!*

Someone swapped Carmina for a placebo dummy doll with a curly red mop on top, silently scrolling through the news on her phone on the corner of her desk, looking for something titled "Moscow Kaputt."

"Are you going to do biology?" I asked carefully, toying with my patriotic pen.

"Nope," she said, busy reading.

"Amoeba is going to eat us up if we don't."

Carmina gave me a quick *oh, please* look and turned back to the newsfeed. "I give a damn about biology so miniscule that even Amoeba won't see it in her microscope."

Fortunately, Pani Salo, aka Amoeba, didn't hear that, or else we would be dead before we knew it. She is so big, that her chin has chins of its own and fills the entire camera view. Her look alone weighs a tonne, and if she gets just a bit taller, she'll probably crush all the sandworms in *Dune*. Still, Carmina preferred her phone.

"Since I was nine, I wanted to write a book," I said out of nowhere.

"Yeah, I remember. About a girl who accidentally got into a fairy world?"

"That was foolish. I want to write a different book now, about Ruzis."

She looked up at me, frowning.

"Yes," I continued, playing with my pen. "About how they got into a fairy world of Ukraine and stole things, tortured people, and shit on carpets. Because they are not people, not anymore, but anti-people, like antimatter. They rot inside and destroy all they touch. But then, something bigger will rise, wise and furious, like the Midgard Serpent that slept for aeons and got shaken from its dreams by bombs and grief. It will open its giant mouth and, with a single blow, burn all Russians off this planet."

"Amen." Carmina gave me a sad smile and returned to her news.

I sighed and went to sit outside with Tofu. As the sun touched the ragged fir tops with its blessing gold, there came the distant sound of a violin. Someone played the national anthem. The wind caught it in its wings and carried it over the roofs and trees. Then a man's voice from some other house joined in, husky and squeaky like a broken instrument. It was so sad and beautiful, I cried. These two didn't even see each other, just set it free for all the killed in Mariupol'. Just to cry to the world, that they can kill us all they like but never break us.

Shrimp was nesting on the log pile just across the lawn. He looked at me. I looked at him and said, "What?"

He said, "Gah-gah." Typical.

Pani Feya joined me on the bench and asked if I was okay. I told her about turning Buddhist, and she gave me this book about chi that penetrates the universe and holds this bunch of cells, thoughts, and illusions called Agnieszka together. If I am just a bunch of something, why would I be this sad about people I don't even know dying a horrible death? About Daddy looking greyer still in the video calls and *kurwa* Liza posting pics of her French boyfriend and her stupid feet in new Crocs like nothing bloody happened?

Oh, my dear pink cappuccino with a heart for twenty-five hryvnias, will we ever meet?

•

18 March 2022, Day 23

Carmina is missing. I woke up alone in the bed with my head hanging down from the mattress, which is bad, very bad for chi flowing according to Pani Feya's *Chi Gong for Stupid Agnieszka*. No, it's not the real title, but it should be because I don't get a thing in this thing about being *condensed energy* in the ocean of chi. Is it like being a piece of butter floating in an ocean of milk? Never mind—Carmina eloped!

The window was open, and her rucky was gone. All the ghastly news about children being kidnapped and sent to the Russian Federasshole flashed through my mind, and in a moment, they flashed through the house, too. Mommy and the Grand Buranas went banging at the neighbours' doors and shutters, not even properly dressed, asking about Carmina. The house buzzed with shock; even photos in the frames grew peaky. All but Pani Feya, who lit a joss stick while smoking a cig and said, "Relax, she'll get hungry and be back." As if Carmina were half a cat and half a rubber band.

Well, she wasn't back for breakfast, and Mommy's temper reached new peaks of explosion. She went all lurid and screamy about that wretched lock on our door, about some girls being snatched right from the streets and sold to brothels and butchers like it was *me* gone, my God. Pani Feya just smoked. Instead of calling the police, she laid out her tarot and said quite casually that she had Knight of Swords and Eight of Wands, and nobody knew what that was supposed to mean.

It was Pan Burana who made the call, finally, and it took him nearly forty years to dial the emergency number on that box with a holey wheel.

Then they grounded me in Carmina's bedroom like I was the accomplice of her crime (me!). I should have turned on the squeaky dolphins and meditated all the way back to an ordinary mess, but with a Drama Mamma like mine, I'll never go Zen unless I leave her castle like Buddha #1 did. Besides, I was worried sick about Carmina. What the hell was going on in her mercury brain? Where did she go? I texted Mara but she didn't reply.

In a panic, I sorted every item on Carma's desk and every sock in her drawers. I put labels on her boxes of shoes and sneakers and lined all her books and journals on the shelf. Then Tofu jumped on the windowsill and paraded left and right, with his tail sticking up. And I had that same brilliant idea that visited my rocket friend: I would get out through the window and go to the woods.

And find Mara who *mierda* never picked up her phone.

I don't know why I decided to go to those scary woods. It just popped into my mind. I was running from Burana's house like a prisoner breaking free, praying to Buddha and all the mighty Cossacks to make me invisible for just a little bit. Sadly, my violet coat flared in front of Shrimp's beady eye like a race flag. He chased me all the way down the road, pinching at my skirt.

"Go away! Go!" I waved my hands at him and kicked my foot in the air, then grabbed my skirt and ran faster. He ran faster too, gah-gah-ing and spreading his wings like a superhero cape. I crossed the street—he crossed the street. I stopped—he stopped and looked up at me. "What?" I asked. "What in the name of holy chi do you want from me?"

He kept me in his beady eye and twitched his tail happily.

"Fine!" I cried. "You can go with me if you like, but if you tell anyone, I'll put you in a soup." He said "gah" and it was like, "Okay, but I'm a goose, and I don't understand what you are talking about unless you said I can bully you, which I will, thank you!"

So we went to Mor. It was the only place Carmina could go, and I was certain she was with Mara and her charming kitty. "Nobody knows about Huttuh. The police might never find her," I said aloud, and Shrimp grunted to that, waddling behind me, sticking his bottom up in the air like he was my personal guard.

The woods felt spooky as we waded through the silent, dense undergrowth of the untrodden paths. The trees in the damp morn-

ing mist seemed formless and full of faces. Many times, I sensed someone's gaze at my back, but when I turned around, there were only swaying nets of branches, sprinkled with rainy beads. On top of all that, I hadn't the slightest idea where I was heading. Every tree looked exactly the same as the next, and all of them seemed pretty *queer* to me.

It was Shrimp, actually, who led me by pinching at my skirt and pulling me left or right. I got tired of beating him off my tormented hem. Then something flicked on the horizon, and for a second, I saw children running behind the trees, laughing. Well, I thought the sharp and bouncy noise was laughter, though it could have been a bird, a deer, or anything woodish. Still, it froze me to the spot. With my heart beating like a hammer, I waited, peeping into the trees.

"Who is there?" I demanded. "Is it Lisovyk?"

Silence.

"I don't wish any harm! I'm looking for my friend!" I cried at the trees. Someone hid there. I could see their pink coat and little almost transparent fingers on the bark. One blink cleaned the vision off, like a wiper cleaning a raindrop from the windshield. To my shock, the drum in my ears turned out to be my heart.

Oh, mierda.

Shrimp clutched my coat with his beak and pulled me away. I ran behind him with my eyes goggling out from fright. Seeing somebody vanishing behind a tree in the thick of wild woods, how spooky is that? Heart-stoppingly spooky, that's how.

I only ceased shaking under my coat when we spotted Huttuh in a strange shape. In fact, it had no shape. It was just a giant wooden… lump. I called Mara's name, but only a faint echo came in response. Then I remembered how Mara said some sort of mantra to "open sesame," and I tried it as best as I could recall, which wasn't good at all, but wow, it worked!

Huttuh lifted itself on its ugly chicken legs, arched a gabled roof like a cat awakened from a doze, and opened one window eye to see who dared bother her. A sash banged open, and Mara's sleepy face poked out, with her black forelock sticking up.

"Agnieszka?" She squinted and looked at the goose standing next to me. "Hello, Shrimp."

"Gah-gah!" said Shrimp lordly.

Momentarily, the reason why I'd run here in the first place evaporated from my mind. "You know him?"

"Of course!" Mara said and rubbed her palm across her eyes. "He's the witch's ally who…" She yawned pleasurably and forgot what she was saying. "What are you doing here this early?"

And I knew Carmina hadn't come around.

•

19 March 2022, Day 24

This is madness, total madness. What happened yesterday is MADNESS. I'm not going to write it down. Not until I am absolutely sure ghosts and shapeshifters don't exist, Mom stops threatening to put grates on all the windows, and I can get back to normal life.

Wait, what normal life? Ben doesn't write. I wear a sweater with a hole in my sleeve, saggy trainers, and two layers of socks. I'm ugly and should be sent to Planet Ugly. And by the way, we're still at war. There was a BOOM, and something smoked behind the church. Then we had our electricity cut till midnight and had to read by candlelight and carry water in iron buckets from the nearest well like total cavemen.

Completo mierda locura.

15

MARA

Agnieszka is standing by my window, desperate to find her missing friend. In a shower of half words, half whoops, she tries to stir the full story into the soup of my dozing brain, and Shrimp adds snippets of this and that like a chorus to a song.

Why are people so obsessed with the worms or whatever it is early birds get? If I unstick my eyelids before midday, I don't want to get anything but back to my bed.

"Why would Carmina escape to Chornoguy?" I finally emerge from the goo of my brain.

Agnieszka gives me a puzzled look. "I don't know where she is. I thought she was here."

She's definitely in Chornoguy, Shrimp quacks. *Because it's the nearest place with a military base.*

"A military base?" I repeat like it makes sense (it doesn't).

"A what?" Agnieszka stares back now in total bewilderment.

Funny sounds break from the goose's beak as Shrimp clears his throat. Then he goes all Sherlock Holmes and says, *All the clues lead there. I don't even need to resort to my spectacular deduction capabilities to know that my little* pani *is about to join the army.*

I slowly melt into the windowsill, listening to him, blinking slowly. "And… I should… stop her?"

Eggs heavens, yes! Shrimp opens his massive wings. *She is in great danger!*

Agnieszka doesn't get a thing, of course. Squinting at me, all pink and glaring, she bursts, "Who are you talking to? What are you saying?"

I yawn. "I'm talking to Shrimp."

"What, to the goose?" She points at him.

"Yep, he's a magic goose." This made them gaze at each other.

Shrimp smiles like only geese do, by opening his beak wide and showing his tiny teeth, which drains all colour from Agnieszka's cheeks. "He's what?"

"Magic," I yawn again. "Shrimp is a shapeshifter."

She frowns. "A what?"

Shrimp shuffles from one foot to the other. *You made me sound like a scary werewolf. Better say I am a helper.*

"Yeah, okay, he's also your ally."

Agnieszka's pretty bluet eyes widen. "My… what?"

"Good grief, stop saying 'what' all the time, or else we'll stick around here till one of us dies," I say. "Shrimp says Carma is in Chornoguy. Now can I go back to sleep?"

"Wait, he TALKS?" She leaps back in a super froggy jump. "Stay away from me! Fork and knife!"

Here we go, Shrimp sighs. *Pray, stay and tell this silly girl I'm sick and tired of her game!*

Ugh, no peace for the wicked. "Just give me a minute." I duck back, determined to use this minute on some constructive "hating the living" in front of my bathroom mirror, but Aidan beats me to it. He darts towards the door and shoots out of it like a liquid torpedo.

"Hi!" I hear his human voice outside. "Enchanted to meet you! I'm Aidan."

I burst out of Huttuh just in time to see him giving the baffled girl his hand to shake. Why would people deliberately touch each other, I wonder? It sends Agnieszka into deeper paralysis, and Aidan fishes her palm out himself and clasps it eagerly. "I see you met Shrimp? He's a good chap, isn't he?"

"Aidan! Get back this instant!" I stomp down the stairs.

Agnieszka bats her fatso eyelashes like fifty times. "You are called Aidan, like Mara's cat?"

"Not *like* my cat, he *is* my…" I start, but Aidan pipes in.

"…Brother! Just arrived from hel… Hellsich." He beams, pulls down the jeans' pockets with his thumbs, and gazes into Agnieszka's eyes like she's the answer to all his meows.

She looks him up and down. "Where is Hellsich?"

"Dunno." Aidan shrugs and picks at the braid on her scarf, just like he did with his tiny paws when he was a cat. "North?"

"Aidan!" I raise my eyebrows at him and open my eyes wide to give him the mental kick he deserves, but he only smiles. Then Shrimp says we're gonna need someone who looks like an adult (i.e., almost kinda beard-ish) not to raise any underage alert on a bus. And I say, "Just great, now I'm using my cat as a bus pass."

A little reminder: next time I yearn for human company, know that it smells like too much trouble early in the morning.

•

The bus is so overcrowded. We ride squashed against each other and I with a goose in my hands. It's cold and slippery outside, and the driver is a madman sacked from the Formula One races for over-speeding. Every pit and bump on the road thrusts us into the air like a bundle of timber.

Naturally, everyone secretly craves killing everyone else except for

Aidan, who's so ecstatic about hugging humans that he actually sings along with the music from the bus stereo. It's a silly pop song with a rough melody and even rougher lyrics. The irritating refrain is "The Russian man is gone…" and my cat yells it out, waving his hands in the air like it's a club party. And I think that our adult-looking chaperone is just about to get us thrown out the window.

But then something super weird happens. Old grannies, kids, men, and mommies catch his mood like the flu, and soon, the entire bus is whooping to the tune, clapping hands and stomping feet, with a periodic quack-quack from the overexcited Shrimp.

What the… I go all agog and ask Agnieszka, "Why are they so happy?"

"Because the Russian man is gone," she says matter-of-factly.

The lads from the back shout to turn it up, and when the song is over, they ask to play it again. The mad bus racer happily loops it, and the chorus strikes up anew. So the Russian man is biting the dust all the way to Chornoguy and quite frankly cheers me up.

When we leave the stuffy bus at last, the frosty air feels like needles biting at my cheeks, and our singing gives away whiffs of steam.

"There is no Russian man, the Russian man is gone," I hum under my breath, striding along the road behind the parading Shrimp. "Nothing left from him, no fucking thing, the other shit his pants."

Artillery is firing, Kozáks're giving hell, Shrimp quacks and skips on his little dancey feet.

"The Russian men are blown to shreds and all their tanks as well!" Aidan and I pipe in and clap to the beat.

Agnieszka throws suspicious glances our way, with her nostrils puffing up. She doesn't sing along and keeps her distance; she must be thinking what total kooks we are, but whatever. It's cool. It's fun. I've never felt this fun before.

We're almost there, Shrimp says. *My super deductive intuition*

tells me she's close.

There is no need for his super deductive or whatever intuition, cos the building in front is swarming with people in khaki, all looking like one, but one. I recognize the slim girl with electroshocked carrot hair, in hiking boots and a deerskin jacket. She waves to us, and Shrimp runs up hissing and beating his wings like the craziest, most nonsensical bird in the universe, which he is. The khaki guys go so pop-eyed-surprised, their bottoms nearly drop off.

The next thing I know, all five of us, including Shrimp, are waiting for the girls' moms in a café with thyme teas and listening to Carmina's grumbling.

She goes, "Our army can be spectacularly dim. I thought they'd choke to death, laughing so much, when I said I wanted to fire a howitzer. And when I insisted I needed a gun, they called Ma instead." Carmina shoves her hand into her hippie rucksack and fishes out a handful of chocolates. "Also, they gave me this. Do I look like a toddler or something?"

Agnieszka stares at the chocolates on the table. "Are they all Nestlé?"

"No idea," she blurts and sips her tea. "What is the matter with soldiers? They are obsessed with my age and gender. They go on and on about it, like darned parrots. Why do they go on and on about it? Why? On and on and on about me being a girl of fourteen. Why?"

I say, "Cos you are a girl of fourteen?"

"So?"

"Why did you go there at all?" Aidan asks as he crunches crisps from a package on the table. I had to buy that so he wouldn't drag in a rat as big as a chicken to snack on.

Carmina sighs and presses her curly head between her palms. "Cos I want to do something to stop this war. If I do nothing, and if many others do nothing, what do you think will happen to Ukraine?"

Aidan gives her a crisp. "Everything will be fine with Ukraine."

Carmina fiddles with the crisp with her long, pointy fingers, then puts it in her mouth. "Also, I don't want my country to keep girls only for home and families." She chews vehemently. "I wanted to join the army to prove that I'm a warrior too and I can fight, I can protect my land, make a difference, be a soldier. I'm fourteen already! All they say about how girls are weak and need protection is bullshit, and I wanted them to know it. I can do better."

"But you do!" Agnieszka opens her eyes wide. "We fight on the home front."

Carmina huffs and rolls her head. "What do you call fighting? Making camouflage nets and gathering donations is an excuse for not being a warrior. Being only forty kilos and not able to carry a sniper's equipment is also an excuse for not being a warrior. Writing encouraging posts on my Instagram—what fighting is this? Nobody takes it seriously."

Agnieszka echoes "Your Pa takes you seriously" and drags one chocolate bar up with two fingers.

"Yeah. When he's around, which is never." Carmina looks away. "Only Ma's home to say, 'you be careful with boys, luv, you know they need only one thing from you.' And I say, 'Ma, I don't give a fig about boys and all they need. Mating is disgusting. Boys are apes obsessed with their dangling sausages...' No offence, Aidan." She raises a hand at him.

"Oh, don't mind me, I'm just a tourist here." Aidan crunches on and rocks his foot under the table.

Carmina blinks. "What does it mean? Ah, never mind. Ma just nods at everything I say like she understands, which she doesn't because she's in her blissful coma every time I open my mouth, listening to God's gospel about Adam and Eve being perfectly designed for each other. Then she finally drops back on sinful earth and says, 'Don't worry, you'll find your perfect one.' And I'm like, holy cow, Ma, why do I even bother talking to you?"

Aidan bursts out laughing. Then Shrimp adds his unforgettable gah-gah-ing, and it's a peal of deafening stereo laughter. Agnieszka bats her pretty eyes at Carmina and says, "Not all boys are apes."

Carmina says, "All of them."

"No, they are not."

"Yes, they are!"

"No, they are not!"

"Yes, THEY ARE."

"No!"

"Yes!"

"Your brother is not an ape."

"Svitlan tries hard to be a man."

"And your dad?"

"He went to the war to stop being an ape. So did your pa."

"The president is not an ape!"

"He is a nice ape."

We follow their verbal gunplay like watching a ball on a tennis court, till Agnieszka goes completely off, grasps the candy bar, and reads from the wrapper most aggressively, "It's Nestlé!"

Carmina cries, "Oh, for Cossack's sake, just eat that!"

"No, I really shouldn't…" she mumbles, blushing and putting it back. Then Shrimp takes it from the table with his beak and drops it on her lap.

I guess they're gonna be good friends.

16

CARMINA

GIVE ME FREEDOM OR GIVE ME DEATH!

From: Carmina Burana   19 March 2022, 21:30

To: Severin Saint   Booguy

Yes, Pa, I did it.

I had to try and join the army, no need to go this hysteric, jeez. Nothing happened. Apart from a few hours of humiliation. Seriously, you soldiers think a woman is a baby till the day she has her first grandchild, and then she's just an old baby.

Major Something (don't remember his sodded name) gave me sweets, asked me to draw them a picture, and promised a soldier would marry me when I grew up! No kidding! Marry me!!! MARry!!? I hope you'll be back soon to shoot him somewhere safe, cos this was the ultimate offence. I'd shoot him myself if they gave me that gun, *caramba*!

THIS IS A MILITARY BASE for chrissakes! Not a ~~brothel~~ registry office.

Ma was surprisingly calm when she came to collect me with Neshka, Shrimp, Mara, and… her weird bro. So many people claimed me, Je-sus. I expected Ma to go wild about the five hundred hryvnias

I snatched from her purse, but she had her eyes only for the officer's chevrons. Whatever floated in the chaos of her bag, she was too busy flirting to notice.

So I suspected Svitlan was home. She can be only this honey-sweet when the man is home.

BINGO. Svitlan is home, staying with his friends in Chornoguy near the animal shelter, where he'll be taking care of all the beasts evacuated from the front. Good grief, how I missed that sweet face! But not when he went all brotherly and preached a miles-long lecture about how irresponsible I acted when I ran away. Seriously, even you sounded less cliché.

"These people are no joke, Carmina," he said. "We are confronting the second-best army in the world."

Holy Cossack's ass. If we kill them, and we'll kill them, we are the first. Svitlan breathed too much British air. Didn't he hear about Chornobaivka? It's the airport near Kherson, aka the black hole that sucks up Ruzis like the Bermuda Triangle. They don't care that this place is cursed. Just keep shoving on, like stupid bio trash. *Look, an airport, let's go there.* BANG! BOO! Everyone got smashed into a pancake. The general scratches his tin-can head. *What's happened? Send more people!* More people die. *Why did they die? They can't die, we're the second-best army in the world! Send more, MORE!* Told ya, they are stupid. Our only problem is that there are too many of them. The Russian army is not scary. It's just long.

Anyway, I'm back to my agonizing routine of reading Dickens, finding a mysterious *x*, and ripping Tofu off the mops that he drags all about the house, imagining himself a mighty superhero fighting Cthulhu. Once, Grandad tried to play catch-a-feather-tip with him, and he bit it in two. Ever since, we've just brought a mop from the closet and let him savage it all he likes. At least the furniture stays safe.

Today, imagine, Tofu didn't crash sofas or eat the linen basket or something, he just fell into some blackhole in the backyard. We sighed with relief, hoping he'd find himself a bear to bite and let us be. Not that I have anything against Tofu (or bears). I like having pets (on my wall on Facebook) and would never harm a living being (unless they go Russian). It's just that I'd like this fluffy ball of joy and fun to go and live his joyful fluffy life elsewhere (on Jupiter) and remember me occasionally (once in a century) by sending me some funny GIFs.

So I was reading this book (not Dickens, meh, Stephen King's *Doctor Sleep*) where all the names sound the same, like John-Jack-Dave-Dan; you never know who's speaking and what's going on, jeez. It rocks me to sleep (so much for Doctor Sleep) but at least gives something magic (don't tell Ma, she thinks Stephen King is scary, which is bullshit). Anyway, I was reading, and someone rang. I went to answer the door cos everyone concluded I was their butler now cos I was *grounded*. There stood Pan Nextdoors, looking like he dropped straight from the front line, i.e., all scratched and furious. He held out his broom with Tofu dangling from the bristles.

"Is this your cat?" he asked.

I said, "Never seen it in my life."

With a deadpan look, he handed me the broom and silently shut the door. I tried to shake Tofu from that stick, but he fought me like a freaking bulldog. We danced hellish hip-hop-break until, finally, I managed to fling him into the window and make a run for it.

"Who was it?" Agnieszka walked into the room in her all-ruffs-and-laces Lolita dress.

"Godly people," I lied my bum off. "Came to say that Jesus loves us, and we should be more compassionate to each other."

Okay, it was bad to lie about her cat, but I did invite her to visit Svitlan at the vet's, which is all her dress is about (silly, right?). After my epic escape, Gran had a long talk with me and said that I could save Ukrainians instead of killing Russians, which would be the same (would it?). They promised to take me with them to Chornoguy on Monday for volunteering.

Ma added that if I cared for my country this mega much, I should take care of the poor animals, too, and help my oh-so-much-smarter brother. In the twilight of her mommy's mind, it looks super great. Everything about Svitlan looks great to her. And I don't care. Much better than sitting around, sleeping through the books, and learning the Beatles' songs Pani Anglia forces us to sing along to with her decrepit tape recorder. Like it can help me in life! Imagine I am in London, buying a ticket on a train. They'll ask me, "Where to, Miss?" And instead of an answer, I'll sing about a yellow submarine… SO helpful.

Agnieszka will probably sleep better, though. She wants boys. I promise there will be plenty of fluffy, meowing boys. She may even flirt with Svitlan; I give her my blessing. He's safe, I guess. Anyway, I've invited Mara and her bro, too. The more, the merrier.

Maybe then, Agnieszka will stop bossing me about my room like it's a king's library. She is so tediously tidy! After practising Buddhism really hard and seriously (for two days), she rummaged through my possessions, and now all my books and toys stand to be shot, socks and panties huddle in the corners of the drawers, and every box with trifles is signed and numbered. I can't take a sodded pencil without her nagging look and all the fuss about *order on your desk is order in your head*.

The order on my desk drives me crazy. I shouted at her that Buddha didn't put stickers on his boxes, he didn't have any boxes, and stickers weren't even invented then. And she shouted back that Buddha was not about stickers and boxes, but clarity of the mind. Then she opened Ma's Zen book and read in her annoying teacher's tone, "Your mind is a crystal ball that reflects the world. Keep it clean, you'll see the truth."

"What on earth does it mean?" I didn't know.

She snapped, "It means clean your poo, and you'll smell the roses."

"Oh, right. That makes sense." I nodded. "Why didn't he just say that?"

"Because." She cleared her throat. "Buddha didn't shit. He was god."

He was a man. All men shit. What's wrong with that? Believing that your mind is a rock is no better. Still, I don't think it's about cleaning desks but about clearing BOYS from your head every time you primp pimples in front of the mirror. Waiting for a prince in shining armour to talk about books and music is a complete waste of time when things like war happen out of the blue.

Agnieszka should be honest right from the get-go. If her adored Timothée Chalamet from *Dune* drops on her head and says "Hey, babe, add me on Facebook!" she'd better tell him right away she doesn't give a rosy poo about his super interesting personality. She wants a boy to tell her how pretty she is fifty times a day, and if he wasn't accidentally born a parrot, he'd better keep walking. All this soul-mating la-di-dah leads nowhere. She wants to be loved. Naturally. The only thing I don't get is how boys can help her with that. Buddha says if you want to be happy, be happy. If you want love, love. Simple!

I love her freely and forever even after she stole all the cosy mess from my room. Why doesn't she get how fortunate she is? I know you love me too, Pa, cos you risk your life for us. No other dude would die for me like that. And if he wouldn't die for me, I'd send his smutty compliments to my butt, cos it's the only thing that gives a crap about it.

Peace to everyone,
Your Zen Skipper

17

AGNIESZKA

20 March 2022, Day 25

I don't think I can stand living with Carmina a day longer. Her room is a primaeval chaos. She steps over all the junk on the floor and calls it *minefield walking*. When she can't solve a math equation, she smashes the book against the wall and yells, "I'm busy making sense you don't have, bye!" How can she think about joining the army with her zero discipline and perfectly barbaric sense of order?

It's Sunday, and we all went to church to pray for Ukraine (people here are really that bonkers about leaving all their troubles to their imaginary friend in heaven). My hands shook when I put on my only pretty dress because I knew Svitlan would come, too. He's so sweet, and he loves animals. He's also Carmina's brother and probably as primitive and untidy. So I'm not using my princess charms on him, nuh-uh; I only do it for myself, to respect the woman in me, as Mommy's fashion magazines say.

Carmina didn't even bother to dry her hair before we went to sleep yesterday. She woke up with what looked like a wild hedgehog on her scalp, and after brushing that slightly, lolloped to church like never-dead Medusa Gorgon.

Dear God.

There were so many people, we might just as well have been celebrating a royal wedding. All solemn and dressed chic and smart.

The priest told us a long story about brave people who drove under gunfire to collect refugees from besieged villages, literally snatching their souls from the claws of death. One ex-prisoner called Ivan got caught by cannibals several times; he was searched, beaten, and threatened to be shot for helping Ukrainians. He put on trainers of a different colour, said *Nobody would recognize me now*, jumped back into his old minivan, and drove for kids, cats, grannies, and everyone else who couldn't break free from Russian terror. I started to pray for this strange man. I wanted him to bring Daddy home, too.

Then someone handed me a paper hanky. I didn't even notice my crying. But somebody did. I raised my head and saw the Mighty God Buddha Dalai Lama land right next to me. Tall, blond, and tanned, with a cool surfer's smile, he gazed down at me with his still, blue eyes and whispered that I'd ruin my good looks if I watered on them. My knees melted into jelly. It was like I was turning into a seal because I stared at him and made this stupid "nguh" sound instead of saying anything human.

"I'm Arman by the way," he said in a low and velvet, very adult voice. He tossed his hair back with a nod of his beautiful head, and the lamps reflected a golden gleam in its fine wave.

I went, "Nguh."

"I came from Odesa with my family."

OHHHHH, I wanted to say, OH MY GODDY GOD ODESA! I SO LOVE ODESA, THE SEA AND DOLPHINS, YAY! But said, "Oh, nguh." No idea what "nguh" meant; it just came out of my nose into the hanky.

Then Carmina nudged me in the ribs. "We're singing psalms, page two hundred."

I fidgeted with my book, still nguhing into his hanky like that snake that bites its tail. My hands got wet and sticky, I could swear Arman sensed me sweating like a pig and was probably looking for more hankies to stop me from flooding the holy temple.

The priest set the tune. His bald head gleamed like a copper bowl, blinding me. And gosh, how bizarrely Voldemort-like he looked because it wasn't a good kind of baldness, like Prince William's, but a "Gee, there is no way to accessorize that" kind of baldness. Everyone sang along, and suddenly, I found the priest's head completely mesmerizing. I mean, what can ever be ugly in this world where God Arman from Odesa offers you a hankie? *Nada!*

I opened my goldfish mouth to merge with all the people in the church as one seamless being, praying as one, loving as one. It raised in me like a tidal wave, the power of many. I felt invincible, and strong enough to crush all tanks and ships and planes and miserable Russian bugs who decided our souls were free to take. My pride enveloped me completely.

But then it happened again, the next most shameful *terrorífico* moment of my life. Amid the second chorus, Carmina gave the loudest, the smelliest, the ugliest in human history… FART. It blasted from her bony frame like a meteorite blow. Everyone heard that! Even statues on the walls fainted inside their stone carcasses. The priest kept singing, though his bald head shone a little shinier now. And people around me sang like they were under heavy helium. The Buranas turned and looked at me, and then everyone turned and looked at me. AT ME! While Carmina kept her perfect poker face like nothing really happened and farting in church is a super holy case.

Estupendo mortificato! I nearly died there, pressing the hanky to my burning face. Carmina always wondered what her superpowers were. Well, I could tell her that right away. No need to join the army and all that. She is a killing *mierda* FART BAZOOKA!

I turned to Arman the God of Grace and Beauty to nguh him that it wasn't me. But he was gone. Vanished, like… like blown off with Carma's powerful gas artillery. How terrible and ludicrous is that? Very terrible and ludicrous, that's how. I'll kill her next time she casts her jacket on the floor.

•

21 March 2022, Day 26

Maths problem. What is the statistical probability of seeing the same star crossing the sky in just two days? I solve it easily. ZERO. NIX. NOUGHT. NADA! There is NO way whatsoever I can see Angel Arman from Odesa in this bumhole again. Fairy tales like this just don't happen. You'd sooner fall underground into a leprechaun's gold pot than meet a Prince Charming of a boy twice in the same rotten spot. It's a one in a gazillion chance. You either catch it or regret it forever. Which is all that's left for me, I suppose. Die an ugly and lonely goblin, probably tomorrow, when Russian pigs go dead *loco* and come fight the secret NATO battle-peckers in the Carpathian woods.

Luckily, I'm a Buddhist now, so nothing in this world breaks me. I accept my destiny. To hell with princess dreams, I'm dedicating myself to volunteering for the sake of my country, like all proper holy spinsters do. It's the Buddhist way. The trick is to let everything go because "death wears no pockets"; you pass away, taking nothing with you. Though I'd very much like to leave a will with, "When I die, bury Arman from Odesa next to me so in the next life we'll be together."

Ow, *mierda*, I think about death again, I always think about death when I don't think about boys. Is this the only choice I've got in my life? Have a boyfriend or die?

Just… *Magnifico.*

The Buranas found the idea of our volunteering fantastic because that's what they have been doing since February (I didn't know that. I thought they flew to the witches' parties). They helped with food and transportation and sold pottery at charity fairs. It's not like giving away all you can, but a real job with a schedule and responsibilities that people's lives depend on.

Today, they took us to the Chornoguy train station, where families fled in packs and often with no luggage, money, or sense of direction. When we arrived, it was a medley mash of people, tents, crates, and cars. Mommy and Pani Feya put fluorescent jackets on us with VOLUNTEER written on the backs, so they wouldn't lose us in the crowd. All the same, I felt like a dead, lost, ugly duckling, jacket or no jacket, because people with bags full of drama came in avalanches, hustling and bustling by like a never-ending waterfall and I was that dry leaf taken by the current.

It wasn't a nuclear physics job. All we needed to do was offer them hygiene kits, water, or food, and point at toilets and tents where they could rest and charge their gadgets. If they asked about lodgings or medical help, we should point to older volunteers. That's it. Still, I went so shy, rambling among the crowd. I didn't know if I did the right thing or said the right thing.

Then I realised, nobody gave a flying pig about what I said or did. They were all shattered and even more lost than me. Seeing their faces shocked and exhausted rattled me. One *pani* with a three-year-old-like child saw my yellow jacket, grabbed my hand and cried, just cried. I didn't know what to do, I went feverish and kept asking what it was that she needed, water? A biscuit for her toddler? A tissue? She muttered that her son was gone. I didn't understand. Her son stood next to her. But when the kid blubbed along, it dawned on me that he lost his brother. I said "Everything will be fine" and didn't believe it myself.

More than anything in the world, I wished her son was back. So, sooo very much, I wished he would be back and knew he couldn't be. Carmina had buzzed my ears with the superpowers she craved. I had laughed at her, but now I'd die to be able to bring dead children back to life. I nearly cried myself and hugged them. The woman felt no taller than me, and the boy was like a doll. Then I led them to the tents with thermoses and pies. I said they needed carbohydrates and hot tea with lots of sugar. People with PSYCHOLOGIST written on their backs came up with better words to say. I felt sad but not like an ugly, lonely goblin anymore. People need to hug each other more. It's wonderful magic, a hug. Not even chocolates or boyfriends. Just a hug.

After this, I looked closer at people and didn't mindlessly shove tissues or water bottles at them. I felt there was something common between us, even if I'd never seen them before or didn't like their faces. And this commonality was Ukraine. We were like… a family that once lost connections but now, in hard times, got together for support and protection.

It was so surreal and not at all like me. Some months ago, I never would have come within a hundred miles of these maniac-looking guys or bitter grannies with reproving eyes who coughed like mummies clearing their throats from ancient dust, sending shivers up and down my spine. I didn't understand when Daddy made such a fuss about smelly old bums or felt sorry for people who couldn't pay for his treatment. Now, I saw a stout *pani* waddle by, leaning on her greasy stick, shaking her giant head with three chins nearly dropping off, and I couldn't disdain her. I saw my biology teacher in her, I saw my aunties, I saw a… a human.

"Do you need anything? Some water?" She didn't reply. Her eyes were still blank as she snatched a bottle and a pack of antiseptic tissues from my hands.

"How much do I owe you?" she snapped and fiddled in her pockets.

I hurried to add, "It's free. You can have a free meal, too, if you are hungry."

The woman turned to stare into my face, awake. "Oh." She smiled and changed completely. Her teeth were brownish yellow, but her smile made her look so nice.

Then I helped a family with huge bags. Three youngsters were almost crushed under the load of their rucksacks. They were looking for a room to stay in, and I sent the mother to the people in charge while I stayed to keep an eye on her kids. I gave them biscuits and chocolate bars, like a big sister. They told me about the small village they came from, and how they couldn't find their doggie. The blasts spooked her, and she ran away, just like Tofu did. I said everything would be okay with their Frosia (I was getting good at little lies). They nodded eagerly, chewing on their Snickers, and made me feel like a superhero. Is it "making a difference?" Do I make a difference? Even being this silly, ugly, and fourteen?

When their mother was back, I ran to ask Pan Burana to take them to their hostel. Carmina caught me on the way back. "How was that?" she asked.

I told the truth. "Great!"

"Did you know they bake those pies themselves?" Carmina chirruped. "All totally free, can you imagine! They come here every day for people they don't even know."

I beamed instead of answering. Carmina pointed at the group of lads smoking cigs in the car park. "Do you see those guys over there?"

"Yeah."

"They buy and repair cars for the army, with their own money. The girl in black with them is the YouTube blogger who collects donations on her *True Tarot* channel to buy clothes, food, drones, power banks, you name it. She gets absolutely anything in a flash. Then puts her helmet on and drives it through the minefields and over Russian corpses right to the front, like a crazy Valkyrie."

I blinked. "She does?"

"Yep. She can get *anything*," Carmina stressed.

"Anything?"

"Yeah. You know why the Holy Grail hasn't been found?"

"Er… Why?"

"They haven't asked our volunteers yet!"

She laughed her crazy ha-ha and I joined in. It felt like we had finally found the right way to fight for Ukraine. I had finally found something OTHER THAN get a boyfriend or die, and it stung me with uber joy. On our break, we went to warm our frozen fingers on plastic teacups and eat a sandwich. Carmina promised not to fart into my lunch and sent me grunting with laughter like a piggy. So loud and weird, I sounded like Shrimp on his goose hunt, and then, OH MY DEAR HOLY BLASTED GOD, I saw Arman.

He strutted into the tent, all elegant and graceful, in a fluorescent jacket with VOLUNTEER on his back, and talked to some lads in the corner. I couldn't believe my eyes. He was here. Helping people like a true angel, aww, bliss *bliss* bliss! NIRVANA!!!

Oh, damn, no! NO!!! I was wearing Gran's ugly feminist pants and a pregnant-troll sweater. Why did I agree to wear those? Why? I looked like mini-Shrek, my god.

"Okay, girls." Mommy rushed towards us. "That was the last train for today. Get ready, we'll drop you at Svitlan's pet shelter now."

ARGH MALDITO MIERDA SEA!

•

22 March 2022, Day 27

I told Carmina all about His Highness (because tall) from Odesa, and she called me a whore.

I asked her, "Don't you ever think about your future boyfriend? How you start a family."

And she said, "Boys are useless at starting anything."

I don't know what's wrong with her, but I'd better not ask.

Her brother is not at all like her. He's kind and gentle. He left his school in London for a swarm of dirty beasts that fled the war from all over the country. He is a vet, and if you think being a vet is oh-so-cuuute, DON'T. Working in a pet shelter is fabulously hard. How Svitlan keeps his brain cells together when dealing with everyday mayhem is a total mystery. No people are hugging and thanking him for a chocolate bar, only a cacophony of barking dogs, meowing cats, baaing goats, neighing ponies, and squealing rabbits. Bigger beasts chomp and scoff food from buckets, mess it up, and poo around. Smaller ones run by the cages, yell, and poo. They all poo as they like, and I come in my Shrek's rags to scrub it out and bring more food which they gulp down and poo out for me to clean! Complete catastrophe! CAPOOSTROPHE!

If hell exists, it looks like a pet shelter. On Doomsday, angels will come with shovels pushing hills of shit and will only take to the heavens those who survive the apoocalypses.

My god. I wrote a whole page about poo. There is too much poo in my life. This is a very *poo*r life I've got indeed. Meet Agnieszka, a devoted and professional Pooddhist!

But what could be done? The war is still burning, and people and animals keep running from it like a forest fire. Svitlan says beasts are scared too. In a way, they are in a much, *much* worse position because they can't come and ask for water or a tissue. They don't understand what's going on and where to go to stop this terror.

It's so very dreadful.

But I stink of poo, and Arman wouldn't talk to me even if a continent of lavender fields lay between us. Today we arrived at the train station at half past nine and could only stay for one train before school. Mara and Aidan were there too, talking to refugees about one million things like they were going to write an encyclopedia about this war. I try not to think about what they said about Shrimp. He doesn't bother me much lately, but the idea of talking magic poultry is perfectly unnerving.

"Hey, how was the bus trip?" I waved at them. "No chorus singing this time?"

Mara grinned and looked around the crowd, huddling near the tents, like they were a unique ant colony she was studying. "Nah, we didn't take the bus. Too long. I'll go and say hi to Carma."

"We have our own ways to travel," Aidan explained. "*Magic* ways." He stressed *magic* like I was supposed to know what that was about.

I only said, "Huh."

His cat's eyes stopped at me. I noticed they changed colour in the sunlight, from dark brown through hazel to almost yellow-green. So bemusing. But his Viking's brows ruined everything. They were so bushy and thick, they reminded me of black centipede nests. Were they still growing? He could get them grown into his sort-of-a-beard by April, and blind himself completely before summer. I must have looked like an idiot, gaping at those brows, because he kept staring at me as if reading it all running across my forehead like a ticker.

Then Arman the God came up and said "Hi."

And dropped me dead right there.

He said hi to me, *my God!* He looked even taller in the sun; he probably borrowed his genes from titans that walked the earth before Zeus and co. I turned to him in my best princess manner, touching my imaginary hair that turned out to be all tucked under my hood, and said, "Yah."

Yah? Like some drunken monkey stole my mouth and talked through it.

And before my burning face could *yup* anything better than this, Aidan jumped in and grabbed his hand to shake. "Well, heyyyy!" he exclaimed. "Do you like cats?"

Hey, do you like cats? What kind of greeting is that?

"Um, yeah, as a matter of fact, I do," Arman said. He tried in vain to get his hand back, still smiling charmingly, and it was like the sun winked from the skies at all the centipedes of Aidan's Viking eyebrows.

"Great! We'll be good friends then. I'm Aidan. Are you here helping refugees?"

"Yes. Arman. And I'll be much more helpful using both my hands."

"Oh, right." Aidan let him go, but immediately grabbed him by his elbow and pulled him to the tents. "Will you show me around, Arman? I'd like a fluorescent jacket like yours. So cool and er... human."

Arman chuckled. "Sure."

Yes, go, don't mind me. I'll just stick here like a traffic sign, waiting for another chance to catch the falling star. Like Buddha, om, om, *ommierda*! Aargh!

Aidan stuck to my prince like a patch and followed him everywhere. If he was a seal, he'd leap into his arms and sleep there all night. I could hardly concentrate on what I was doing, because every time I heard laughter, it sounded like them laughing. Every time I saw a mess of black curls attached to a boy's face, I wanted to hit him with my water bottle.

Why does life have to be this bloody unfair?

18

MARA

At the Chornoguy train station, I feel like Alice, forever falling into the rabbit hole, but instead of seeing the stars flashing by, I get attacked by all the chaos of the situation. People jostle and hustle, loud and messy, wrapped in clouds of confusion, exhaustion, rage, and despair. They remind me of a hundred supernovas, blown into phantasmagoric flowers of emotion, bringing both death of the old order and the birth of the next—a phoenix in the ashes.

Talking to them is not the same as taking them through The Slit when they stay in the orbit of their lost lives and can't see anything else but the shine of their broken chains. A month ago, I was certain only the dead could see me, but I was wrong. They saw me as a shadow on the screen, where their memoir theatre played their lives' dramas backwards, unwinding the glowing history thread circle by circle until nothing remained. Dust in the wind.

The living don't know it, but they are dust in the wind. Though, unlike the ghostly butterflies in my woods, volunteers here *hold on* to something so subtle and vast like the air you never notice until it's gone. I could break down to pieces their disarrayed thoughts and weigh every feeling, I could grope the basements of their convictions, the solid skeletons of their habits and experiences that filled their minds like cluttered shelves and cabinets of their command post. However, to be brutally honest, I couldn't find the core, that initial push, that power that made them leave their convictions, habits, and experiences and come here to feed the strangers in shock and disruption.

And the refugees... Dirt and blood on their coats and haze in their eyes, stone faces, stilled looks, constant calls and all the same questions: *Are you okay? Where are you? Do you need money?* Eating out of habit, sleeping whenever they fall. Hands covering their heads, erratic gulps of air, grips on their humble possessions, leaps of fear and leaps of faith, chuckles stopped abruptly, out of respect. Musicians playing the *bandura* in a trance, little children surrounding them, singing the national songs, and the beating, this cutting through, unstoppable beating of a heart, like a bird fluttering in a cage of invisible strings, the heart of something bigger than people in the trains and tents and the battles and graves. The heart of Earth that grieves with them all.

They may be just dust in the wind, but now, here, I can see them glow. They may hate it, and, well, they actually do, yet they glow like Christmas fairy lights finally connected to the source and each other. And they think I am one of them, which, I won't lie, feels pretty good.

I help one old lady to get off the train (in her case—fall off the train) and get nearly smashed to the ground by her bulky body in a bulky black fur coat smelling of naphthalene, soil, and one hundred and one recipes for apple pie. For a second, I feel attacked by a sweaty grizzly bear who snatches me by the hands and peeps into my face through glasses like two cups of lemonade.

"Dima! It's you, Dima!" she grins, showing an even line of fake golden teeth. In a flash, I see her son, Dima, in khaki, standing on his knees with his hands behind his head somewhere on the dirty road of a shelled village, surrounded by the swearing Russians, brandishing guns.

The houses behind him are just walls riddled with bullets with blind-eyes windows and roofs sunken to the ground. Dima and three other Ukrainian soldiers are stiff and weary, watching the soil, the trash rotting in it, the broken glass, flinders, bricks, shells, the melting snow, the grass pushing through like it doesn't know about the war and death hunting in the shambles of hopes. Their faces are grey with *knowing* what's coming. Life in their chests quivers like a string that lets the arrow fly. *Fascinating,* Dima thinks about the grass that keeps growing no matter what. Green and fresh, so young, so free, so joyful. It sways a little when the shots pierce the air, throwing a bunch of birds into the sky, and four bodies fall into the dirt face down.

I see Nyura, too, the old woman in a bear fur coat, a week later in a room she rents with her friends, getting a call from a sergeant who delivers the news in a cold voice that stutters when he reads the name from the list, then coughs violently into the receiver and begs his pardon. Nyura gulps without a sound like a fish trying to breathe the air and grips her chest where the air can no longer go. She lives for a few moments longer, and her heart quivers like a string that lets the arrow fly, aching for another arrow, the one that once was part of her. Then stops.

"Oh, dear, sorry, darling…" Nyura chuckles, snapping me back to the present, and her breath smells of all the rotting hopes. "I thought you were my son Dmytro. You look so much like him." She lets out another smelly chuckle and leans on my arm with all her whale weight.

"It's okay," I say, swallowing the remnants of the vision. "How was your trip?"

"Ghastly! But I made new friends, and that was worth it, dear. Oh, I remember once in Italy, I got lost in that damn Minotaur's labyrinth of their narrow stone streets. People were the only red thread to get to my hotel, dear. Even if I only knew how to say 'hi' and 'bye' in Italian, which is one word, mind you. Ah. Making friends is such fun… Like, on my first job in Kyiv, when I was only nineteen, a student, and in love with a moron. Do you think my family helped me? No, my friends were there for me…" She kept talking without pauses, leaping from one memory to another, overwhelming me with stories that flickered past me like a high-speed train, blurred into one giant long serpent on rails.

I try to remember every window on that train cos she is trusting me with her life, slipping away from her. She knows, she *feels* it is running down like water from a slanted roof, and she is in a hurry to leave all her acquired treasures in the hands of someone who can pass them on.

In the tent, I make her black tea with lemon and two sugars (her favourite), and she sips it with her eyes closed, smacking with her tongue. "The taste of heaven! Oh, how long I haven't had it. With all this modern cry for green teas and sugar-free diets, I think I was dead more than alive trying to live healthier." Nyura smiles at me, and I smile back.

She's happy. At least now, here. She'll die in a week but now she lives and it seems like all that matters to her. She won't be as happy tomorrow, but nothing will wipe out this moment of her life. It's a solid gemstone, and I'll keep it for her.

I used to be a death gates keeper. Now, I'm a memories connoisseur. Cool.

My first impulse is to find Aidan and share my discovery with him, but my scout has scooted off and clawed into some model-looking guy named Arman with a smile that charms and eyes that kill. Now my cat follows him everywhere and gapes at him like Arman is another Mona Lisa in a frame, and he was the one who painted it in the colours of his deepest meows and purrs. So, mostly, I hang out with the girls and other volunteers.

We don't just deal with the refugees, but also people coming from everywhere to offer their help. One elderly lady hobbles to our tents on two aching legs and two sticks and says she keeps a cow and a goat and makes cheese. I look at her face which reads "I haven't seen your twenty-first century yet, but I disapprove of it already" and ask what we shall do with her cheese.

"Why, give it to the kids of course!" she retorts and I have no guts to refuse. There are at least five kilos of it in her rucksack, and we all end up eating it on our next tea break.

It turns out so delicious that the senior volunteer asks Pani Varvara (the lady with two sticks) to bring us more tomorrow and gives her some of our extras, like flour, potatoes, and sugar. And I know Varvara will be here with the first roosters' cries carrying a giant pot of *varenyky* on her back, the dumplings that is, made with mashed potatoes and cottage cheese. It's the most famous local dish that will gather endless queues of hungry travellers (and I'll be one in the tail). And the day after that, one of our drivers will give her a lift, an even larger pot, and a shine to her grey days.

Then the vans with supplies arrive and we unload and sort the products, and it's shitloads of water bottles, tin cans, packs of nappies, napkins, hygienic products, and candies. In a few hours, I can see the people around me completely exhausted. One *pani* barely stands, and her eyes, even if open, don't see much over those grey bags of fatigue. I take the crate from her before it falls on the ground, and she smiles wearily at me with a short spasm of her cheek.

"I should probably go and rest," she adds apologetically.

"Yeah, you should." I sense her coming here right after her eight-hour work shift, and can't help asking her why she does it. She gives me another spasmodic smile.

"My husband is in captivity," her voice wobbles like surfing on a wave. "My dad and brother are serving, and my niece keeps asking me when they will be back. I think I just… I just can't stay home, do nothing, read the news, and fret. I need to help someone, at least… It keeps my mind off things. Otherwise, it'll crush me."

"This crate will crush you if you don't rest." I lift it a bit to highlight my reasoning.

She nods obediently. "Yes…"

"The world won't go anywhere if you sleep a little."

"No." She shrugs her puny shoulders as if shaking off a pressing burden. "I guess I'm just afraid to not wake up."

I stop midway with another crate in my hands. "What do you mean?"

"I mean… This is how life works. It goes on and if you can't go along, you get ill or die."

I've never heard anyone saying this so easily. "Um, yeah… but I thought people, they try to avoid discomfort and pain at any cause, and mostly they live for pleasure and entertainment."

Now her smile is genuine. "You're young. It's enough motivation for youngsters, but you'll know one day that pleasure and entertainment are only side effects."

"Excuse me?" I tilt my head, taking another load from her.

"Side effects," she repeats as if it can help. "When you do something right, I mean… when everything is balanced in your life, pleasure comes, and you enjoy it."

I meditate on her words, wandering by the windy streets of drowsy Booguy. If Aidan were here, we'd discuss human quirks, but he's taken his new friend to a picnic in Mor and is probably playing him his silly Italian songs. I wish he didn't get attached to someone whose destiny is to die, and also change their mind, forget, and break their words when convenient.

This would have sounded far more powerful and intimidating in my head were I not rambling around the town of mortals contemplating all the things they said at the refugee camp. It's illogical. It makes no sense. Suddenly, people are not what they've always been to me.

I stop at the playground and sit on a swing, remembering how fun it was to eat bananas with the wind blowing in my face as I swayed. Some kids are playing in the damp sandbox, building a castle where they put their plastic soldiers, call them Russians, and smash it all to the ground with their tiny spatulas. Their parents talk on or watch their phones with tired faces, crossed legs, and crossed arms. I take mine out and text in our mutual chat.

Mara

> *Hey, wanna hang out?*

Carmina Burana

> *YAS! I need 2 get out. This perfectly even line of books on my shelf is killing me!*

Agnieszka Aniol

> *It's called order, silly (⌣ ^ ⌣) And yes, can we see Aidan the cat? (* ‾ ⌣ ‾)*

Er, I take my eyes off the screen and look at a couple on the bench with their heads leaned toward each other, watching something on one phone. How shall I put it?

Mara

> *It's March, and my cat is on his sacred mating mission. I doubt you'd like to see that.*

Agnieszka Aniol

> *Ew! (> ‿ <)*

Carmina Burana

> *What? I thought u liked it. True love & romance from the films, gentle kisses, etc.*

Agnieszka Aniol

> *ʃ ⊃ ●_● ʅ ⊃ It's different!*

Carmina Burana

> *How exactly is it different?*

Agnieszka Aniol

> *Well, I'm not a cat, am I? I have a human body, and I'm entitled to human love (✿ ^ ‿ ^)*

I kinda want to write that Aidan has a human body, too, and is obviously after human love, but then decide that there are enough dramatic revelations for one day.

19

AGNIESZKA

23 March 2022, Day 28

War is ugly. War is heaps of bags and bundles that smell like Gran's wardrobe, cries and curses, a crowd of phantom-like kids that get sick on your coat, and tides, tides of dirt. Volunteering is not just about being a superhero with the superpower of a cuddly teddy bear. I'm not just on duty at the tents, making lists, serving food, giving directions, and doing other noble stuff, but also doing something really, really disgusting. Like cleaning up someone's vomit.

Today was our turn to tidy up. We washed up greasy-as-hell cauldrons outside, in the cold wind, without any detergents, while crowds of people with bags and children and cats and their griefs and traumas pushed past us in grim silence. Then we tidied the tents after some hundred people had littered there all day. It smelled like the devil's mouth. My princess coat now looks like a gypsy's welcome mat that someone accidentally threw over my shoulders. But even this dirty tent, which is now a little bit less dirty, is better than Russia.

Ben wrote me an ever-scrolling letter. I can only understand one word in ten. Even Google Translate converted it into complete gibberish. Who does he think I am? An English professor? Now I need to answer something clever, cool, funny, and seven pages long so as not to look like a stupid blondie. Ah, forget it. It's irrelevant what he thinks as I don't love him anymore. I have Arman now, who speaks the most melodic Ukrainian I've ever heard.

The only problem is that he does that mostly to Aidan-the-Shaggy-Eyebrows.

When I complained about that to Carma, she said it was because they were gay. Why does she always have to be this spectacularly irritating? I gulped air to look all oracle-wise and like I was a super expert on the matter. I didn't really know a thing about gays, but I improvised (lied), "Boys don't go gay when they talk to each other. Gays are those who wear one earring."

"Are they really?" she asked mockingly. "I thought those were pirates. They wore one earring."

"Pirates were gay, then."

I thought Carmina would choke herself to death from laughing so hard, but sadly, she didn't. Why do I even bother telling her stuff? She thinks men are Nature's biggest blunder. Anyway, Arman can't be gay; he has no right to be gay because I'm a useless zero-dater as a girl already. My chances to get him to fancy my boyish side are don't-even-think-about-thinking-about-it.

So, I shoved my best friend on the shoulder and said she wasn't helping.

"Helping with what?" she promptly switched her laughter to yelling. "Getting laid? Stop thinking about boys, blimey. There are thousands of zombies on our land, raping, robbing, and ruining lives. Do you really think dating is super necessary right now? Will it help anyone?"

I snapped, "And will not loving help?"

"Loving helps, I didn't say it doesn't. Mating is not loving. Don't you see the difference?"

What? *What* difference is she talking about? Carma must have gained another superpower of seeing invisible things, like nonexistent differences. In any case, I had no desire to discuss raping and killing. It's too horrid. I can't stand it so much that my head goes blank, gets sucked inside, and then all the victims I see on the news turn into plastic mannequins. So I won't feel their pain and horror. Men tend to go mad and do so much damage to this world, and somehow it always smells of S**.

Every time I think about S**, Pan Borov and his squeaky mattress come to mind, and my upper lip curls up in disgust. When actors kiss each other in the movies, I suddenly find a gazillion more interesting spots BUT THE SCREEN to rest my eyes on. If I watch it with Carmina, we go "Ewwww! Erlack!" and then I talk, talk like a cursed talking bot, and I wonder truly wondrous wonders like if veggies are dead or alive when we drag them from the soil. And why has nobody gone back to the moon in the last fifty years? But then those stupid lovers move to bed, and I want to move far-far-far away from them (like the moon, unless someone f*cks there, too).

What they do between the sheets doesn't differ much from the butcher's job, only this time, the meat yells and moans. But I don't think I need to worry about it because I'm going to marry a boy who will stay dressed with me even on a beach. Our love will be one thousand and one percent pure…

"And utopic," Carmina added when I voiced my thoughts. "You should marry a book character. You'll love it cos there's plenty of choices but also hate it cos the best are already taken."

"Book characters don't exist," I pout.

"Neither do boys who swim in suits and ties."

Ow, this was sensationally wicked. Never again will I talk about boys with Her Feministic Genius.

Back in Booguy, I sat to do algebra (algebore) but mostly stared out of the window, watching Shrimp stalking in the backyard. He perched himself on top of the woodpile and preened his feathers. Amazingly, this goose found a military base in the big city and Carma in it, and I can't even find x in this goddamned equation. How stupid and useless am I? Very stupid and useless, that's how. Why do I think Arman would date a sweet-natured little elf that exists only in my stupid head? I turned to my spiritual guidebook for consolation. Buddha said our pure crystal mind is always within us, under thick layers of dust that cover the shine of our true selves. Great! Now, I'm also a rock inside a dirty pig.

•

24 March 2022, Day 29

I must do something to stop being this ordinary silly girl. And not just for Arman, for Ukraine, for my shiny true Buddha self. We did our usual bid at the train station, and it was better than Maths because there were no xs or ys but real people with real stories.

Today we met a train from Severodonets'k. The stuffed-up-to-the-ceiling carriages brought like one million families; even the upper shelves for the luggage were occupied by children and pets. They slugged down on the platform and panted like they had actually run all the way across the country. "They fired at us. We had to evacuate people from the back carriage and detach it on the go. Sorry, may I have tea?"

All of them asked for candies and put three sugars in a cup. Kids wolfed cupcakes in such a hurry, literally stuffing themselves, and fell flat on the ground when the train made the loud CLINK sound on the rails. The elders grabbed me by the shoulder every time any noise came and asked if it was really safe here. And when I said it was, nobody believed it.

People from the centre or north of the country are not like that. They come with smiles and money, joking about liqueur in their coffee and picking lodgings meticulously. People from the east don't care where they sleep, their phones are always uncharged, and their things are lost or destroyed. They are looking for their relatives and cry when I bring them sweets. I keep telling them "It's okay, you'll be fine" and think about broken porcelain vases that will forever carry cracks no matter how neatly we glue them back in one piece. About a pebble thrown in a pond. The ripples on the surface will eventually stop, but the pebble will stay on the bottom. Forever.

It aches so much that I can't do anything more for them. We only help them hold together and collect their stories as proof of Russian crimes. Mara collected one million and one horrors from the front line, and Carmina told us one million and one ways to become a superhero.

She said everyone did that, and it was no big deal. You don't have to be able to fly to save lives. A boy of nine sang songs in the city square, and a girl of eleven played draughts and won every single time. They raised heaps of money for bulletproof vests for our soldiers. People gifted coffees, cooked dinners, knitted socks, adopted orphans, took sick animals off the streets, and went out on the balconies of ruined houses playing *Nay, thou art not dead, Ukraine* on sax.

So inspiring.

Carmina called it magic even though there were no elves or witches, just ordinary people. One girl of sixteen got shot in the back, fell, and pretended to be dead when the Russian cannibal grabbed her phone and silver cross and kicked her in the leg. When he left, she crawled and crawled and crawled, leaving a blood trail on the ground all the way across the street to her gran's car. She survived by a miracle. Because she had *something* to live for. I don't know why my eyes welled up hearing this story. Maybe because I have nothing really to crawl across the street for? Magic never happens to me; boyfriends go gay or write incomprehensible letters about UFOs.

I went all completely soppy when Mara passed a story about two postmen, killed by the Russian army while driving money to pensioners in the suburbs. Shot point blank and robbed. She said the next day, two more postmen drove there, knowing that could be their last trip. One *pani* in Genichesk gave sunflower seeds to a Russian soldier so he'd give life to sunflowers when he rots in our soil.

I thought, like, could I be this brave? They weren't immortal superhumans; none waited for any help from Krypton. Is this what makes people stand out? Would Arman fall for me if I were this brave, too?

"And then there was this sapper, Jumper," Mara continued with her eyes sparkling, "who saw the prevailing number of the enemy gathering at the river and knew there was nothing to be done to stop them. He'd really little time to think and blew up the bridge with himself on it."

I burst into tears, like a drama princess.

Mara stared back at me and asked why I was crying, was he a friend? I sobbed "N-no, I've never met Pa-pan Jumper, it's just s-so very… sad" and her eyes went all truck-headlights round.

"Don't mind her." Carmina gave me a napkin. "She's that sensitive. It's her superpower."

Then she suggested that we help more, do more, do something super great, something just as heroic. Mara said she could try and ask the dead to rise against all vicious minds on our land, and we gawped at her like she'd just sent trees to fly. "What?" She looked from one blank face to the other. "Come on, haven't you heard about restless souls and poltergeists?"

Carmina said, "I was actually thinking about selling something to raise money for drones."

"Hmm." Mara squinted at her.

"Tarot, voodoo, white magic, and all that is cool, but seriously, we need something solid to answer the aggressor," Carmina went on. "I'd raise the dead if we were attacked by the dead."

Mara fixed her in her gaze for a moment but then shrugged. "As you say. I'll go and unstick my stupid bro from his new catnip boytoy before Arman kicks the bucket and rests in my hut forever."

My God, she's *loca*. I won't be surprised if she turns into a wolf one day and carries me to the moon and back (still thinking about what's hiding there because NASA fell suddenly on their heads and said we should build air farms there. What are air farms?).

Anyway, I'm perfectly determined to make more of a difference by selling my soaps and such to raise money and save lives. So the next time I meet with Arman, I won't be a silly seal, I'll be a super charitable businesswoman. Even *kurwa* Liza will acknowledge my big heart. I'll tell Daddy how much I care, just like him, for our nation. Then

Pan President will call me personally and invite me to his castle to dine with his family, because if not for me, Ukraine would fall.

·

25 March 2022, Day 30

Gran Bozhena let me work in her studio and take all I need to make my soap masterpieces. So very kind of her. It's a lovely little place, a gentle blend of a glasshouse and a fantasy smithy, with long shelves of pretty pots and strange-looking figurines.

They gave me the creeps at first, but then, after Bozhena fiddled with each little gnome in her wrinkled fingers and told me their stories, they seemed rather exotic and not at all spooky. She spoke of them like they were living alien beings with their own characters, like my dolls.

Once, I believed my dolls were alive. I heard them talking to each other at night. Through the veil of my daze, I kinda saw them finish the interrupted game at my bed. Mommy said I just dreamt it, but when I told Bozhena, she chuckled and said, "Many things pass unnoticed because we think it's really nothing."

Hmm. Hmmmm.

I have my own desk near the fire and plenty of materials like honey, oils, and herbs. I can buy ingredients online; Mommy doesn't mind since it's for the greater good. Bozhena gave me her newly baked pots, too, so I can paint them all I like. I wish I could save lives with it; I wish I were magic. Not just *Harry Potter* fantasy, but *really* magic.

·

We returned from the Chornoguy train station with a Varus shopping cart filled with the remnants of the aid supplies. Nobody knew what to do with that load. Eventually, volunteers decided to give it to the animal shelter. So, we took it with us on the way to Svitlan's clinic. Our way meandered through the woods, coated in fluffy haze, still and silent.

Even though Arman was stuck in my head like a pebble in a shoe, the fog beat off the desire to talk about boys, somehow. Besides, I didn't want to spike the crazy feminist in Carmina again. I thought about my soaps and pots and wondered if she believed in magic.

"Like what Mara said? About the living dead?" Carmina asked as she swung a branch in front of her like a Cossack's sabre while I pushed the cart.

"And curses, and bewitching. Do you think Shrimp can talk?"

She giggled. "He talks all right. I just don't get goose language."

"No, I mean… You know what I mean."

Carmina slowed down and looked around the empty road. "It might be nothing but… I think I saw a ghost," she whispered.

"What ghost?" I hiccupped as my heart jumped in my chest.

"I don't know. Like little children? I didn't *really* see them, but heard them romping about, you know, like kids do. Then someone small and quick skipped behind the trees and vanished."

I couldn't believe my ears. She described exactly what I saw the day I ran into the woods with Shrimp. "Are you sure?" My knuckles went white from gripping the cart handle.

"Yeah! I told Mara about them, and she said they were the kids killed in the bombing. They're kinda stuck because they don't know that they died, so they can't really die."

I didn't say another word, too afraid I was of seeing the ghosts again. The sound of our steps shuffling on the damp asphalt and the squeak of the cart's wheels were the only answers. I was thinking about Mara, living alone in the woods, swarmed by ghosts, spirits, and God knows what else. I'd go crackers if I were her. She's always calm, though, never afraid. Nothing seemed to throw her for a loop. How brave she must be!

"Look!" Carmina pulled at my sleeve. "Another victim running from the war."

I jumped at the thought of meeting a dead child, but it was just a dog pissing on a tree stump. He looked thin, almost transparent, with dishevelled patches of grey fur on the sides. We felt sorry for the poor animal, who must have escaped here from the blasts and shelling.

"Let's take him to Dr Svitlan," Carmina said, and I already imagined telling Arman about our brave deed of saving a living soul from the cruelty of the war. We could even get on the news! The reporter would comment "Ukrainians are truly amazing. Two girls rescued a dying husky from the forest and returned him to his grieving owner, who lost her pet after Russians bombed her house in Vinnytsia." The footage is of a crying old *pani* and her dog running up to lick her face. Everyone is happy, happy, happy. And smitten by my kindness, Arman asks me to be his girlfriend.

We spent another half hour trying to catch the stupid beast. He wasn't at all happy to get saved, as I could tell. Whoever taught him dog manners failed to bash any sense into his head. He grinned with his fangs and growled at us and only paid us some respect when we swung a pack of *cabanossi* at his nose. I tied my belt around his chest as a sort of leash, and we dragged him to the shopping cart left on the road. With inhuman effort (and more *cabanossi*), we sat him in the cart.

The rest of the trip was less stressful. Our new friend enjoyed the ride, and we nicknamed him Ryder, like a shopping cart cowboy, yeehaw. I even started sort-of-maybe liking dogs (but only huskies); he was so sweet when he howled at the passing cars. But upon arriving at the shelter, he went completely feral. This poor, wretched war victim started a bloody bedlam.

We took the front door leading to the vet reception area because he obviously needed a check first, and who knew it was staffed with animals and owners like a hive of wild bees? They all jerked, their dogs barked, cats leapt up the walls, rabbits ran, and parrots savaged the cages. People cried, and it all looked like a road straight to hell, not pending fame in the evening news with a lurking wedding altar in Odesa for all my virtues.

Svitlan ran out of his clinic to see what the hell was going on. He looked at us with the husky and knew exactly what the hell it was. "What the… Carmina!" he yelled. "By God, why did you bring a WOLF here?"

20

CARMINA

SHADOWS ON THE CAVE WALL

From: Carmina Burana   25 March 2022, 14:01

To: Severin Saint   Chornoguy

Dear Dad,

Do you know how to tell a husky from a wolf? I don't even know how to tell my head from a kamikaze drone buzzing like one hundred mopeds in the sky, it aches so much after Svitlan yelled at me at the vet. I mean, jeez, why the *kurwa* fuss? Once in a millenary, a *BRILLIANT IDEA* entered my mind, and this time, I did something superheroic for the country. I rescued a dying animal, helped Nature, and expressed truly Buddhist compassion. So what if he turned out to be a wild beast and not at all dying? Even wild beasts don't mind a little adventure in a shopping cart with a snack. Life is too short to waste a chance to show your bros on a leash what it's like to be wild, free, and dangerous. (No, he didn't bite. He was nice and civil, just like a doggie. Don't believe Ma if she says I fell prey to a forest monster.)

Apart from going a little Mowgli, working with Svitlan in a pet shelter is much better than joining the army (surprise!) cos nobody tells me that I'm too young, or too much of a girl. The army will never take me seriously, I suppose. They'll always put me in a box labelled "female" like it makes any difference in the fight. Death has no signed boxes; it takes us equally. I am the great-granddaughter of Cossacks. They carried their intent through centuries to put this cry for freedom into my lungs. I have the equal right to fight and carry the spirit of my nation.

Ukraine is not about men. Girls are not about having boyfriends and kids. Blimey, I don't want to sit in a box all my life!

Animals have no such crap in their heads. They never squander their time trying to figure out who you are. They don't give a dead rat's crap about who you are. They only care if you have good intentions, and their radar never fails. Agnieszka says beasts are dumb and really lack purpose. But if by "purpose," she means labelling boxes, I'd rather doze with Svitlan's cats forever, thank you.

We don't do anything serious on this "home front," just feed, clean, play with pets, and teach them their names: super relaxing. It helps me forget about the war and all the injustice in the world.

Yesterday I sat on a crate and used my sleeping superpowers to throw a ball. It hit the floor, then the opposite wall, and flew back to me. A swarm of doggies ran after it, barking like mad. The luckiest, who caught it before it boomeranged into my hands, got the biscuit. It went on for hours cos I was literally pinned to the spot with Mimi the cat on my lap. Whenever I come, she nests on me like I'm her personal chair.

Anyway, I was throwing the ball. Mimi cuddled like a fluffy bread loaf on my lap and watched the bunch of loony dopes of doggies. She didn't meow anything, just squinted around and growled resentfully when I moved my legs. Then it hit me—BAM!—like a ball at the wall. I realized, with utmost clarity, that there was a living being tucked into my belly. Not a cat. A cat is just a "box" called a "cat."

She was a… creature. She felt pain and joy; she was a character like us and saw the same world we did but understood it in some way inconceivable to us. In other words, a total mystery sat on my lap and, blimey, you can never tell the same about people!

Because you come to them to stroke their hair or play with a ball, and they're like "Stop dumping your dirty socks under the bed, it's disgusting!"

Or worse still: "Hey cutie, are you on Facebook?"

Or they grab you and hang you on the nearest tree cos of the bracelet in the colours of your country. No, wait. Russians don't count. They aren't quite people.

It's sort of okay here. Still, we hear distant explosions and never feel safe, only hopeful. I don't put anything on the windowsill, and I estimate roughly the direction of the glass shards' blast wave. Finally, I understand a lot from physics. And when there are no sirens for hours, and it's quiet, a bit *too* quiet, the silence stresses us even more: we think, like, what are those fuckers up to?

I can't stop hating them, Dad. Torturing and shooting helpless civilians is normal to them. No, not normal. "Normal" is the wrong word, rather "routine." And not just killing. I heard so many stories of them raping mothers in front of their kids, roaming around the village searching for girls under ten and then hanging their savaged bodies like trophies outside, or burning them in a heap like garbage. Pan Tolstoy, what did you, *kurwa*, write about love, peace, and compassion? Did it help? There are towns in the east with not a single hut that survived the bombing. My pen pals keep asking why, why they do it. If they want that land so badly, why do they blast, rob, rape, and shit on every little bit of it? I wish they were *just* rapists, *just* killers, *just* looters. That would mean they are people, bad and wicked, but still people. Who are they now? Who the fuck are they now?

I don't think others know it as Ukrainians know. Cos many say there are more humane ways to resolve this "conflict" and keep the great Russian face clean. The world is bound to "stay positive" and "open-minded." They get outraged by what they do to us but not too much cos poor great Russia! We can't cast any bad light on Pushkin and Tolstoy, can we? And all those innocent Russians who don't do any evil, just watch us die in slow agony online, then go back to enjoying their ballet and balalaikas. At first, I thought they were idiots. They are not. They are accomplices.

Kids I met at the Chornoguy train station, hungry, shocked, and hurt, never said "Let's give up to stop this war." Their homes are gone, and their lives are in pieces like a jigsaw puzzle, broken and half-burnt. Still, they chant *Glory to Ukraine!* instead of thanks for the candy.

So don't get mad if I go bananas and fart fire from every pore when I hear about "peace talks." Who talks peace with maniacs? We will only start thinking about thinking about halftones with the cannibals when the last living, dead, or unborn Russian leaves our land.

But. Even after they get what they deserve, I won't forgive them. How can I? Like, okay, let Putin go to prison, and like, nothing happened. Fuck Buddhist compassion. Ruzis take *pleasure* and *pride* in shedding our blood. Let their blood now wash it away. It's only fair.

I wish women ruled the world. Nobody would kill for gas and oil or invent nukes. Women would go all magic, care for the planet, and look into the future. They'd take us to the stars, not show off their rockets and bombs. Agnieszka thinks it's too feminist (i.e., bad). And sitting in a bomb shelter while a bunch of barmy gorillas rattle guns over your head is like okay? Let's be honest and admit at last that men made the world as it is, including nukes and wars. MEN.

I went so mad biscuit about it, really. I saw the dudes getting off the train and wanted to yell at them, *What in the dragon's fart are you doing here? Go back and fight in your stupid war! Everyone will call you a hero.*

Today, I was sorting packs of warm clothes at the volunteer centre and really, really fuming. So when Aidan came to ask me where to get no-sugar, no-gluten, no-lactose food for refugees with special needs, I looked at his stupid boy face on top of his stupid boy torso on top of his stupid boy legs, and yelled, "Go to hell!"

I thought he'd never talk to me after that. But he grinned and said, "So, that's where all healthy food comes from?"

Actually, I don't think Aidan is stupid. He's fine like, probably, some other boys. Sometimes I look at the macaroni blast of his hair and think he must be suffering through brushing that just like I do. He's got a forever-laughing mouth and no idea what to do with his hands if not shoving them into his pockets. When I don't think about Ruzis and stuff, my rage subsides, and things appear different. Clear and transparent. Like with Mimi, I see that the world is not just about war, politics, and men going all ape-y, it's much, MUCH bigger.

And, damn, how I want to break free and run away into this big world!

Once I saw three little ghosts in the woods. Real blimey ghosts! Do you think I went mad? But the girls saw them too, so ha! They exist, Pa, they do, it's not my fantasy!

But that's not all.

The other fabulously warm day, we were walking home with Mara and the gang. Aidan and Arman strode in front, so I caught their shadows on the asphalt. Dad, I can swear I saw one long boy's shadow and one short cat's imprint, shimmering in the light. The pointy ears and a tail looked like a little devil on all fours. I nudged the girls in the ribs and pointed at that nonsense. Mara grinned with her ragged line of sharp teeth and said, "Yeah, he's a cat. Some people are

just like that. Look at mine."

I turned and saw two long shadows behind us, mine and Agnieszka's. Cold crept down my spine, and my stomach ached like it had been punched. Cos, holy dickens, Pa, Mara HAD NO SHADOW, none whatsoever, like she was… a ghost from the woods!

We giggled stupidly like it was nothing, but inside I screamed WTF?

When we got home, Nesha said it was just an optical illusion and asked me never to mention it again. So, I'm writing this to you, cos it will blow me up if I don't.

Now. You know what I think? I think, why would people kill each other most brutally for a toilet pan or gas when they can walk down the road, turn their heads, and see something that will turn their world upside down?

Do you believe in wonders, Captain Papa?

Your slightly shocked Skipper

21

MARA

Aidan drives me up the wall with his silly songs. Every day, after we return from volunteering, he comes up with a new poem about his Arman-the-Golden-Sun, and that guitar never shuts up. SO annoying. I run outside with my book for some peace and quiet, sit on the mossy log of a fallen tree, and read about Mayan pyramids. No sooner do I reach page two than I hear it coming.

> *Caramel fingers, shaped and round,*
> *Amazing grace in every lovely turn.*
> *I once was lost but now I'm found,*
> *Was freezing cold but now I burn…*

Aidan winds between the trees like a tipsy medieval bard with a guitar over his shoulder, singing his heart away,

> *Your touch set light to the dark night,*
> *Your touch has set my fears free.*
> *I burnt candles but you are the sunlight,*
> *I was so blind but now I see.*

He straddles the log next to me. I do my best to ignore him but fail to read a single line. Aidan hoists his instrument up his red-shirted chest and says, "Wait for the best part, you'll cry when you hear it."

"Good luck with that," I grumble and turn the page. He sings,

In every strand of golden hair,
In every curve of the godly face,
I see my joy and my despair,
I see your amazing grace.

My eyes shoot up. I say "Bravo, kitten. Now if you don't mind, I'll get on with reading something deep and meaningful" and return to my book.

Aidan gets tangled up somewhere in the full eclipse of his in-love mind, then pops up with, "Do you think Arman will like my songs?"

"Gosh, give me a rest!"

Aidan scratches his head, looking up dreamily at the tree crowns. "He is so intelligent and beautiful, but also proud. He is a fighter. All his life, he's trying to be what he is, not what others expect him to be. I was just wondering… what's that about? He is always what he is. I mean, who else can he be? I just don't get it. I never saw him turning into a bat or something."

I open my mouth to explain it but I might just as well be talking to a bug and if I dressed this log in my hoodie, he would talk to it for hours.

"His parents are tyrants," Aidan goes on ignoring my attempts. "Not like Russians, small-size tyrants. Arman says they control his every move even though he's already sixteen. Like… get this, they don't let him have a kitten!" He gives it a thought and then asks, "How old am I, Mara?"

I take a guess. "Two hundred and sixty-four?" Merely a teen by the sound of him.

"You won't mind if I have a human, will you?" He beams at me.

"Pardon?"

"Arman could live with us in Huttuh! We could travel the world together, visit mermaids and griffins, *mavkas* and Daddy Lisovyk. I could introduce him to our swamp lady, *Pani Kikimora*. Get this! He thinks it's a swear word, like, you old *kikimora!*" he bellows with laughter. "She'll crack in half if I tell her."

"What are you talking about? He can't live in Huttuh. He's not dead or a *molfar!*"

Aidan stops giggling and gives me a serious look. "Then I'll stay with Arman."

It catches me in the throat, like a swallowed hedgehog. I lower my book on my lap. "What do you mean, *stay* with Arman?"

Aidan leans his guitar on the log and moves his bum closer to me. "I mean, my heart belongs to this charming young human. I will go wherever he goes. It's my destiny."

I slam my book shut. "Your destiny is to help the dead pass The Slit, remember?"

"Not anymore. I love Arman, Mara. I want to stay with him." His gaze is gleaming and adamant.

Unbelievable! I can feel my insides getting sucked out. "Aidan… you are…a cat," I say with long pauses as if explaining economics to a dolphin.

"I know!" He thrusts his hands in the air. "Arman adores cats. We could make a good team."

I sigh. What he says is a crime against common sense, a brutal violation of the order of orders, and simply mean. "Are you seriously leaving your Baba Yaga? Just like that?" I stare at him.

"Look, I'm sorry. I'm sure your mother will send you a better sidekick." Silence on both sides. Aidan hides his fists in his pockets. "Come on, say you won't keep me against my will. We are friends. You don't own your friends, right?"

I honestly can't think of anything to say. Well, I could, but it would only make sense to someone with brains not blended into a love soup. "You are not going anywhere," I finally say. "The war will be over, and Arman will get back to his beautiful, intelligent, and proud life. He'll forget about you; they all do. They come and go and don't notice a bloody thing under their noses unless it's on their silly little screens."

"Arman is not like that," Aidan protests. "He seriously wants to widen his horizons. He says this war changed him and made him get out of his golden shell and do something. He volunteers, not just to help those in need but also to revolt against his family and their rules, any rules in fact."

"But the war will end, and he will return to his golden shell. He widens his horizons only until his world smashes into college, money, friends, family, love, and success. Then he'll die. End of story. Your friendship will turn into an odd blotch on his memory, drowned in many daily troubles and dreams and desires and regrets and fears and all that crap. I don't want to hurt you, kitty, but people are just like that. He will never love you as much as you love him. Because he never really *sees* you."

Aidan lowers his eyes, bitterly. "But he does now. Something happened, and people see us." He mumbles to the log between us, "They got united in their grief. Many forget about things you say and reach out to each other. Many remember what they are really living for. Maybe we, too, should come out and really *see* them?"

"There is nothing to see. I know them very well," I blurt out, although I don't believe it anymore. My voice whiffles like a fizzled balloon. After flashing through so many shaken minds on the train station, singing with strangers on a bus, seeing Carmina doing cartwheels just cos the morning turned sunny, and listening to Agnieszka's twaddle about her magic dolls, I can't call it bollocks and retreat into my books. To tell the truth, I enjoy their company, even if all they do is extremely silly.

I don't just sweep along their lives and dump them into The Slit like a candy wrapper in a waste bin; I share the moment. It's not just me and Aidan against the living anymore. Why didn't I see it this way before? All of a sudden, people are no longer my enemies. Because now, death is no longer a blind spot for them. "You are right." I stand up.

"Am I?" Aidan looks up. His face is so childish when he's sad.

"Yes. Yes! It's that simple. I know why they can't get through The Slit! Come on, it's almost time." I grab his guitar, beckon him with my book in hand, and run back to Huttuh.

Aidan leapfrogs off the log and skips behind me in his cat shape.

"These people die in agony; they are shocked and shuttered," I say on the go, "like those refugees on the train. They don't know what to do! And I was such an ass not to assist them. I thought, like, it's all their problem, I'm just a gatekeeper. Gosh, and I marvelled at why they were so stupid, why they never looked my way or never wondered about death and stuff. Well, I was only interested in their stories, not *them*. Death was hiding, too, that's why!"

This is all very interesting, but what the heck do you mean? Aidan meows as we enter the hut, and he hops on top of the armchair.

I sweep all my lemonade bottles from the pantry and trot around the room. "We must broaden our horizons, kitty, and break our habits, too. We'll do what witches do when the time changes."

What do the witches do? He widens his eyes at me.

"They move."

The floor under my feet vibrates from anticipation. Huttuh gets my thoughts, all right.

•

In half an hour, the crack between day and night opens: the sun sinks behind the flat clouds like a heavy ball of fire, a yolk drowning in a glass of water. Aidan and I are on the second-floor balcony, which still smells of fresh wood and varnish, newly crafted by my masterful hut. She marches through the forest, proudly swinging her legs and puffing through her chimney.

We can see the liquid haze of the dead in the ravine. It's growing like a tide. The voices of hundreds of lost souls join into a monotonous, mournful call. It lifts into the skies in a sonorous howl of a phantom organ. My heart turns into stone, heavy and sharp, as I look around the simmering ocean of the dead. Damn, I hope it'll work!

"We'll park here." I swallow the lump in my throat. "Now, kitty, grab a lemonade, tissues, and toys for kids. We're getting poor refugees to settle at last."

"Oh, cool! We play volunteers!"

Aidan can't help smiling when we drag out a table with a thermos and a box of ham-and- cheese sandwiches, just like we did at the train station.

I tsk. "We don't *play* volunteers, we *are* volunteers. That's our mission. We don't *keep* the gates from them. I finally got it. We *show* the gates!"

"Oh… right," Aidan agrees, still smiling carelessly. Such a nincompoop. He can't care less about what our sacred job is about, as long as he plays human in it.

I open The Slit, but instead of the beacon, I take a bottle of lemonade and shuffle out into the mist. Aidan is making hot coffee at the skull circle. He cheers me by beaming from ear to ear and double-thumbing up. Still, my courage fails me. My legs turn into dough sticks, and I totter along like an octopus learning to walk on land. My heart is pounding so hard, it moves up to my head. Because now, I must look them in the eyes. *Look them in the eyes*, I mumble under my breath. *Look the dead in the eyes.*

Save me.

When I finally touch one cloud-like woman on the shoulder, breath fills my lungs again: she looks just like many more on the Chornoguy train platform, scared, lost, and hopeless. Her eyes reflect sadness, unbearable sadness.

"I can't find Misha." She trembles. Shivers run along her ghostly body like ripples on the water's surface. "Did you see my dog? I've lost my baby."

"I'm sure we'll find him," I tell her. She gives me a mystified gaze, probably taking me for an emergency worker, so I act like one. "You are cold and must be hungry. I'll make you hot tea."

As she leans on my arm, I drown in the whirlpool of the short twenty-five years of her life, wrapped into one single minute of our stroll to the table with snacks.

I am a girl called Zoriana, and I was born to sing. I sang when I was four, prancing by the cobbled lane, pulling at Mom's warm, firm hand. It was just a silly two-line song about flying away on a big air balloon, but so fun and enticing that it possessed me. I sang in my parents' car every time we drove somewhere far on holiday. Oh, I loved singing in the car, because my parents always joined in, and baby Sasha tried hard to accompany us by banging on his toy drum.

Even Opera, my silly dachshund, wailed happily to the tune and once nearly fell out of the window.

I sang pop songs exactly as my guiding stars did. It was a game I played at school. I would go like Evanescence, Lady Gaga, and Whitney Houston. My pals nicknamed me Parrot for this. I sang in the conservatory, too, mostly opera, and my teachers kept telling me I had talent. It explained why nobody in the concert hall moved when I let my alien voice free. They gaped at me in disbelief, an ocean of wide-open eyes. It's because the sound I gave went so low, vast, and powerful, that it hardly fit in my lungs and rushed out like a giant tornado. It only took a song to untie any knot in my chest. When I was sad, or angry, I set my tornado free, and it crushed all the walls in my way.

I don't have talent, I must say, I have JOY in singing. I have a purpose. This is what I tell myself, hiding down in the Mariupol' theatre with my husband and dog. Misha is resting his head on my lap, snoring, as I solve Sudoku on my phone. Many people I know are here, my mates and family. We cuddle together on the mats and benches in the empty halls like stray cats, hoping to get through another day. Can't help dozing off. I'm still sleeping when the blast of a tornado stronger than mine collapses the roof on top of our heads. I've never heard a scream as loud and high as this. But I can't waste a note. Where is Misha? He was with me. Where did he go? I find myself alone among the debris of the crushed concrete, dust, and metal. Where is *anybody!?*

Then I see myself lying there, unnaturally twisted and silent.

Zoriana lifts her eyes from the steaming cup in her hands and looks at me.

"Am I dead?"

I nod. "And my family? Misha?" Her eyes get intense.

"I will find your dog," I promise. "You need to rest. When you are

ready, the light will guide you."

She presses her lips tight and nods. I leave her with Aidan and dive back into the mist. It's gonna be the longest hour in my memory.

•

Time steals the dying seconds away, one by one, as the room dips slowly into darkness. Silence gathers around the fire and three candles on the coffee table. I deliberately leave the electric lights off because they make me sad, and I'm super sad already. Sensing my mood precisely, Huttuh puts a glass of milk and a cookie on the table. Aidan jumps on my lap, purring like a living generator. He tucks his tiny paws under himself and lies on his belly. I stroke his silky fur gratefully and think about Misha, the lost dog. My heart would blow to pieces if I lost Aidan. I wish he never met that Arman from Odesa.

Do you still think that people are stupid and useless? And make no sense? he asks, looking into the fire.

"No. Now I think they make sense." I pet him behind the ears. "But most of them never think about making sense, never look for it until it's too late."

Shall I tell Arman about this? So he can… get prepared?

My hand halts on his back. "If you wish."

I miss him so much, and there are still hours before I see him again. I've just composed another poem. Would you like to hear it? He tilts his head back and stares at me with his big green eyes.

"If I must," I sigh wearily.

> *Being lonely was my biggest fear*
> *Before you made it disappear*
> *By simply being,*
> *Even if not here*

Oh dear, this is not about Arman. This is so much about me.

22

AGNIESZKA

26 March 2022, Day 31

Smetana went mad. We tried all available trademarks in the local shops, and they all tasted like a bomb blasted in a milk jar. The cows probably produced it under gunfire, in the storm and smoke of the blows. It's bitter and sour from their blood, sweat, and tears. I found it rather romantic and was ready to eat it with my eyes shut for the sake of Ukrainian economics, but the Buranas said no, and now, they only buy it from the local farmers. I don't mind as long as they pay taxes and donate to the army.

Gran Bozhena took my patriotic soaps and pots with my ornaments to the charity fair, and they all sold out. She said people, even foreigners, loved them so much, they asked if I kept a special shop. A shop! Me? *Fantasticamus!* Mommy promised to open business accounts on all social media for my works, sell them online, and send them by post. All money raised will go to the hospitals on the front line helping doctors do their sacred duty. I could hardly breathe from excitement when I texted Daddy the news. He'll be so proud of his little princess. I think of others, too, see? I'm a true Buddhist.

NOT thinking about Arman, though, nuh-uh. He hadn't popped into my head once, with his piano-long fingers casually skittering over his iPhone's screen, scanning the news scroll. And I definitely didn't walk past his rented cottage six times on my afternoon promenade in case he was there (which he wasn't). I wish I'd brought at least two more Lolita dresses to save him (his refined taste) from running screaming into the woods once my ogre looks lurk in the distance.

You know what? I feel comfy in my sweater and strident feminist pants. It won't roll out a red carpet under my feet or blind me with camera flashes, but nothing aches in my ribs or steals my warmth. I am a happy, happy, comfy ugly ogre. If Arman doesn't fancy my Shrek, he will never get me, the princess. Wow, it sounded so, like, brilliant that I spilt the beans to Carma as we nested in our bed to read.

She gave a loud horse grunt. "Just for once, can you think about anything BUT Arman?"

And I thought about Aidan, a different pot of borscht, but maybe, just maybe, he could be my boyfriend instead. He seems handsome but wild and really unpredictable. One minute, he discusses music quite seriously, then suddenly "Oh, look, a bug! Quick, let's catch it!"

Once he fell asleep right on the platform bench because he said it was so warm and sunny, why not take a nap? Who naps in the chaos of the train station just because it's sunny? Only country bumpkins with extra eyebrows on top of their eyebrows, and hair living on its own. I could only figure out his features when he tied it up in a bun on the back of his head.

If he kisses me, I won't be able to tell it from a brush of Mommy's fur coat against my face. Oh God, no, why did I think that? It's in my brain now, ewwwww! A gazillion and one mosquito bites of his BEARD!!!! Yuk! yuk! yuk! Fork and knife! Fork and knife!

"Fork and knife!" I yelled.

Carmina jumped on the bed and hit the shelf above her head.

"*Caramba*! I'm reading a Jesus-horrible horror. Nearly shit my pants, you nut. What's the matter with you?"

I stuck my nose back into *Great Expectations.* "Nothing." How to get smart in one minute? Just talk like you dropped from Venus and saw all the rules in the arse. "I just thought it's bad, very bad feng shui to have a window in the bedroom facing west. It will take us like forty goldfish and a dream catcher made with dragon hairs to smooth our karma. I can lose my Arman if I don't wake up to the waking sun."

"Good!" Carmina turned back to her horrors. "You better lose him before he puts his parts into you, and you lose your mind over it."

How rude! "He's not a putting-his-parts kind of man, stop it," I said, blushing.

"Oh, really?" Carmina glared at me. "What's he gonna do with his parts then?"

I pulled the blanket over my knees and my book up to my nose, and mumbled, "Nothing."

"Nothing?" She squinted.

"Nothing! Just…" I muffled it through the blanket, "Piss."

"Well, tell him to piss off then when he dares to paw your tits. And I can tell you exactly what he'll do." Carmina was in her fizzy drink bottle mode and thoroughly shaken.

"Well, don't!"

"He will pi…"

"Don't!" I kicked her in the leg.

She snapped, "Well, I won't then!"

"Well, don't."

"I won't."

"Yes, don't."

"I won't!"

"DON'T!"

There stretched a rubber band of electrified silence. Then the lid popped off Carma's bottle. "He'll piss off to snog someone else. Someone who's not such a booby about it."

Good God. Next time I raise the question of boys with her, I am SO throwing myself down the stairs. "You are cruel," I complained. "Why are you so cruel to me?"

"I'm not cruel, I'm just being factual. You don't buy a cake just to look at it, do you?"

I pouted. "So?"

"So boys don't date girls just to hold hands with them."

"I see nothing wrong with just holding hands! Neither does Arman," I snapped, switching off the lamp on my side and burying myself under blankets, leaving Carmina to her stinking horrors.

There's no way to convince her that dating is not about s**. Arman is different. He never looked at me *that way*, like in the films when the characters suddenly find the perfect moment to suck at each other. Maybe he doesn't need it at all. He might even be magic. What if he's come from the stars and has the power to turn Russians into dust? Hmm. Why would he hide in this hole then? Oh well, he might be just an ordinary cool guy with a big lion's heart. He might just as well be the psychopathic rapist waiting for a chance to stick his hand under my sweater. Or worse… he might be Russian! Aaaah, shut up, brain!

•

27 March 2022, Day 32

At church again, listening to Eggie's speech (his name is Father Yashko, but I'll never remember that). His head is so sleek that all the candles of the shrine gleam off it like the shield of Archangel

Michael. He could be a Buddhist monk in disguise. They all go Jason Statham and proud because it's bad, very bad karma to have hair like Carmina's. Carmina, who doesn't give a curly pig about talking eggs and almost fell from the bench in her sleep.

I try to look *artful* in my vulgar shapeless jumper because Arman is two rows behind me, and my neck is about to crack from too much turning around. I couldn't wait to talk to him, get him mesmerised by my soap success, blind him with the shine of my talent and loving heart when he learns about my "shop." Well, before I had any chance to stun him, Mommy dragged me to Pan Egg to have his blessing.

"How about we get baptised, Pumpkin Pie?" she asked as we made our way through the crowd between the benches. "Father Yashko says it wards off bad luck. What do you think if he does it?"

Maldito mierda poo is what I think. "Mom, I'm a Buddhist!"

She tutted. "You can be a baptised Buddhist; nobody dies from that."

Well, I'll be the first. I could die right there listening to her telling and retelling how much we suffered back home, what a total purgatory Daddy is going through, etcetera, etcetera. Her voice swam tipsily from one word to another, then sank midway into snivelling. I felt stupid. She never cried before me. Why would she do it for some egg man? People gathered around with their pitying oh-s and ah-s and talked to Mommy like nannies to a kindergartener. I wished they'd shut up and stop going on about my dad in that sorry way. Like he was dead already.

Daddy didn't reply to my message yet. Too busy saving lives, I suppose. And why would he talk to me about soaps? Why would Mommy talk to me when she has a perfectly round egg in Father Yashko? Well, FINE.

I ran to join Carmina on the benches. She was with Arman, showing him pics on her phone. My heart immediately started drum-diboom-booming as I plopped my bum next to His Highness. There are times when my thoughts spin quite fast, like a washing machine on spin-dry mode. However, there are also times when they don't move, but sit there in a confused silence, shrugging at me. Like now. My princess gloss faded beside Arman as if it were a fake gilding next to a solid gold piece. They say love gives wings, but I didn't feel any wings. I was rather Icarus who instead of drowning in the sea, fell accidentally on this bench.

We had a lovely chat though. Well, he and Carmina did. I just did my best to come up with two words of sense put together to prove my parents did teach me to speak. Every time I thought of something cute and clever to adorn their conversation with, it was all about poo, Buddha, and in a stupid Spanish accent. I pulled my sweater over my nose and wished to stay there till the day I died. By the time I was finally ready to produce something a little bit more sophisticated, I was so high on my deodorant fumes that my powers of speaking were only enough to say, "You know I make soaps. Really, you should buy one."

Arman looked back at me, abashed. Entire galaxies went crashing down and the damned world set on fire. It did sound like I called him dirty. *Mierda.*

Better die now!

•

28 March 2022, Day 33

Dad still didn't reply to my string of messages, didn't even see it. I start worrying if he's all right. When I asked Mommy if she heard from him, she snapped, "Do I look like his secretary?" Meaning she had no news but won't talk to me about it. She believes if she doesn't talk about something, it doesn't happen. And who's the child among the two of us?

I texted Maví. She said she and her folks moved to Dnipro because hardly anything worked back in Zapahorb, and enemy fire fell like never-ending hail. *My God.*

Ran around the house looking for Tofu and his magic cuddles, but he fell through the ground and now was probably halfway to the cat universe where everyone is too busy sleeping twenty hours a day to fight in stinking wars. Shrimp, perched on top of the woodpile, watched my convulsive scurry like a kitty would watch a laser dot. Exhausted, I plopped beside him and stroked his back. "Shush, pretend to be a cat. I need to pet a cat, or else I'll cry and never stop."

Did I imagine it, or did he really say "Meow?"

Meeting trains with new waves of refugees felt exhausting. I couldn't stop being shocked by all the grief these people carried along, like dirty coats that had grown into their skin. One guy in a too-thin summer jacket with blots and cuts came up smoking and talked like a robot to the empty space between us. I stared at his reddish neck with pimples, old jeans like buggy sails, and stinky cig between his trembling, dirty fingers. He was freezing but didn't seem to even notice. And I was choking, but not from the smoke—from his story.

About a family that Russians shot in front of his eyes. A girl and a boy no older than twelve, their parents. Pushed them out of their house, shot them in the head, and left them on the doorstep.

About bodies lying in the off-road, slowly turning into dirt in the snowy drizzle. Because of the bombing, people couldn't get out of the cellars to bury them. Someone covered the dead with old carpets so that kids wouldn't see them. But kids, they are so curious…

About a bloodied sneaker in a puddle. It flew off with the blast wave, only a sneaker.

I didn't know what to say, or what to think. I smelled the burning plastic of the neighbours' flats I saw back home, the crumbled skeletons of houses, and blood on dirty snow. Every Russian I knew suddenly grew sort of transparent, and ugly sneering goblins showed through their faces.

"Even now, I close my eyes and see the bodies," the man kept moaning. "I see that sneaker. Every time I close my eyes, I see it. Like it's here, in a time loop."

I showed him to the tents and wobbled back to my duties, still smelling smoke and thinking about Daddy back in that hell. I went so shuttered and depressed that my head ached like a cracked melon. I dropped the box of nappies when sorting the supplies, and Mara picked it up for me.

"Hey," she said to my greenish face. "You look tired, would you like some tea?" Like I was one of those lost travellers. She took me by the arm, very grown-up-ish, and led me to the table with the thermos flasks.

Her touch was firm and steady, like Daddy's on our park strolls on the big holidays. When I got the flu, wherever he was, even in the *complete circus* of the hospital, Daddy found a minute to sit by my bed and say things like "No flu can break you unless you agree with it" and other medical enigmas which I didn't get and didn't have to because his mere presence was enough to make things fine again. If only he was here, safe, my head would immediately heal back into one piece.

"Everything will be all right with your dad." Mara tapped into my thoughts as if there were a back door for all the willing bums to read my mind. Her eyes, fixed on me, were so black, it felt like they could suck me in. Brr.

I nodded and sipped my tea nervously. Earth is nice (between wars), but right now, I'd prefer to join a dying star on its silent drift to Complete Nothing. Suddenly, I wanted to talk about something else, *anything* else, just like Mommy who goes into her panic wardrobe revision every time something truly alarming bangs at her door. I came up with the superiorly intelligent "Do you have a boyfriend?"

Mara raised her eyebrow, just one, and said, "I have a cat."

Mmm, makes sense. I sulked for about ten seconds more then found it too gross and thought about ice-cream-cool Arman. With my nose catching the fragrant steam from my cup, I set my bucket mouth loose. "You know what's weird? Every time I see this boy, I wait for the butterflies to dance in my stomach or what it is they call butterflies, but I only go queasy. Is love a kind of sickness? Like smoking cigarettes? You start with coughing, end up a pathetic addict, and die from lung cancer but proud you were cool enough to do it? I really don't get the fun of it, but if Carmina is right and dating is all about snogging, I only hope I won't vomit while doing it with my future boyfriend."

Mara flashed me a lopsided smile. "Why do you need a boyfriend at all?"

"Why? What do you mean *why?*" My lungs suddenly ran short of air. "It's… Well, it's obvious!"

"Not for me." She shrugged

"Really." I crossed my arms over my chest and blinked one million times, trying to process a totally unprocessable equation. "I just need a boyfriend, or I'll be an old spinster and loser. Yes. And I need him to be magic, kind, intelligent, and cute. But if his armpits stink, he draws dicks on the toilet tiles, or says 'bitch' to sound cool, I'll suggest he go straight to the Buddhist monastery to monk himself out for the next forty years of his life."

Mara chuckled. "You've just sent the entire boy population there."

"All but one. My perfect future boyfriend." I saw Arman with Aidan coming to the platform. "I'll go and say 'hi' to Arman and your brother."

Arman noticed me and smiled, granting me a ticket to ride on a cloud. In less than a fairy's twinkle, my head went light, my fatigue turned to joy. Aww, Arman, I could eat you alive, but I won't because it would be terribly awkward to marry you afterwards.

Shining with the light of a million smug fairies, I squeezed into their conversation about cats. Ah, finally, a subject I could handle! I almost completely made sense, telling how Tofu climbed the bathroom door to look scornfully down at us all, then panicked and cried to take his freaked-out bum down. They laughed. I snickered alone and thought about all forty-three muscles in the human face because I made such an unnatural sound, some of them must have snapped.

Aidan said, "The worst of all is hair, hair everywhere. Mara runs amuck when she finds hair in places hair should not be, like her cup of cocoa. I say it is completely not my fault, and she goes 'QUITE!' Because it's my hair's fault, and so she's gonna shave me bald cos she has already 'HAD IT UP TO HERE.'"

"Oh, no," His Highness said. "Nothing is wrong with your lovely hair."

And I said "Er," clapped my eyes stupidly and added "Errrrr," even stupider. And before I had a chance to join my shocked brain cells together and figure out how the hell it all became about Aidan's mane, Arman reached his hand out and touched his black curls, very fondly and sweetly.

I felt like screaming and throwing my arms above my head. But I only smiled a psychopath's grin like it was so, like, fine to touch Aidan's hair very fondly and sweetly. Like I was sticking there just for the mere chance to see his very fond and sweet touch of Aidan's hair!

But what I really, *really* wished was to crabwalk back to the tent and drown myself in a teacup with seven kilos of sugar.

They didn't pay any attention. I suppose they wouldn't notice me even if I turned into a donkey and bit their heads off. They just stood there and chuckled at each other like two loving dolts, emanating the tenderness and affection of true Buddha hearts. And I was that hard apple piece stuck in between their teeth, only instead of being an apple piece, I was the ugly troll, and instead of being in their teeth, I was in a state of complete disaster.

Okay, breathe, Agnieszka. I need a break from being a Buddha princess for a tad and… MIERDA BLOODY POOOOOOO!

Once I believed that the Cold War happened in Iceland, that brothels were where broths came from, and that Arman was designed by the gods of the heavens specially for my *magnifico* princess heart. Now, I wished he would just die in the arms of Pan Bushy Brows and leave me *mierda* alone.

They didn't leave me alone, of course not (too shoot-me-gentlemen). We walked to the tent together. I lolloped along, trying to add my usual malarkey in the pauses and NOT sound like a gays-eating

Nazi. Then I said, "Do you plan to stay here for long, Arman?" Oh, brilliant!

"No, actually… My family is moving back to Odesa." Arman flipped his golden hair back without touching it. (*Aww*… no, shut up! It's too gay.) "Father has a business to keep, and I must get back to study for Oxford. Besides, there are also people in need. I can volunteer from there."

I think Aidan died a little. "But it's war," he said in a voice of panic.

"Yes but… Odesa is a fortress. No matter how the Russians try, they will never in a million years get it. We'll fight, we'll survive. Everything will be fine." Arman looked back at us, smiling reassuringly, with his hands in his pockets. "I feel I must go home and be where my heart is."

Yes, go. And leave *my* heart where it should be.

•

29 March 2022, Day 34

I may know little in life. There is no way to predict when this war will finally crush into our victory or to say if Cossacks really caught bullets with bare hands. But I know a lot about being in love. And, really, none of it smiles at me. I went back to being a soap-making, trash-wearing bucket of soppy jelly, and guess what? I love it. Waddling around in muddy boots with my not-so-blonde-already hair tied in a bun is oh my God, such freedom. Why did I even care about looking fairy-like, walking fairy-like, talking fairy-like? Whenever Arman glimmered on the horizon like a glorious rising sun, a little flicker of electricity shot through my brain and turned all my fairies into Frankenstein's monster. And I hate it. I hate hating myself for hating this. Enough! *Basta!* If this is love, I'm taking the next spaceship out of this sh…

And anyway, I have a war to fight. People to help. So, it's decided. I'm gonna join some happy virgin nun clan!

Breaking the news about it to the brutal rottweiler with slightly better manners, i.e., Carma, was a minefield to cross. Really, I didn't want to spend hours ripping a psycho-feminist off the ceiling. But there was really little choice when she burst through the bathroom door in an explosion of bright orange trainers with blots of dirt from Jackie Chan-ing in the rainy backyard. And my virgin nun clan meditation balloon blew flat.

"Can you knock?" I snapped, still in my lotus pose with fingers in the mudra of peace.

She plopped on the toilet. "No. I need to pee, and this is the bathroom. Can you go Zen somewhere else? It's an emergency."

Charming. Everything she does is an emergency and needs to be done yesterday. Soon I might only see the flickering light of her moving around. I stomped out of the bathroom, slamming the door shut, very un-Buddha-like, and grabbed my *Burda* magazine.

"What's up? Arman dumped you or what?" came from the bathroom.

"No, *I* dumped him! I dumped all boys in this world for the sake of shapeless sweaters."

Water flashed and splashed, and then Carmina burst out with, "So he *is* gay?"

I sensed my inner chi moving not quite harmonized at that moment. To be utterly honest, Buddha so died in me, that I felt like hurling *Burda* at Carmina's face. She plopped next to me on the bed, totally unaware of my killing mood.

"Yes," I mumbled, and, without any notice, stupid tears ran down my cheeks. "And he's going back to Odesa."

I thought my heart would blow like a Russian rocket, destroying everything for miles around. Carma immediately started the anti-panic operation and rushed in search of Tofu but brought Mommy instead. She flipped-flopped in her pink bathrobe, with her hair pinned up and a moisturizing mask turning her into a leper, but happy as a jumping ball.

"Bunny, it's Dad. I've got news!" she exclaimed, then paused. "Ow, sweetheart, don't cry, Daddy is fine. I contacted Doctor Oko, his colleague, and he said they moved to the hospital. Half of Zapahorb is under blackout, so they moved there and worked on diesel generators. Martin's phone battery died, that's all."

My tears drained so quickly that my head felt like it could float away. "He's fine?"

"He's fine! He promised to call us in a few hours. Dear me, I must go have a haircut and perm. No volunteering for today, girls." Mommy shot out of the room faster than I've ever seen her shooting out of anything.

Oh well, I wasn't in the mood to see the glamorous prince of Odesa anyway. In fact, I wasn't in the mood to move at all. Better spend the rest of the war growing roots into that bed. Tofu padded in silently, jumped on the windowsill, and sat there watching sparrows in the window, pretending like he didn't give a fig if I existed. Then Shrimp waddled his way in, very mannerly and wary, flew up to the bed, grazing me with his massive wing, and settled there next to me.

I brushed my ruffled hair from my eyes and said, "What?"

He cackled "Gah" and rested his head on my lap.

That was actually nice. So calming. I petted his white feathers like he was a big, goosy cat. And my helium balloon head finally landed. I took my phone and texted Mara, hoping she hadn't thrown hers at Lisovyk in self-defense.

Agnieszka Aniol

> *Do you ever feel lonely?* (´ ° __ ° `)

She responded in seconds.

Mara

> *I have Aidan.*

Agnieszka Aniol

> *Yes, but... He's your brother and I mean someone dear to you* (●' ⌣ ' ●) *Someone you could talk to for hours and tell your deepest secrets* (❀ ⌣ __ ⌣)

Mara

> *What do these symbols mean in your text?*

Agnieszka Aniol

> *What symbols?* (⊙_⊙)?

Mara

> *The ones in parentheses.*

Agnieszka Aniol

> o(≧∀≦)o *Lol, they are not symbols!* (¬ ‿ ¬) *They are emojis! It's like faces. They tell you how I look when I write the message.*

Mara

> *They don't even look human.*

Agnieszka Aniol

> *No, but... They express emotion. Haven't you ever used them?* (.' ⌣ '.)

Mara

> *No. And I'm pretty sure people don't smile when they send a face with a smile.*

Agnieszka Aniol

> *No, but they smile on the inside. It's... the feeling that we share* (~ ̄ ▽ ̄)~

Mara

> *Right. Yes, I do feel lonely sometimes, but not cos I have nobody to talk to. Talking is boring. And predictable. Sit for hours, looking at each other, what's the point?*

Agnieszka Aniol

> *Er... in... knowing each other better?* ‾\\(_°o)/‾

Mara

> *And?*

Agnieszka Aniol

> *And...* (°—° //) *being together, being friends...*

Mara

> *Yes, and?*

Agnieszka Aniol

> *Don't you want to have friends* (´·ω·`)?

Mara

> *I do, but not to chat with them. I wish I had friends who would have the same aim as me, go where I go, do stuff together, make discoveries, and share our experiences. Together we could go further, do more, understand better, you see what I mean?*

Agnieszka Aniol

> *Erm, yeah, I guess so* (°_°)

I stared at the screen for like a million years, at the killingly correct spelling and punctuation in Mara's message, imagining her reading some boring history book in her lonely hut in the woods, looking like a hole in time and space. How she must be... sad. I so wanted to cheer her up and say something wise, cool, and supportive. And by wise, cool, and supportive I didn't mean my silly dolls or anything as ridiculous, but then I texted:

Agnieszka Aniol

> *Would you like to play dolls with me someday?* (❀´‿`❀)

She took time to write back.

Mara

         ヽ(*°▽°*)ﾉ

Oh, my God. I smiled like a dolt, seeing it. Being this miserable and still smiling. How crazy is that? I must be a schizophrenic with two minds that use my facial expressions by turns.

•

Mommy primped herself into a s** bomb just for the call, and it all went wasted because we weren't yet online for ten seconds when she started to cry and flushed it all down the drain. Imagine Marilyn Monroe, who instead of singing *I wanna be loved by you*, sobbed to the mic. Exactly. That was my mom.

But it was all irrelevant because Daddy was cosmically happy to see us.

He looked different, though. I hardly recognized him in that haggard, thin face with hollow cheeks and stubbly grey chin. The shadows under his eyes darkened like bruises, and he wore like ten layers of bum's clothes and a bum's hat. Because of the blackout. He said they had to save every bit of power for running the medical equipment and heating the surgeries.

"We sleep in coats for three or four hours a day because people come in crowds. The mobile connection is failing, and I think it's gonna get worse. But we gotta fight this fight."

"No, you gotta shut up and evacuate," Mommy fired back. "You hear me? Get on that train!"

Daddy rubbed his chin. "Well… I'm afraid the railway is blocked but don't worry, the army has come. They promised to open the green corridor and take us in their cars to the nearest station."

The army has come, yay, YAY! Blessed be the Ukrainian Army.

Daddy said that before they waded their glorious way into Zapahorb, people defended their homes with pure rage and fate itself. Because the rains swelled the lands around, and the river rose just in time to see the Russian tanks sink into the bog.

"There were only the police and the territorial defence battalion. We had no weapons, no armoured vehicles, nothing," Daddy continued. "Only several tons of industrial explosives."

I asked, "What is that?"

"Dynamite, Poppet. We are a mining city, remember? We mined every road and tunnel and blew down the only bridge connecting us to the west. They kept bombing us like mad; there wasn't a single day without the bombing, and people, children died in my arms before we could even get them on the table..." He stopped and nodded, looking down. We only saw his hat in the camera.

"Oh, honey..." Mommy sighed, patting her eyes with a hanky.

"And do you think we gave up? Do you think we are ever giving in?" he went on in an iron tone I never knew he had. "We cut trees to jam the roads, block the airport with trucks, change road signs to *Go to Hell, Ruzies*, make Bandera cocktails, patrol the streets. One of our brigades, sent to Donbas, left two tanks that couldn't shoot or even move but looked okay. We loaded them on platforms and dragged them all around the city. Freaked-out locals took pics and texted each other. The enemy monitored it and trembled, thinking we've got a full armoured division here. Yeah... Power and road engineers never rest in this place, trust me; if they did, they'd still fix it in their sleep. Girls, I've never seen my people so angry and awake. And scared. God, I was so scared, but then the army came at last. I mean, just a hundred or so soldiers, but you should have seen how we cheered when they arrived. And the volunteers? Do you know what they do here?"

Daddy didn't give us a chance to ask what. "Wonders, absolute wonders. Bring stuff, find food, water, tools, batteries, and warm clothes in this mess when the world is crashing down. *Panis* from the neighbourhood cook for us on the open fire, and if not for them, I don't know if we'd keep half of our patients afloat. I ask them, why didn't you leave? They knew it was coming, they *know* it's gonna go to hell. They say, what will happen to the medical personnel then? What will happen to the patients? What will happen to their confined parents, pets, or friends in the army or railway or utility services? They sent their kids to safety, but not everyone should leave, they say. And I thought it was like a safety net. We are a safety net. Everything is connected, and we care for every chain, see? I don't even *know* these guys! I think I just love them. God, I don't know why I'm talking this much, I just miss you so… I just want you to remember what we are standing for here."

And I, all tearful and rabid, wanted him to remember that he was my father and I needed him. Here. And quick.

•

30 March 2022, Day 35

After losing my almost-boyfriend, seeing hell in Daddy's eyes, and feeling peace is gone forever, it's really nice to return to the state of serene normality where the world makes sense.

One day, I'll work out exactly where it is.

Today, on a bus to Chornoguy with Carmina, I was thinking about my life being a random collection of bloopers with Russian missiles blasting in the background. I must have given such a thousand-mile stare, like a doll in a plastic box on the shop shelf, that Carmina asked, "Did you sleep last night?"

"I had a solid thirty minutes. It's okay, you're not even that blurry. All three of you."

She looked at me like I'd just gotten smashed by a car. "How long?"

I started bending my fingers, counting sleepless nights. "I need more fingers."

"You need to sleep!"

I don't need to sleep. I need Arman-the-God to stop being this magnificently mega-gorge. It's annoying. Love is annoying. It's not anything *good*, it's a sodding ocean: sink just a tad deeper, and you drown. And I mean not in a nice way, like drowning in a bath of jelly bears, no, you bloody choke to death!

We saw him sashaying near the tents, still tall like my standards, still not mine. He put on a refined air as if plugged into an invisible player, listening to something inexplicably divine inside his head. Again, I felt my legs turn jelloid, and a smile crept back to my face.

"Hi!" Carmina gave him a high five. "No VOLUNTEER jacket today?"

He shook his head gracefully. "No, I'm here just to say goodbye. I'm leaving on Friday."

"Oh." My smile vanished. He's not just gay; he's a faraway gay. How terrible and disastrous was that? Very terrible and disastrous, that's how.

Then all terrible and disastrous things went pronto oh-my-God *magnifico,* when he said, "I'll miss you girls. Was really cool to meet you. Are you on Instagram?" Yes, he did say that, he did.

We exchanged Instagram handles and scrolled each other's profiles, giggling at the photos. He even updated his story with our group selfie, and I didn't mind my face looking like an old potato in a sock. Because it was an old potato next to His Highness. I couldn't believe Arman was this, um... easy? He said he felt at home with us because we weren't die-or-date-me sort of chicks who really put him out. That's when Carmina broke into hysteric ha-has, and I had to jab her in the ribs to keep her from ruining the moment.

"So we'll be friends forever then?" I asked.

He said, "I'd love to." And the sun suddenly shone a little sunnier. He's my friend. Arman is my friend! And I don't need to stuff myself into two-size-smaller skirts or kill my hair blonde for that. *Excelente!*

I was in blissful spirits for about five seconds when the day promptly decided to take a turn. Because Arman left us to say good-bye to others, and it was like somebody turned off the lights. "Others" were mostly girls who surrounded him and snickered at his every word, no matter what he said, even if he said nothing, just coughed. I wondered if he praised them for being this natural and homely, too. In any case, they didn't take any selfies together, so there!

Then Aidan arrived in such a terrible mood, I didn't have the heart or—quite honestly— the courage to shine a smile on his angry mafioso face. He confined himself to the food tent, scribbling away on a paper napkin. I took a moment off from sorting supplies to look over his shoulder at his scrawls, written as if with his left tail.

I met you and realized

You've always been around,

Hidden in my mind,

Waiting to be found

Again

"It's a nice little poem." I nodded, keeping my hands locked behind my back.

Aidan shot me a look with his alarmed hazel eyes. "Do you think Arman will like it?"

"Dunno, but you better hurry up to find out because he's leaving quite soon."

"Oh, no!" He rushed out so hurricane-hurriedly, I had to pick up the stuff dropped from the tabletop.

Through the flap in the tent, I could see him catching up with Arman. His lips said, *Blah blah don't go, I have a gift for you.* Arman stared down at it in dismay, *Oh, a napkin! How sweet.* Aidan stepped

closer, and they nearly bumped their heads together (because personal space was Aidan's personal enemy). *No. Open it.* Arman opened it,
and by the flare on his tanned cheeks, I could say his world crushed
against that napkin for one heartbeat.

(Deep sigh) Okay, it was my first ever love story, and I'd had
enough of it. I'll never be able to love Arman like Aidan does. I'm
not even sure I *want* to love Arman or boys altogether. Let's admit
it, my life will never be this giddy-tiddlywinks romantic. Magic always happens to someone else because being a total loser is what I
really excel at. Not even my soaps, pots, dresses, dolls or embroidery,
and definitely not my immaculate common sense (and I know it be-

cause I'm writing this, sitting behind the stinking crates).

Hiding from my problems behind rubbish probably wasn't the best decision, but nothing else rushed through my blendered brain. They say that in crucial situations, like wars and stress, people break their limits and go beyond. Well, I guess my beyond meant hiding, and that was a problem. First, because everyone knew I was there. Half the tent saw me drop to my knees and crawl away. Second, because it's so crowded I will be needing a Ring of Power to deal with the consequences, and finally, Carmina could recognize my sticking-out boots anywhere.

"Hey!" She peeped over the crates, like a serial killer playing hide and seek and finding his victim. "What's up? People over there need your help."

"I'm not going there," I whined.

Carmina crawled in and pushed me aside to fit her minus-twenty-five kilos of weight. "Okay, spit it out. What's going on? I've got tissues in case you feel like crying."

"It's just… I dunno." I rubbed my eyes with my sleeves. "Arman is leaving, Aidan is his forever after, and I think like… Is this all? I'm not dating him, and I just realised I'll never date anyone. And if I don't, what is there for me?"

She goggled at me. "What is there where?"

"There. In my life. I'll finish school. Maybe. When we win. I'll study law or medicine or business or anything as boring to make my parents happy, then what? I'll open my craft shop and… and what? It was so easy before the war. I knew what had to come next, or maybe, just didn't think about it. But now that I think about it… You see, there is no magic in this world, only boys with their parts to put in others and this stupid, stinking war!"

"Holy cow, Nesha, a hut on bird's legs cooks and makes cushions, Mara casts no shadow, some guys can't see her, my dad goes through hell, dancing, and you say there is no magic?" She stared at me hard for a few moments.

"Well, it's not magic, it's delusion. Buddha said that."

"Why would he say that?" Carmina's brow furrowed.

"Because there is no magic in Buddhaland!" I cried. "It never happens like that. You wait for a miracle, or just sleep and know one day you'll wake up to a magic kiss and the wonderland will just drop you on the head, but all you get on your head is a *mierda* Russian bomb."

Carmina frowned at me so hard her eyebrows creased into an accordion. "But the miracle did happen! You saw Aidan's shadow."

"No, I did not. We imagined that. The shadows, elven world, fairies, ghosts, dolls, Narnia and *Harry Potter*—all that, it's just childish make-believing. Grow up, Carmina. It's called wishful thinking."

She stared at me with a blank expression as my logic wormed its way in. After a few seconds of nothing, she finally snapped, "You've just said you wanted magic, and now you say it's all bollocks and it never happens. Decide already what it is that you want."

I flung my jazz hands in the air. "Gosh, as if I knew. The day I suss that out, there'll probably be Armageddon. But I do know… I know that…" I cast about for any sort of words to translate that weight on my chest. "There are six-year-olds winning Olympic medals and rising stars strutting on red carpets by nine. And I'm a fourteen-year-old useless bucket of plankton even gorgeous boys can't fix. I thought I felt like a loser because I was all magic inside, you know, like Spiderman or Cinderella; they had a secret. Even if they were losers, they had this magic sparkle. What if there is no such thing? What if it's only a fiction? There is no sparkle. I'm just a loser inside a loser."

"Agnieszka… What is it all about? We are at war. It has nothing to do with your sparkles."

"That's the point!" I raved, then sighed. "Look. I don't want to sound whiney and, like, ungrateful. I know Ukrainians die awful deaths all around, and it's really so very shocking and gross, but, in fairness, it doesn't change a thing. They just die. Nothing can be done about that because some dicks in Moscow say so, and *basta*. And when I think about it, I think, is this all? We just die? No secret? No magic? The world is tedious. It's full of kindness and beauty, too, but duh, it's tedious. I want… more. It so cracks me up that nobody notices something is really missing in this life."

I finally managed to shut up before people got freaked out by the talking crates and ripped the entire tent to shreds, because, God help me, it was mostly in Russian.

Carmina gave me an extremely bizarre look.

"What?" I said and felt like a blown-off dandelion, ex-dandelion, barely anything anymore.

"You are really losing it, ain't you? Relax, breathe, Zen, omm." She patted me on my knee. "Do you know what Gran said when I went psycho about the army and told her almost the same things?"

I fiddled with my hair, braiding and unbraiding my braids; dang if I knew why. A dandelion with no fluff and no meaning. "Let me guess," I stammered, jumping over the lumps in my throat like the enemy block posts. "She went, 'Back in my days, blah blah blah' and ding! You were back in the Middle Ages?"

"No-o," she tinkled with laughter. "Well, yes. But right after the Middle Ages, she said I was that little fish in search of the ocean."

I stopped torturing my hair. "What little fish?"

"A little fish was looking for the ocean." Carmina tuned her narrator's voice. "It swam from one place to another, from one fish to another, asking directions. It wanted it big, wanted it epic, wanted it exactly as in all those books and films, and poems and songs." Her voice went higher as if she were singing an opera. "Finally, one old fish swam up to it, waved around, and said, '*This* is the ocean, you dumbo.' 'This?' said the little fish indignantly. 'This is just water. What I want is *the ocean*.'"

My heartbeat pulsed. "Um… That's gripping. But what does it mean for me?"

"Hell if I know, you tell me." Carmina shot me a smile. "But how I see it is that magic or whatever you meant by 'more' is not wishful thinking, cos it's not in our heads. It's over there." She nodded at the legs shuffling in the tent we could see through the holes in the crates. "Too big and too obvious to notice."

"Call me thick, but I still don't get it," I lied because my face now pulsed like a red emergency button, so I definitely got something.

Carmina chewed at her plump lips. "You know we call the guys who work on the railway People of Steel for a reason," she said in a miles-distant voice. "These trains come from the cities torn to pieces by Ruzi sadists. But none of the workers fled. They keep packing refugees and bringing them out of hell. Then they go back to hell for every single breathing soul to save, or to fix the railway lines in the fire rain. Do you think they aren't scared? Like shit they are. But when the siren wails, the train stops, and the bombs blast, the conductors can't cuddle into little human balls with the rest and pray. They find the guts to get up and answer those prayers like, *It's okay, all will be fine, don't worry.* Then they get caught for just doing their duty, get tortured and killed, and maybe they'd rather run, but there is yet another whimpering kid, a freaked-out mother, a shell-shocked dog, or even a goldfish in a plastic bag. They don't think their lives are more important than that fish. And if they die, they'd rather sell their souls for one little living being."

The tears welling in her eyes froze me. I couldn't remember Carmina ever crying.

"These people are like those losers in *The Wizard of Oz*, who had wits, courage, and heart even if they didn't know they had it. Even if they needed to go through the horror of a Russian meat mincer to know they had it all this time. Is it tedious for you, too?" She turned her face to me, and her eyes glittered like diamonds.

I focused on my fingers going white from gripping my knees. "Maybe not."

"Of course, there are also people like Dorothy and Toto," she continued, "who only wanted to go back."

I whimpered, "I want to go back."

"Nobody is going back. There is no going back, no more home as it used to be."

"Then what is there?"

She tugged at her tangled curls. "Dunno. Do you remember the train that arrived the other day, all riddled with shrapnel?" Now her voice reached dramatic peaks. "The driver said he took the risk to sneak the entire six carriages of people past an enemy tank. He said it was certain death, but the people all shrunk there in terror gave him this magic kick to do the impossible. This is just... beyond everything. Doesn't it look like the 'secret sparkle' you want? True superhuman superpower."

"Superpower just to... survive?" I managed to squeeze through my throat lumps.

"Yeah, okay, it does look like we're just trying to survive to do the same damn thing we did before, but we are not just surviving. We are getting tempered. We discover our hearts and courage and wits. And when we are ready, nothing will be the same again."

By the time we finished this earthquake eruption talk, I felt a bit like Bilbo in *The Hobbit* when thirteen brash and shameless dwarfs broke into his hut and pulled him out of his cosy tree hole for the biggest adventure of his life. Which at first seemed as cheesy as my stupid diary scribbles.

Then there was no time for magic talk or discovering our hearts and wits because the train from Mariupol' arrived, and many passengers came from Zapahorb, too. We met Pan Doopa from Carma's block, with his arm and head plastered. He was the kind of man even angels wouldn't talk to. Every time his bulldog head moved in my direction, I found the asphalt so very interesting. But today I almost hugged that troll, I missed home so, so, so much.

He looked like many separate pieces barely holding together. Displaying earth-shattering amounts of self-control, he said that our house caught the blast. "Half the building crumbled… only a few sets of flats left," he added with canyon-deep pauses and gave me an ice-still gaze. "Your dad is fine, he patched me up. But many died, many…"

Oh. My. God. Oh my God, my dolls, my dresses, my stuff. Oh my god, Daddy! I felt, like, stuck inside the cut-off elevator, falling fifty stories in a second. My stomach wasn't even remotely attached to my belly. And I didn't think I could breathe any more.

There is no going back, Carma said. *There is no home as it used to be.* We are homeless bums now.

Carmina fixed me with her warrior glare. "Now, all cosmopolitan pacifists who dare say Russians are people with hearts like ours can straight-up go suck a lemon!"

23

CARMINA

I AM DEATH

From: Carmina Burana   30 March 2022, 23:50

To: Severin Saint   Booguy

Dad,

My rage is so Ukrainian, it doesn't translate. Russians will burn in hell forever. Nah, what am I talking about? They are already in hell; they came from hell. That place around Moscow is a damned demons' den. Russia is where the demons rise, but since nobody believes in it now, we just call them terrorists.

Gosh, I'm so angry, and Ma is like, *Don't be angry, it ruins your karma.* And lying that I'm happy like a dope doesn't? Anyway, whatever, I'm not gonna waste my letter talking about Ruzis cos my laptop will just burn. And also, I'm tired of it.

I'm tired of people who never lost anything, too. They are really silly because they feel guilty for being, like, okay when I'm not. Every time I tell anyone here about you on the front line, in dirty, cold trenches, literally holding demons off from tidy houses with lacy curtains and Jesuses in the frames, they look like someone's brought flowers to their graves. I DON'T NEED THEIR SORRY FACES just cos they are sorry themselves for not being sorry enough.

On the other hand, there are people like Liza, so naïve and stupid, first-level goblins with zero intellect. They talk about freedom like it's a gift. But nobody gives or sells it. You can't expect it from anyone, anything, anywhere. There are no fabrics of freedom, no places that connect you to freedom like free Wi-Fi. You take it yourself, you fight for it, you ache for it: this is true freedom. You can't move to France or the States or the bloody moon and there, you are free. Bullshit. That Russian bomb will get you anywhere. In your head.

Did Ma tell you? Our home is gone. All of it. The stuff I collected for years is gone, and people I knew are in hospital or squashed under the ruins. It's like, all our life is crushed into dust, but do you think I cry for it? Duh! Cities will be rebuilt, things will be remade, Cossacks will rise from ashes because our roots stretch so deep, our spirit soars so high, stupid heartless terrorists can't even imagine. Sadly, they never will cos they'll all die here. One way or another, demons fall back to their pit.

I miss my kung fu weapons, though, staff and nunchaku. Grandad promised to remake them, but my darling first weapon… You never forget your first weapon, so familiar to my palms it hurts. Agnieszka keeps listing to me all sixty (or however many, I forgot) dolls from her doll pantheon, their names, their characters, their looks, their skills, their stories, like they were real people sharing her room. Which, if you are wondering, which you are probably not, but anyway, is pretty scary. Then she stirs up our ex-neighbours into this doll soup, and I'm quite lost.

I am lost in any case, cos since we've learnt about tragedy at home, everyone's gone psycho and babbles without breathing, blah blah blah. Never shut up about how terrible it is and how we're all gonna die. And I really wanna shout *Cut it out! We are Cossacks. We'll cover each other's backs through thick and thin, fire and rain and all that.*

Cos, seriously, it's toxic. Am I the only soldier around who can stand it but, bah, is not allowed to?

Oh, by the way, do you know our city is a hero? I used to laugh at the phrase "hero city." Sounded like Ironman with iron for his clothes (a *Fe*-male!). What a dolt I was! Dr Aniol, Agnieszka's dad, told us on the phone about our army's feats when the soil dried enough for zombie tanks to propel through all the mines on the way. On our side, there were only a bunch of freshly conscripted boys and volunteers armed with basically just rifles. No armoured machinery, no optics, no tools, no artillery except for a few trophy Grads and 152-calibre howitzers with little ammunition. Doc said they'd just recently finished building fortifications and digging the ditches. Many hadn't even got proper helmets and uniforms. And you know what? They kicked the second bloody strongest army in the world thirty bloody kilometres away!

The brigadier general (forgot his name) personally wormed across the muddy fields, spying on Ruzi block posts and taking the coordinates (because no optics and no armoured cars). Because there were only enough rockets to fry their asses and watch them running like stinking rats.

Then orcs whimpered all over the media about special NATO forces. Special NATO forces my ass! Ex-shop security guards, postmen, and plumbers, so "special" it burns, hahahah. Poor little Russia is at war with big, bad NATO. Yeah, over seventeen thousand Russian soldiers rot in their tanks and cars, and NATO hasn't even arrived yet. Probably they never will. The biggest military alliance on the planet is so chicken that if Ruzis attack one of them, they'll just kick that country out of NATO and say it's not their problem now.

But whatever. Maybe they are Buddhist, kinda the best fight is an avoided fight, so *let Ukrainians die all they like. We are peaceful people and won't give them weapons to hit the fucking Kremlin, only tools to scratch their itching backs because it helps release stress.*

Never mind, we're not afraid of dirty jobs, we know what to do, and we'll do it. Alone if needed. Let the world smell their coffee, whine about their bills, and pay their shrinks to deal with "too much negativity" on the web. Ukrainians will bring down Russian drones with their slippers while singing national songs, and post funny memes during the air alerts. And if China farts at Taiwan, or Israel at all who hate them, or the USA gets sick in the head and attacks its neighbours, or Iran, or Syria, or Pakistan, or Mighty God himself in some unforeseen future, and everyone starts screaming, their coffee spills on the floor, and shrinks faint, we'll brush shrapnel off our shoulders and say, CHILLAX, GUYS, IT'S ONLY THE WAR.

But that's not the important thing I was gonna tell ya.

The important thing is… (I don't know why I wrote you all that bullshit about No-Actions-Talks-Only. I don't know shit, it's just raving. Ctrl-A-delete is always an option, but frig it. Let's roll on!). Putting that in parentheses was also stupid.

I've kind of slipped off the topic (again!). Okay, the thing is… What I was about to write is so big, gross, and crazy, it's really hard to explain. It's just the war, Pa, these many deaths, fear, twisted bloodied bodies leaking into the news, stories of violent rapes and tortures, and people's strange, vacant faces on the evacuation trains—it moved me out of my home but also moved home out of me. Something shifted, and the solid building of the world I knew or thought I knew collapsed and bye-bye roof.

Maybe this is the point? Am I going mad?

I'm definitely going mad, Pa, cos I think death is the only goal we live for. We die anyway, right? We die now in the rocket terror, or in some fifty pointless years of trying to figure out who I am and where I go. Okay, maybe I'm too much of a baby to understand life yet and also too elephant thick to give a damn about *who* and *where*, but I watch Ma and Granny, and they seem not to give a damn either.

But if I had, like, a daughter of fourteen, and she asked me the same question, dang, I know exactly what I'd tell her: "We are mighty free Cossacks who live to die with honour and dignity. Probably while killing some demon." *YAY. (YAY?)*

Now the crazy part, and holy cow, it was my worst *BRILLIANT IDEA* since the wolf ride in the shopping cart. Buckle your seat belt cos we are in for a rocky ride, Pa. If you see the light at the end of this tunnel, don't go for this trap. It's my driving insanity that's switched on the headlamp.

It all started with Nesha and me behind the trash crates, talking about life (don't ask). Then the bathroom genius fixer Pan Doopa from the flat next door arrived, grieving for his dolphin tiles more than anything else, poor sod. And I went mental. Okay, not exactly medical-grade mental, but definitely off. Not even cos of our blasted home, but Mama. Back at Gran's, she started true Shakespearian mayhem and cried for that stupid sugar bowl of fine porcelain that had stood in our glass cupboard since the Big Bang times. We never kept sugar in it, so fine it was, actually, too fine to keep anything in it, but gosh, HOW SACRED. Ma went on and on and on about how it was a piece of family history and meant so much to us. Just for the record, Pa, it meant *nothing* to me, and I'd much rather live in a place where things like porcelain sugar bowls don't exist.

So Nesha and I retired gracefully to the gang's quarters, i.e., my bedroom, took the window-escape route and ran to Mor forest. I was dying to ask Mara about ghosts, death, and anything BUT sugar bowls. I mean, she lives in the creepy woods with creepy skulls, candles, and a black cat, so she must know something about death, right?

We did our best to look for the *queer* trees, but we really didn't have to cos the first path we took led us straight to Huttuh as if popped up from underground, and her roof did a bit remind me of a mushroom cap. Mara stood up from the porch and beckoned us inside like she knew all about our trashed home and was waiting for us.

"It's unbearable!" Agnieszka exclaimed, falling into a chair near the fire. "Death is hunting us. I feel like it got into my room and turned everything to ashes in rage at me for running off."

"Death does no such thing," Mara said firmly, bestriding a bar stool. "She knows exactly where you are. No need to *hunt*, it's always here, waiting for the right moment to touch you."

We stare at her with our hearts on halt. It wasn't her words that poured liquid ice into my veins, but her tone. So cold, smooth, and nonchalant.

"How do you know?" I swallowed.

Guess what. She said "Because I AM death" and killed herself laughing while slapping her leg. Then she stopped abruptly and added with a smile, "Sorry. Always wanted to say that. So epic. But for real, I'm only the guide. I guide people to the gates between the worlds of *Yav'* and *Nav'*, living and dead, or 'The Slit' for short."

"No shit," I burst out, and Nesha stopped pulling at sleepy Aidan to say, "Don't feed us this nonsense. People die every day—this is reality, not your fantasy about ghosts and gates."

"Well, Princess"—Mara spun around on her bar stool—"dying people is only *part* of reality, just as fantasy is part of it, too."

"Fantasy doesn't exist!" Agnieszka straightened up. Her nostrils flared like wings.

Mara shrugged. "Maybe it does, but you don't see it? Because someone said it's not there?"

"Maybe it's not there?" Agnieszka insisted. "If I don't see it."

"Or maybe it is and you know it, deep down. You *want* to see it but, for some reason, you keep it away, sealed in a glass ball of your imagination." She dropped her voice to almost a whisper. "A little ball that has nothing to do with the real world. A world inside a world, inside a world… A dream within a dream. Within a dream. *Within a dream.*"

Then it trailed away with soothing hissing, like the spell song of a snake. Mara didn't stir, with all her blackness in the dim light, giving an impression of a hollow in the space. I felt cold creeping up my spine, and my hair stood up on the back of my neck. It moved as if somebody brushed their fingers up my neck. My first reaction was

to leap and run. Well, I leapt, grazing my shins on the coffee table and… and that was pretty much as far as I went.

Mara was faster.

She rose from her seat: not standing up—wafting up in the air with her legs fusing into streaming, jellyfish-like black palps. Then it all went a bit *Lord of the Rings*, like when Gandalf traced the ring of power to Hobbiton and went mad at Bilbo. Cos the ceiling dome swelled and expanded, and darkness crept in like black clouds of ink in clear water. The floor rippled, the walls bulged— we were inside a giant throbbing balloon! But the most horrid and hideous and *caramba* CRAZY thing was Mara. She'd turned into a monstrous Nazgul! A Harry Potter Dementor! She was a shapeless shadow floating in the air on her jellyfish tentacles with just one big, shiny eye in the middle of her head. If that was a head, that is. Which could be anything, in fact. No kidding!

Bless Agnieszka who screamed at it like all those blond gals in the cheap horrors, and her cry pierced it like a needle. The balloon-hut deflated like it was exhaling, and the jelly-Nazgul sank, launched forward, and grabbed Nesha by the shoulders with familiar human hands in woven bracelets with tiny skulls. "It's okay, it's just me, Mara," it said, and suddenly I saw the girl I knew.

Agnieszka gaped at her, going all Snow White, then squeaked, "D-daddy? Is that… you?"

Now you are gonna ask me *what the frig?* I'll tell you what the frig. Later, when I described to Neshka that guts-twisting piece of flying eye in the black rugs, she said there was no such thing because what she saw was a gigantic blimey spider. Y'know how she's afraid of spiders? No, you probably don't. She's not just afraid of them. She turns back to cosmic dust at the mere idea of a spider. Of course, she says the same about rats, snakes, bugs, and children with gaps in their teeth, but spiders… Spiders are the worst. And guess what, she saw a black widow as big as a room!

I'll tell you what the frig else. After the cheerful hi from her worst nightmare, it wasn't even a giant spider, but her dad. Agnieszka stared at Mara for, like, two light-years, while we took her by the arms and sat her in a suddenly popped-out-from-nowhere chair.

"Agnieszka, it's Mara." I waved across her face. She blinked and looked at me.

"I think… Daddy was here," she mumbled. "Not the one from the video calls but… Daddy I remember."

I shoved Mara on the shoulder, crying "What the hell!" and she said she just wanted to show us her true self. Which one, I wondered? The Nazgul, spider, or… Dr Aniol?

Then Aidan's voice said, *Stop scaring the souls out of them. Je-sus, Mara.* But he was nowhere around. The only other living being in the room was the black cat on the pillow. Aidan the cat. And he yawned at us sweetly.

"They are fine!" Mara waved away. "You're fine, right?"

Good question. A rhetorical one. It hung in the air like cigarette smoke. We goggled at the cat as he watched us back, swishing his tail lazily, a black ink blot with two shiny green eyes. And the silence was so thick I could eat it, should I be interested in eating anything at that moment. Then he spoke again. The cat spoke. THE CAT!

Do I have something stuck to my whiskers, or what?

"Aaaaaaah!" That was Agnieszka. She burst out of the house like all six hundred sixty-six demons were chasing her. One of them was probably riding me.

I can't believe I wrote you this. It's too big, bigger than the war or our blasted flat, bigger than anything. Okay, you must be thinking, *Holy crap, another *BRILLIANT IDEA* from my brilliant psycho kid. Am I into the next episode of the* My Daughter Goes Nuts *show?* Yes. And you are welcome :)

Could it be some kind of black magic? Like voodoo or witch-craft? Must ask Gran tomorrow. We talked for hours about it with Agnieszka cos she was still afraid of the spider, and I was afraid of losing my blimey marbles. I kept prattling about hypnosis and war stress to hold my shit and be supportive, but inside, I was yelling, *WHAT THE FUCK!*

Seriously, what the fuck? We are at war with Russian zombie cannibals, and my house was bombed into the trash, my father is catching bullets with his chest, Ukrainians die every day, and my new friend turns into a one-eyed, flying black jellyfish who sees the dead! Ah, almost forgot. Her cat TALKS! Talks like her brother. In fact, he IS her brother. I need some water.

In films and books, they always bring water to people in a state of shock, and I was so shocked I needed buckets of it.

•

Okay, I had a full litre. It didn't help: I am still in shock, but now, I also want to pee.

You see, Agnieszka is right about something being missing here. Like… superpowers? At times, I think superpowers are real, then I think they're bullshit. And sometimes—a lot of times—I just don't know. Today I know they are real, but all I knew about them is bull-shit.

It's nearly midnight, and I'm still in this excitedly spooked mode. I hope you are safe. Don't believe giant black spiders, Pa. Giant black spiders are not what they really are.

Hug you,
Your mad Skipper

24

AGNIESZKA

31 March 2022, Day 36

Mara is a giant black spider! A spider, my God. I'm so freaked out I jump from every shadow and will probably do that for the rest of my short and jumpy life. And I can't even tell anyone because, hello, they'll go all Men in Black and lock me in one room with Napoleons, flying spiritist tables, and people talking to their socks. This wasn't the Narnia I expected. The wardrobe is all wrong.

It gets better in daylight, however; I totally forget it. I painted Gran Bozhena's pot today, and the sun rays beaming from the tall windows were so golden, they made the dust sparkle. Three big glass pyramids from the windowsill cast jolly little pools of rainbows, stretched across my desk. I was so happy thinking about Dad being back soon-soon-soon-soon. He promised to leave Zapahorb right after all his patients got transported out of that hell. Like the captain of his ship, he'll be the last to abandon the hospital.

Then the events of yesterday night popped up, and the brush in my jellied hands jerked. The pot rolled off, hit the tiled floor, and fell to shards with a loud crash. I was shaking so much, Gran must have thought I went all vampire and burnt in the sunlight with hissing convulsions. She asked me if everything was okay. And the honest answer would have been: no, nothing is okay, nothing will be ever okay after I saw my friend turn into a giant *mierda* spider!

It chopped my whole world into two, like, bubbles, one inside the other: the inner one, where everything IS okay (even war), and things like giant spiders sit only in bad dreams, and the outer one, which is the bad dream. And these two worlds, they never merge. Never merge, damn it! You either sit in your cosy comfort zone and wait for the imaginary letters from Hogwarts or get out into the never-ending madness of flying tables and talking cats nobody can explain. You don't even, like, do anything; it still bobs up and breaks your pots.

That would sound quite insane, so I said, "I'm so sorry, Gran. It's just the war."

Works every time.

Maybe it's the lack of sleep? I don't know what is real anymore. Is my home real? Pan Borov from upstairs and his creaky mattress, Pani Lyudmila and her flower pots, Pani Iryna and her inner voices… Are they all dead? I'm scared even to ask. And my darling dolls! Is it just Helga and me again, like in the old times? Floral patterns on the carpet, quilted duvets on the beds and the cup with the bunny face, pink unicorns on the walls and frills on the curtains—every little nook I remember, they are solid in my mind. But Daddy said Russians shelled our house days ago. He didn't write about it because he didn't want to worry us. Worry us? Worry us??? Oh, Daddy. Like I'm made of gruel!

I am probably made of gruel. My brain is definitely gruel. I am so gruel I don't think I'll ever sleep. Writing helps. It distracts me from the long shadows creeping by the walls and ceiling. Every barking dog outside, every rustle of the wind is the voice of pure, utter evil.

"Okay," I said bravely, put my phone away, studied sleeping Carma, and tried meditation to let it do whatever it does to all the great

Buddha-minds, which is, apparently, to gut me with more fright. Because I suddenly remembered The Toilet Rat. It shot up like a bobber on the river surface: Daddy telling me a story about big hairy rats running through the sewage system. A silly suckling back then, I really, like, saw them swarming in the pipes, getting into our toilet. Since it was but a little tiled room, I supposed the rat lurked inside the pan, in that little water pool. It could come out any time to snap at my bum!

At night, I imagined the gleam of its beastly red eyes in the dull reflection of the balcony door in my room. The swift motion of the shadows from the driving-past busses across the wall, weird noises in the pipes, the suspicious, inexplicable rustle coming from the neighbours… The Toilet Rat was everywhere, watching me, biding its time to catch me and drag me into the sewage, to live in the Kingdom of Crap forever.

In a convulsive jerk, I clawed into Carma's foot and made her jump. "Ah? What? Russians?"

"No… I want to pee," I squeaked.

She stared at me in silence. "…And?"

Cold shivers ran over my froggy skin. "I can't go there, I'm too scared."

"Of what?"

"Of The Toilet Rat!"

"Je-sus." Carmina sighed, fell back on her pillow, and pulled the blanket over her head.

I tugged on it. "Will you come with me?"

"Are you five or what? There are no rats in our toilet," she mumbled and turned to the wall.

"Like there are no talking cats in shaking huts?"

That got her to sit up with eyes wide open. "Holy moly," she said and swung her legs over. She bent to get her socks and pulled them on. "Let's have a double toilet trip then. I'll protect you from your rats, and you stand on the lookout for the flying Nazguls."

"Deal."

Before sleep, I plugged into YouTube to get lulled by Molfarka Marichka's hoarse lisping, in the hope that she won't talk about Russians being dicks because they are possessed by demons from the upside-down reality where all black is white. I'm sick and tired of Russians! It doesn't matter who they are: Nazis, terrorists, demons, space invaders, simply morons, whatever. I wish they'd just get lost.

The interviewer was obviously sick and tired of Russians, too. He asked Molfarka other stuff, about magic things. "Why can't people see it?" Good question.

The witch blew a *mierda* raspberry, and her grey head wobbled on her broad shoulders like on a wonky spring. "People see only what they notice," she said and sucked on a long, funny pipe just like Bilbo's. "And they notice only what is already in their memory. So they don't really see anything. If you want to see, you need to open your mind."

Open my mind, huh? How freaking dangerous is it? Very! Open up to see your friends turning into big black widows, that's how *mortificato* dangerous it is! Now how do I shut it up, please? I want my unicorns and fairies back, I want my home, I want my Daddy.

25

MARA

Damn, I messed it all up. The girls will def ignore me at the station and will never come to see me again. For the first time, I find the living amazing and want to be true and honest with them, and they run away screaming. Is the world indeed a theatre like Aidan says? Where everyone pretends to be someone else, lies, lies, lies, and ignores the obvious until it hits them in the face and they run away screaming?

People surprise me. I still think they are lazy bums most of the time, like cats dozing when the sun is shining. But then something shakes the ground under their feet, and the kraken awakes. Who are the real humans, I wonder? Those who appear by day, when everything is okay and makes sense even if they don't see or give a shit about it? Or those who appear by night, when the world crumbles to pieces, and rise, grabbing at all the strings they thought were guiding them somewhere. If the strings snap, they just die, falling apart with the rest of the toppling world. But if they don't, I see a giant luminous heart inside a boring grey shell.

And it mesmerizes me.

It mesmerizes me so much my head turns into a box filled with jumpy tennis balls, and I try to hit them all out by talking to Aidan even if he's busy staring into the void or sleeping. He's sleeping quite a lot today, I finally notice. And he has barely touched his coffee and pizza.

"Are you ill?" I pat him on the scruff, and he growls, shaking his ears at me. "Yes, Arman is leaving, but that was inevitable," I say in a voice that sounds like I swallowed it.

He says nothing.

"You'll get over it," I promise. "Everything will be back to our usual lovely mess."

He still flounders silently somewhere in the cosmos of his frets.

I swallow hard and give in a little bit. "You'll meet a dozen more Armans at the train station. You may befriend them all for as long as they stay. Isn't it nice to be in a constant flux of friends?"

No reaction.

"Fine. Sulk here if you want." I spring to my feet. "And I'll go and do things that bring me joy, a sense of direction, and also save this world and you in it from collapsing into a total void."

I pick up my beacons and tramp out, slamming the door behind me. The door doesn't slam as loudly as I expect. Huttuh must have taken care of her creaky joints. So I open and shut it again to make up for it. Once I'm out and building the fence, I start to feel ever so slightly ashamed of myself. My little kitty has his little kitty heart broken, and I act like a bitch. Mentally, I swear to be a tad on the nicer side and do magic to cheer him up. Like asking Huttuh to put some music on, go party with *rusalkas* in the lake, *mavkas* in the trees (they adore Aidan!), maybe *kikimora* even if she hates me for befriending humans, drop in on Lisovyk for a mug of kvass, and chase squirrels up the giant elms.

The plan seems impeccable. The only problem with impeccable plans is that they tend to crack in the most unexpected ways. Like tonight. Carried along by sincere goodwill, filled with peace and compassion, I fling myself dramatically into the house with my flashing ta-da hands and cry, "Guess what, kitty, we're having a party tonight!"

Aidan lifts his sleepy head a little, just enough to indicate he's noticed me coming, but files it under "B" for buzz off and goes back to sleep.

My face drops like a mudslide. "Come on, you can't sulk forever!" I kick off my boots, rip my hoodie off, and throw myself on the floor next to his armchair. "I'm sorry I didn't let you join that beanpole, but it's for your own good."

Seriously? He talks at last. *Wow. Get a medal for that.* Well, sort of.

I sigh a long, don't-be-a-moron sigh, burrow my face into my arms crossed on top of my bent knees, and say, "More dead came today. Shredded. It's not just a violent death, it's a violent death for the violent death's sake, and it's so nauseating to walk them through those memories."

Aidan's belly puffs and drops erratically as he squints harder. But still, he says nothing. I drop my arms and struggle to my feet. Whatever. *At least I tried*, I think on my way to my room. Let him sleep this out. Huttuh will cuddle him into blissful oblivion as only she can. And tomorrow, he'll be himself again, barely remembering some blue-eyed, doll-faced mountain of a boy.

I fall on my bed, my face hitting the pillow, and the world starts to slowly rock. Okay, not exactly the whole world, just my bed. Its four legs curve into rockers that lull me to sleep like the ever-waving sea. The last thought on my drowning mind is Aidan, a miserable, cold, wet little creature, meowing and scratching at my door one stormy August night. He fits easily in my palms, he is so small. But, damn, he scampers like hell around the hut on his little legs, messing with the carpets no matter how hard Huttuh tries to keep them tidy, and plops on his round bum every so often. Funny, silly Aidan.

Naturally, he is also the first thought on my mind when I wake up. Ever since Aidan invaded here, raising an avalanche of both panic and rapture about sharing my life with another living being, I've woken up to his meows, whoops, jumps, and shakes at my shoulder. Sometimes songs, sometimes dead birds or mice plopped on my pillow. He takes all sorts of little corpses from the forest and places them next to me. That is his way of getting them to Mother Death. Which, with all due respect to my kitty partner, is rather dirty.

I wake up to none of that today. The silence in the house is so complete it eats my calmness away. "Aidan?" My voice is muffled by the pillow. I toss around in the bed, drag my body upright, and call for my cat again. "Are you still angry, fluffy bun? It's no time for hide and seek. Let's have breakfast."

I stagger from room to room, look under every chair and wardrobe, and peek into every pot and basket. Huttuh kindly obliges me with ever so many new pots and baskets to peek into. After countless times of looking into the same vase always popping up in another place, my sleepy brain finally gets on the rails.

"Wait a minute!" I cry and bang the vase back in its place. "HUT-TUH?"

I swing back on my heels and feel the room around me zoom out, then in, like a camera lens. "He's gone, hasn't he? Escaped! You lost my kitten, you old cauldron!"

A jolt runs through the chimney rocks as she shrinks, dread in her every window, picture, and tapestry. Still, I press for the answer. "Did you?"

She hastily tosses a log into the chimney, sets fire to it, and shrinks down at me.

"I can't believe it. You let him out!" I bellow, stomping my foot.

Huttuh pops a glass of lemonade on the table, the bubbly one that humans produce and seal like a genie in a bottle. She has never done that before, out of stupid pride. Each bottle of bought lemonade carried inside, she received with unconcealed contempt, hurt by me loving something *outside* of her magic. Now her pride is tucked under the cellar, and the glass of fragrant, fizzy drink lures me to the table. But it's like a splash of icy water on the red-hot brick of my anger. I grab the glass and smash it against the floor. The shards fly, scattering all over, and the blot on the rug looks like a frozen explosion.

If Huttuh could cry, she probably would right now. Meanwhile, I cry for both of us because she has betrayed me and has taken away the only person I truly cared for, now that I finally learnt what caring is.

"Where did he go?" I demand and raise my voice. "Where did he go, Huttuh!"

There is only my frantic face in the mirror over the fireplace, where she shows me places and people on my command. She adds a log to the pile, and the fire gets bigger than the one in my chest. "You'll take me to him, then."

Huttuh shrinks even shrinkier, and I go off my rails completely. "Don't you forget that I am your witch, I am Baba Yaga," bursts out of my chest. "I am your boss!"

I stomp upstairs to the balcony pilothouse Huttuh has built for our travels. My bare feet thud heavily on every step. Somewhere amid my impressive climb, I bend over the handrail and yell, "And I mean NOW."

She moves at last, warily, dragging her feet and wobbling like a ship in troubled waters. It takes her only a few more wobbles to gain the speed of a running deer. Still, I think it's too slow. "You can go faster! You can fly," I snarl, and the wind snaps the words out of my mouth.

In a moment, I can see feathery shadows growing by each side of the hut.

The woods are getting thinner. The trees flash by like film frames merging into one single smudge. The verge in the distance rapidly approaches, and the blast of air hits my face, flapping my oversized black T-shirt like a pirate flag. Huttuh leaps off the edge and dives down the valley, sliding gracefully on her brownish eagle's wings. Oh, yes. My hut might have chicken legs, but she's got the heart of an eagle.

My own heart seems to drop to my feet and get whipped out of me. I can't help whooping freakishly and thrusting my arms in the air. "We fly! Whooo, we fly, Huttuh! You did it! You rock, baby!!! Aidan, I'm coming!"

Well, no, I'm not. Immediately, the sonorous, raving yowl of the air siren pierces the air, and I curse under my breath. Oh, sodding air defence, they have probably taken us for an enemy airpoop, I mean… jet. Carma calls it *airpoop,* and it's bloody contagious.

"Down, Huttuh, down," I command and see the landscape below sweep by at a fantastic speed. "We are gonna get blown to molecules by the Ukrainian air defence."

I look around the balcony. Why didn't I think about a steering wheel? There is no steering wheel on my ship! Neither is there an option for a noiseless landing. We have practically reached the town, and I see people from the closest farms pouring out of their houses and pointing our way.

Instinctively, I throw myself to the left side of Huttuh's balcony and press with my whole body for her to turn around. She catches my drift immediately, makes a sharp loop, and soars down. I keep chanting "Lower, lower, lower" until we glide a few metres above the fields, and the tall grass whips Huttuh at her legs and the front door.

There is a shabby-looking barn on the field's border with a rusty old car rotting behind. I suggest we cling to them and pray people will be more on the stupid side today and not notice any difference.

Huttuh spreads her feet in front and turns her wings against the wind, flapping and dropping speed. The first touch comes with a thud. I almost topple on the floor when she jumps back up, fluttering with her wings.

Finally, Huttuh grips the land, hops, runs, and gradually comes to a stop. She folds her wings and drops her bum on the ground with another big thud that sends my teeth clattering.

I look down at the path running right from under the front door and cry, "No, Huttuh, not in the middle of the road!"

She makes one funny leap to the side, like a frog ballerina, and plops down. Huttuh shuts her eyes and sits silently, like she's nothing more than a child, hiding from her friends behind a transparent curtain. I rush downstairs, break out of the door, and quickly assess the situation.

Nobody is running in our direction with grenades and rifles (considering the war situation), and the air-raid wail has stopped. "Okay, we're safe. For now. But you really need to blend with the surroundings." I cast an anxious glance around. "Turn into something ... normal."

Huttuh opens her windows wide in amazement, then squints them back shut and tenses with her every brick and shingle. She shudders and pulses like she's really ready to flare up, and then—poof!—a cloud of fumes rises, and she's not a hut anymore. She's a red-and-white striped circus tent with flags and fairy lights.

Facepalm. "No, I mean... normal and *boring*." I point at the barn and the car wreck next to her. "Like this."

Another moment of tense trembling of the jolly big top tent, and in a cloud of fumes, there already stands a barn JUST like the one I pointed at, with cracked windows, bolted doors, and bundles of grass growing from the roof. Help me, God.

"Okay, fine. Twin barns, let's do twin barns. Just... Don't move." I shake my finger at her. "Aidan is in Booguy, right?" No answer. Then I recall I'd just asked her not to move and add, "Just say yes or no, and then don't move."

Huttuh blinks with one window, and I nod, then run in the direction of the town, hoping once again that people's crappy memory and focus will be a little crappier just this once.

Arman did say his family rented a cottage in Booguy. They are leaving this morning, so there will have to be some big parents' car parked at some big parents' house among some five hundred houses around. Piece of cake. All I need is to find the right shadow.

The sun is high as I scud down the road and across lawns and gardens, skipping past wooden fences, sliding up walls, leaping on top of roofs, silently, like a cat, and sweeping along unnoticed. Because I don't leave traces. Yaga is never available.

Carmina asked me once why I cast no shadow. Simple. I *am* the shadow, looming in the corner of everyone's eye. I am the reflection of the light that the living let slide out of view every so often. I can be anyone's shadow. I can be of any shape and hue. When silence falls and thoughts are still like glazed waters in the winter night, someone's curious mind might catch me looming behind their left shoulder. *Just my shadow*, they'll think, and they will be right. Death is only their shadow.

It takes me a wink to locate the right house, and not cos I'm incredibly quick. I just know Arman. His family always takes the best, so I run to the most luxurious house, and the car parked beside it turns out to be a glossy, posh BMW. Without a minute wasted, I spot a little skittish black ball dashing under it. Gotcha!

"What do you think you are doing? Traitor!" I jump down to pick Aidan out of there.

But this little shit is fast, furious, and fighting me back like a crazy Ukrainian soldier against a tyrant. With impressive hissing,

snarling, snapping, and skittering all about under the car.

"Ouch! What the fff... You've gotta be kidding me!" I yell at him.

Finally, I manage to grab my kitty by the scruff and pull him out. Then the house doors are flung open, spitting out Arman himself, and I get distracted for a split second. Enough for Aidan to break free and dart away bullet fast.

He sprints up the driveway and leaps at Arman, nearly knocking him flying. "What the…" he yells at first, dropping whatever he's holding in his hands on the pavement. Then Aidan safely settles on his shoulders and curls up around his neck like a living fur collar. Arman comes around so quickly that before I can crawl out from under that darn car and flip my forelock back, his hand is already stroking my cat's glossy coat, and Aidan tunes his generator's purr.

"Oh, hi!" Arman takes a look at his new fur collar and smiles at me. "Is this your cat?"

I stare daggers at Aidan. He stares swords back at me and claws into Arman's creamy jersey with his tail coiled around his neck. We get sucked into this silent eye battle, and I think, I think hard. I hold my breath and then burst, "No. Actually…" The pressure in my chest crashes through the metaphorical dam, and I pant. "He's your cat."

Aidan raises his head in bemusement and opens his ears wide. *Are you for real?* he meows.

"If you want it. Of course," I add and stick my fists into the pockets of my pants.

"Um…" Arman gives me a look of bafflement, then disbelief, and then bafflement again.

Deep down, I hope he will say no, he can't, it's not in his perfect parents' perfect plans for perfect life and blah blah blah. Then Aidan will see he doesn't care for him. But Arman tears him off his shoulder and looks at that cute, funny face, holding him at arm's length with the childish delight of dead-and-went-to-heaven Christmas morning. "My cat. My very own cat?" he murmurs.

Aidan meows and stretches his paws to hug him.

"I was looking for, er… a new home for him." I break the awkward silence hanging over us. Awkward probably for me only. Those two are too thrilled with each other to notice anything.

Arman cuddles him up and pets him lovingly. "I always wanted to have a cat..."

"Good. He's cool. You won't have any troubles with him," I say with the confidence of an experienced PR manager and rock on my bare feet, listing Aidan's many virtues. "He really loves cuddles. Also coffee. And make sure he eats pizza at least once in a while cos he fancies himself Italian. He sings and plays guitar, so give him a guitar, or he'll play on your nerves."

I spot a little fold, breaking Arman's perfect brow line, and his jaw drops. Now, he probably thinks I went utterly stark raving crackers, and my bare feet don't help me in any way. Welcome to the real world, boy, a place where logic goes to die.

"He plays the guitar?" he repeats with a slow nod, still stroking Aidan.

"Yep!"

You let me go, seriously? No Russian trap? You know they always say one thing and do the opposite, comes from my cat, and I add, "He also talks. Like a newsreader. He really needs a kind of net stretched between his brain and mouth to catch at least some of that. So talk to him, or he'll get bored."

The furrows on Arman's forehead deepen. The logic is struggling to die.

"And you can hear him talking once you shut up all the other voices in your head."

Arman looks at his new (old) friend, scratching behind his ears. "What's his name?"

Aidan! Aidan meows.

"Aidan."

"Aidan?" Arman shoots his eyes back at me, animated. Their starry glitter pricks me in the very heart. He does love my cat! "Like your brother?"

"Yes. *Exactly* like my brother," I stress it, and Aidan meows desperately.

Ignoring all the hints, however, Arman shifts the cat to one hand and digs inside his pocket to get his phone out. "He didn't leave me his number, could you just…"

Gosh, sorry, in the whirl of the war, the dead falling like snow, finding and losing friends, and my probably first-ever life crisis, I forgot to buy a smartphone for my cat. I grant him a lopsided grin and say, "Don't worry, he has yours. I'm sure you'll hear from him *quite soon*."

Then the cottage doors fly open, revealing a huge, elegant-looking *pani* in a dark blue suit and high heels coming towards us. Her legs are so long, she could overstep continents. "Arman, why are the boxes on the ground?" The woman's voice squeaks like the hinges of an old window. Her perfect pearl-white hair is brushed into a bun, leaving out just one little strand that shakes with every squeak. She holds back, noticing Aidan, and the corners of her lips sink into a sad bow. If she didn't use foundation in kilo jars, I'd probably see the rest of her expression. "Put that dirty animal down. You'll ruin your sweater and will probably catch fleas."

Arman turns his torso towards her, manfully, like a gladiator to the lion. "This dirty animal is my cat, Mother. He comes with me, and that's final. My friend Mara is giving him to me."

The giant lady assesses him in stony silence, and I can't help but think of Atlanteans who used to be as tall, cold, and cruel. Or Egyptian statues in tombs. She could have been one of them! Not a single line moves under the buckets of her foundation. Then she glances at me briefly, sees the skull print on my black T-shirt, and pretends I'm not even there. "Pick up the boxes," she says in a cold, lazy tone and climbs into the front seat of her car.

Arman beams. "Yes, Mother." He passes Aidan to me and runs to gather up the packages.

I give my kitty a final hug. "Be a goodie. And be happy, little silly furball."

Oh, Mara, I'll miss you so much. Promise to walk Huttuh to Odesa one day? Aidan purrs as he brushes his face against my cheek.

"I'll *fly* Huttuh to Odesa. After the war, for sure."

Aw, I love you, Yaga.

"I love you too, kitty." I give him back to his beloved human, who smiles sheepishly at me for talking with a meowing cat.

Then the doors burst open again, and a rock of a man strides out, swinging his arms wide and jingling his car keys. He flashes a look at his Atlantean offspring with a cat in his hands, misses me altogether, and says, "I'm not cleaning his shit from the seat. Get in."

The BMW moves slowly away, gleaming under the sun, and the funny little face peeking over Arman's shoulder and watching me is getting smaller and smaller. I wave at Aidan with my hand held high, as people do in those tearful romantic films when someone leaves and they are so depressed that they keep doing weird things. Like waving hands.

Time stops for that moment, then moves on, crawling like mud. I drag my feet along the dusty path, hoping to get back at least by October. *Aidan was my friend. My only friend. Carmina and Neshka are spooked by me. Who's gonna be my friend now?*

As the twin barns loom on the horizon, I sigh, then throw myself at Huttuh's mossy wall, press my face into the wooden beam, and mumble, "I'm sorry I was a bitch to you. You were right about letting Aidan go. He wasn't really happy with me, was he?"

A giant wing from somewhere behind me brushes gently at my hair and spine. I yank my head, turn, and realize I've just hugged the wrong hut. "Ugh, meh, meh, rotten barn!"

Huttuh shakes in giggles. "Not funny," I grumble, but my traitor mouth twists in a smile.

26

MARA

We hit the road back to the woods, taking the longest, safest way around the town. I make ten of my longest strides to match Huttuh's single little skip behind me. She keeps nudging me on the shoulder to give me a ride, but I shake my head and mimic Zelenskyy's legendary quote: "The war against fat is here. I need exercise, not a ride."

So she gets back to hopping behind me, and I get back to hating my life. "This is stupid, so stupid," I mutter under my breath, with my eyes fixed on the path sweeping under my feet. "If Mother Death, or whoever it was, sent me Aidan, why would they take him away? Okay, he needed a temporary shelter. But why wouldn't they send me some other refugee instead?"

Suddenly, Huttuh puffs a cloud of signal smoke, falls on her base, and closes up. I raise my eyes and notice two little figures frozen in the distance. Then the thinner and taller of them waves at me. "It's the girls!" Before I finish yelling this, I'm already rushing to say hi.

Huttuh's gay scamper behind me almost spoils my joy cos Agnieszka gets so pale that she could go all British lady in the costume dramas and faint. And pop-eyed Carmina would drop her jaw and never find it in this tall grass. "Hey. Are you still talking to me? Sorry about that... circus with showing my true face and all that."

I scratch the back of my neck and try a little harder. "And don't mind Huttuh; she's a bit skittish today."

They goggle like two goldfish at me, then at Huttuh, back at me, and then at Huttuh again. Finally, Carmina gets her balls together and says, "What are you doing?"

"Just going home."

They go even more goggly.

I take a glance over my shoulder and add, "Well, yeah, my home is here. I mean, to our usual place in Mor." Another long silence threatens to drop Neshka into that dramatic costume-drama swoon, after all, so I have to be quick. "Would you like a glass of lemonade?"

"Only if you don't turn into spiders, please?" Princess Agnieszka mumbles.

I raise my right hand and give her my promise.

Lemonade is magic. Agnieszka drains barely half the glass before her cheeks flush with rosy patches, and she looks around the house, curious about its size, always bigger inside than it seems from outside.

I put mine back on the table untouched, though, and look at the wet stain on the floor. "Thanks, Huttuh, but I'd prefer a, how you call it, 'much healthier, rich, deep, and fragrant bread brew of my ancestors' or kvass in short."

This makes Huttuh burst with delight. The floor ripples like water. Immediately, my lemonade leaps in the air and lands back as a mug of foamy brew—dark and champagne-bubbly kvass. Carmina claps her hands and cries, "Wow! Bravo! Can you do it again?"

But instead of more magic tricks, Huttuh tinkles the little silver bells over her front door. I wipe the foam off my lips. "Ugh, I have guests."

Agnieszka's seat scrapes at the floorboards as she leaps up and scoots to the window, probably looking out for fairies. "I don't see anyone," she exclaims in disappointment.

I explain, "That's cos Huttuh jingles me before they even touch that darned bell."

Even if we all talk Ukrainian, Carmina looks for the translation somewhere on the ceiling, rolling her eyes around and up, then back at me. "Why would she do that?"

"Why, so I could prepare my fake smiles!" I stomp to the door. "Wait, I'll send them back to hell."

I fling the door open. The girls' curious faces peek out from behind my shoulders, and together we stare down at three little kids and a dog. THE little kids and THE dog. They are shivering cold and look a little more on the dead side than the first time I saw them. I can see their bones through their tight and dry, faint skin. And the West Highland White Terrier is so dirty he could almost change his breed to Big Black Brush.

"We want to go to our Mommies," says the girl with a scratched face.

"Oh my, you're still here!" I jump downstairs to take them by the hands. "Come inside, let's have some cocoa, eh? I'll take you to your mommies, promise. Bring your dog with you."

"It's not our dog," comes from the little boy from Sumy while we climb the teeny-weeny steps Huttuh built for their teeny-weeny legs and paws. "We found him in the woods. He was alone and scared…"

"Oh, that must be Misha from Mariupol'!" I suggest, and the dog barks, wagging his tail in circles like the blades of an electric fan.

When we are back in the hut, Carma holds a broom like a weapon, and Agnieszka is nowhere to be seen. But her boots sticking out from under the old tapestry give her away. "It's okay. They are just kids killed in this war," I say as I help the children take their coats off.

"You mean, *ghosts?*" Carmina points the broom at them, still in her warrior stance. The children gaze at her inquisitively. "These are… dead little people? And a dead dog?"

I can't hold my laughter. "They won't bite. Will you, kiddos? Come, let's have a snack."

We gather around the table, where I serve pancakes, biscuits, hot chocolate, and a plate of chopped lamb for Misha. Carmina joins us cautiously and pets the dog (she has a soft spot for animals). The little girl who sits hugging Misha around the neck grins at her, and she grins back, not that scared anymore because grins smell like friendship. Then Agnieszka slips from behind the tapestry because it also smells like chocolate. I pass her a cup and pat a stool next to me.

A bit jittery, Neshka sits and stares over her cup at the children. "H-how did it happen?" she asks in a lost voice. "How did you…" She can't say "die" and instead says, "Turn up here?"

The eldest, Arsen from Kherson, says he died in a car from a road mine.

"I think I died there," he adds timidly. "I saw my elder brother drag our mom and sister out of the car, crying like he never did. Then I walked with him and Mom and Diana a long, long, long way, till we came to a river, and Mom said it was the only way. Oleg is a bad swimmer; he never liked going to the beach. But Mom was bleeding, Diana is four, and I am six. Oleg looked at the water, like, very funny, and then he walked into it. It was so cold and muddy. I saw him start to drown. I cried for help, for anyone to help. I didn't want him to drown."

Everyone stopped eating. Even Misha seemed to be listening.

Arsen sniffed and continued, "Then I saw a boat and started shaking it. Two men turned and saw him spluttering. They fetched him out and wanted to bring him to the hospital at once, but he begged them to go across and save Mom and my sister, mostly by pointing fingers and gurgling, because he couldn't talk. The water did something bad to my brother. He made these funny noises with his mouth, and his lungs hurt him badly. So it was me talking. I told them about Mom and Diana, and they went back for them. I thought I was with Oleg in a boat, but then… I was here."

"I wasn't in a boat. I was on my playground!" Vlas, the youngest, piped in, unsticking his mouth from his cup. "I was building a sandcastle because the sand was wet, and Mamma said I could make one, only quick. And I was very, very quick. I made a very quick castle." He glanced proudly around the table. "But then there was… boom! And I saw a black cat. I thought he could live in my castle."

"That was Aidan," I explain to the girls. "He found them."

Carmina turns to the silent, double-faced girl, Olesia. "And what happened to you?"

She only shrugged. "Dunno. I was waiting for my parents in our cellar, but nobody came. I ran out looking for them, and some men chased me and shot at me."

Carmina frowned. "What men?"

Olesia shrugged again. "Green men! With guns. They cried in Russian, 'Shoot her in her legs, shoot her in her legs.' I was so afraid they'd shoot me in the legs. I didn't see the car coming when I ran on the road. Then BANG, and suddenly, I was sleeping back in the cellar, waiting for my parents. I thought… the boys and the cat were just a dream. I'm still in the cellar, and one day Mom and Dad will come for me."

She looks at me pleadingly. "But they won't, will they?"

Instead of answering, I brush her spine gently.

The silence falls so jelly-thick that I hear the wind behind the windows. It's still a few hours before The Slit opens, so I slap my hand on my lap and say in a jolly tone, "How about we play a little? There is a bit of Narnia in my room."

"Narnia?" Agnieszka drops the candy she was unwrapping.

I point at the back door. "Yep, over there."

Excited, they turn around to see the sparkling electric light leaking through under it. Huttuh is cooking something colossal there. I walk up to it and with a dramatic *abracadabra* wave of my hand swing it open. Instead of my bed, wardrobe, and stuff, there are swings, trampolines, and slides.

"A playground!" Vlas cries while Arsen squints into the distance. "And what's behind it? Disneyland?"

Beyond the playground, there lies a brand-new world, drifting in space like on the back of a giant turtle. A castle is lurking in the background, mounting lordly over a serpentine road, gleaming in the sun. Which, I suppose, used to be my ceiling lamp. The clouds float by like smaller islands, each with a land of its own on top, with rivers, hills, and villages. They moor at the highest sequoia trees, and anybody could climb there by the funny spiral elven stairs that grow out from the bark.

With a cry of rapture, kids scoot to the magic world, and Agnieszka is ahead of them all.

I close the door and glance at Carmina playing with Misha, talking to him as if he is magic. What I'm gonna say next will probably be the Mistake of the Year and will win the Prize of the Worst Baba Yaga in the Universe. But I'm so thrilled with having Carma and Nesha as my friends, that, before I know it, I blurt out, "Hey, would you like to see the crack between the worlds?"

27

AGNIESZKA

1 April 2022, Day 37

And I thought Russian bombs, giant spiders, maybe boyfriends turning into gays, and huts with whole countries inside turning into Eyes of Sauron were the worst anyone could possibly survive.

No. Those weren't even nearly bad enough.

You know how in horror films, there is eventually a moment when time slows down, the music creeps like a hunting cat, and you find your heart suddenly everywhere—ears, neck, and stomach? The heroes feel it coming. It's closer and closer, just around the corner; it's gonna get them. Any moment now. It's always totally predictable and always totally expected, yet they keep on in the hope it will just pass. I mean, how dense *are* these people? Couldn't they sense danger hovering over them? Couldn't they just run, never open that door, never peek under that bed, never listen to that vicious voice?

I've been living like this for thirty-seven days of war, and to-day, when it finally gets to me, the horrors make sense. Sometimes, it's not about the impending danger you should run and hide from. Sometimes you just feel your doom coming. And you can't *not* open that door.

Daddy's hospital was bombed in the night. Carma and I read

about it in the morning news on Telegram, and the gasp got stuck in my throat like a big, dry pill. I called Daddy immediately (he didn't pick up), then ran to tell Mommy, but she was already on the phone and yelling. Then more calls were made, more news was seen, and more people talked to. For hours, we picked through the crumbs of what happened, and the spring in my chest tightened with every twist of dying hope.

Finally, we reached Dr Oko, Daddy's colleague. In the short

voicemail from the ambulance bay, he said that many were evacuated, but if Dad was among them or still under the wreckage, he didn't know. And nobody knew because the shelling was still on, and the rescuers couldn't get to the area. "It's on fire," he said, panting. "I'm sorry, but it seems nobody could survive that blow, Pani Aniol. Our surgery was on the basement floor, and since a few upper floors collapsed, it's… It's almost impossible to stay in one piece down there."

That was it, my doom door.

Mommy made an odd noise with her mouth, as if a lion had broken free from her chest, and the phone slipped out of her fingers. She was crying now. When I picked up the phone, and we heard the voice of Dr Oko promising to get his *body* no matter what, she practically wailed and squeezed her head in her hands like it was about to burst. All the Buranas fussing around her made it look like Mommy had gone psycho. With a gentle touch, Carma stroked my shoulders. She probably thought I would go just as mad, and oh *maldita*, instead of crying like I properly should have, I hiccupped with a crazy little laugh.

Okay, I am mad. I'm so mad because I can't cry. My eyes burn dry, and my body's petrified into a lump of granite, so hard that if I move my finger, I'll break it. And I laugh like Liza's silly little yappy dog. Oh my god, my god, this is so big, so big! It's going to crush my little birdie heart into a million dying embers. Didn't I beg Daddy to come with us? Didn't I tell him? We asked him so many times to run, why didn't he? Stupid, stupid, stupid Father!

Mommy cried all day. I sat with her on her bed and brushed her beautiful silky-wheat hair with the silver brush. She used to love it. Now, she didn't even seem to notice me. "I'm sorry, my little cherry bun, your mommy is an idiot," she mumbled, with her head still leaning against the carpeted wall and eyes fixed on the incense lamp Gran Bozhena left to "purify" the room.

The silver brush froze over her curls. "You are not," I said.

Mommy blew her nose.

"I didn't talk to you about serious things. About Martin. Because I was afraid the worst would happen. It was a bargain with the devil, you see? I don't talk about it—it doesn't happen. I should have been wiser in dealing with the devils. They never keep their promises."

"Mom, it's not your fault."

She ignored it. "But what have I done, Bunny? I haven't talked nice to him ever since this bloody war broke out. Now he'll never know how much I loved him…"

"Daddy isn't stupid," I murmured distractedly. "He knows, and he always knew it."

There was something in my words that made her cry again. Her gurgling and sobbing stilled my heart. I was sitting behind her with my legs crossed, studying the brush like I was going to paint it in oil. Tears froze dry in my eyes, two beads of ice. "If you want… we can get baptized?" I offered gingerly.

"How does it matter now!" Mommy blubbered.

Then the door cracked open, and Carmina peeped in. She made a sign of an imaginary tea bag dipping into an imaginary cup in her hand, and I nodded. Thanks to our volunteering, we knew exactly what Mommy needed now—sweet tea and low carbohydrates.

·

Later, in bed with Carmina, Helga the teddy bear, and dozing cat and goose, we scrolled on our phones to a background noise of lamenting dogs' songs. One beast wailed from afar so drearily, I wondered if he knew about my dad. If he had also lost a dad. If he felt just like me, lonely and lost.

I received another letter from Ben, asking if everything was okay, which it's not, but no chance I'd write that, not even to Arman in our group chat where he posts funny pics with Aidan. Any words I picked became a salad of stupid clichés. So many times, I heard people whining at the train station about their lost folks. Now, it felt like talking about Daddy would be some pathetic parody, an echo of someone else's grief. I didn't want it to sound like anything at all, to be honest. Maybe Mommy's right: if I don't talk about it, it will just… disappear?

But too many things have disappeared already.

First, my pretty princess looks and Lolita style, then home, now Daddy. My life is like a broken suitcase rolling down a mountain, losing all its contents on the way. How terrible and unfair is this? Ghastly terrible and unfair, that's how. What would Buddha say to this, huh? What?

•

2 April 2022, Day 38

I woke up to Tofu scratching at the door, and I wished I never did. Before yesterday rebuilt itself in my mind in a typhoon of sadness, everything seemed to be okay. But then, I am a homeless orphan again. Why can't I go somewhere where nothing of this happened and never will?

Still no news about the *body*. Which is good news as a missing person isn't always dead. I stuck with "missing" and went totally off my hinges when people in the market, where we went for our veggies, stopped to give Mommy their condolences. Why won't they just shut their sorry faces up and mind their own sorry business? Daddy will come back! I can't believe he won't.

Okay, maybe I just *want* it that way, but we must stay positive, must we not? There is still hope that it's just some stupid misunderstanding. I just opened the wrong door, missed my turn, and mistook the route. Maybe I got lost in a forest filled with ghosts, and my home and all in it is still there, somewhere behind the queer trees.

Everything now feels wrong, and too surreal. Huttuh, phantoms, the giant spider, Ben, and Arman are lost dreams now. It's all so far away that it's no longer true.

Dying for a boyfriend just days ago, was that even me? So stupid, so tremendously stupid, now that I think about it. Why did I even need somebody to love me in my dresses when Daddy loved me in pyjamas and chicken pox, dumb as I am and a wimpy wet weed as I am? No matter how ugly, useless, or bad, I've always been his magic princess. And he was my gracious king.

So. There is the deal. If the best-ever super mega boyfriend from some glamourous Paris or even Sirius flies in through my window, I'll slap him with a fly swatter and sell the rest of him by auction for just one day of having Daddy around.

Carmina's ma and grandad took a train to Dnipro to ask around the evacuees from Zapahorb. Someone has to know about Dr Aniol. They might even meet Daddy himself, perfectly fine but thinking he is a football player from sunny Argentina, coming here in search of his insane wife who lost their baby in a plane crash or something. Like in those soap dramas because why not? Too much crying means roaring laughter in the end, right?

After all, there *has to be* some balance to it.

Mommy didn't go anywhere and hardly even left her room. Gran Bozhena nurses her with "special" teas that smell funny. When I snuggled with the pets and Carma in our bed, I felt like a missing person myself. Or probably dead. I felt like there would be no tomorrow.

•

3 April 2022, Day 39

Is this tomorrow? Sunday again. Like it matters. Absolutely NOT going to church. I told Mommy that I had a lot of homework to do, but I mostly scrolled through the news and chatted with Aidan on Instagram. He had sneaked Arman's phone and sent music to cheer me up. *A cat. Sent me music.* Two months ago, I'd piss acid from the mere thought of it. Now it's just… normal?

Nothing about Daddy. Time ticked itself to a total stop. I tried to study, but it's the same as trying to jump over a fence with your feet still on the ground. Like, the molecular formula of water is H_2O. Why do they think I need to know that? It's just water, it's always been water, no matter what I call it. Then I need to cook this water with another bunch of letters and digits to get something I can't see or touch because chemistry is just like that. You don't mix, shake, boil, and freeze funny-looking substances with your hair sticking up and eyes goggling mad, but sit and try to get imaginary water from drawing imaginary formulas.

Ohhh, there are nine more chemistry problems on the list, but one call from Dad would have solved all two hundred of them.

Carmina was texting Captain Severin with the eyes of a psychotic murderer on a face creased up like a big, damp ginger sock. I dared not talk for fear her rib cage would crack and a monstrous red dragon would fly out of it, spitting fire all around. I'd be needing buckets of H_2O to keep my second home.

So I did a bit of tidying up to calm my chemistried nerves. Took Daddy's magic *vyshyvanka* shirt from the dresser and eyed the intricate ornament I made to save him. There are many things people are afraid of, but if you think about it, they all come from one thing. Death. Daddy wasn't even afraid of death. Some might call that a bad idea. Some might call Daddy a fool. Some DID call him a fool, loudly, but he barely heard them over the rhythmic sound of his big, generous heart. I was proud of what he did for the people, but I couldn't help hating them for stealing my father. Russians would rot in prisons for killing him. Or did they? The suspense and uncertainty were killing me.

"Are you thinking what I'm thinking?" Carmina put away her phone and gave me a witty smile.

"I'm thinking about Daddy," I said. "If he really died, if I'll ever see him again."

Her smile got a little wittier. "Remember the ghost kids going into the *other side*?"

"Yes. Why?"

"I was just thinking… It's not just about ghosts, is it? It's where all people go after they die. Mara gets the dead across the—whatsit—Slit!"

I rallied. "You think we could ask her if Daddy is there or not?"

"Worth a try." She shrugged.

I looked at the window: there was just a window to look at, and nothing behind it. "Mara won't pick up her phone again. You know, she hates chatting. And it's too dark already. We'll never in a million years find the way to Huttuh."

"No." Carmina untwined her rubbery legs from some unbelievable yoga pose on her chair and stood up. "But I know who will."

28

CARMINA

TO DO OR NOT TO DO, THAT IS THE QUESTION

From: Carmina Burana — 3 April 2022, 20:51
To: Severin Saint — Booguy

Okay, Pa,

You don't believe me when I talk about magic huts, shadows, and all that. Is this cos of my super hidden superpowers I poured into my letters ever so often? I don't blame you. After scrolling through all those pics of the blood-chilling massacre in Bucha, I felt so rotten I wouldn't believe in daylight behind my window. The world as I see it, what I imagine it should be, and what it really is, are suddenly *three different things*. And I'm not sure I know what thing is what now.

But never mind. Forget the superpowers. It was too childish anyway to pretend I was born a hero in the state of cryo-sleep but ready to rise in shining glory and save the planet. The bitter truth is that my inherent power is either not there, like, at all or is never gonna come out, like the last bit of toothpaste from the tube. Perhaps it has nothing to do with toxic people or bad luck; I might be a whimper inside a wannabe warrior. Perhaps I'm just a scared gal, like everyone else.

Between just you and me, Pa, I'm scared to bits. For Ukraine, for you, for us all. After the morons destroyed our home and Dr Aniol (maybe) died, I sort of got caught inside a toy box that was shaken-shaken-shaken and put down. I've replaced everything on the shelves and swept up the debris and everything seems fine, but the

vibration lingers, deep in my bones. Life is so fragile, so evanescent, but across the threshold of death, I don't see any heavens or hells as they call them. It doesn't matter if you believe it or not: there is nothing human there. Not *nothing*, just nothing we could understand, and that frightens me terribly.

Do warriors feel it? Do warriors fear it? Do they ever lose their grip, like I do?

I thought being all tough and snappy would make me immune to this. To despair, to sorrow, to regret, to plain and primal fear. But it's not about what you say; it's not about what you think. It's not about what you feel. *It's about what you do.*

So much has been thought and said and feared. All these epic posts and crying headlines, pompous slogans, catchwords, hashtags #bravelikeukraine #standwith #prayfor #nowar #peace… lamentations, donations, banging at every door, cries, pleas, protests and demonstrations, signed petitions and national symbols burnt into the skin. The tragedy grew into a farce. It doesn't work! Russians are killing us in all possible ways, and all I can do to react in return is a mass repost on Facebook. Pathetic!

I must act, *do something*, Pa. I'll go bonkers if I don't do anything about this stupid dying man's world. Simply helping the refugees and babysitting the pets won't bring back the dead, won't stop people from dying, and won't change anything before we just… just die. I don't know what has to be done, but I'll do it. At any cost, the screw will turn.

And you'll be the first to know. Just stay safe out there. Please.

Your freaked-out Skipper

29

MARA

Huttuh is so quiet, I can hear the tick of the clock from upstairs (and I didn't realise we had any clocks). There is only so much focus I need to read the words in the book on my lap without really following the idea, and I use the rest of my mind to ardently hate this life.

My jaws lock in a yawn, and my eyes blink the sleep away. Slowly, I get rocked between the waving lines on the page into a doze, but then a turn of the page brings a curious illustration of a Mayan warrior riding a dinosaur. I arch my eyebrows, swing my legs off the arm of my chair, and turn it back to read the passage again. The words take a moment longer to sink in. Mayans appeared to have lived long before people managed to tame fire and invent wheels, working tools, and bloody volunteers who steal Baba Yaga's cats. I hurl the book at Aidan's empty seat and start picking at loose threads on my armchair.

There were times when I cherished the quiet hours of the day. Nothing soothed my mind like moments of stillness, an antidote to the windstorm of Aidan's rushing about the hut singing, scratching, and toppling pots. Now, I feel like some chaos will do me good.

The doorbell rings, and I grumble to Huttuh, "What now? Turn into something scary and tell them to get lost, will you?" But instead,

Huttuh shakes me off my chair onto the rug, and the bell ding-dongs again.

"We forgot the password. You there, Mara?" comes a voice from outside.

I go, "I'm not anywhere!"

"And who's talking then?" The voice rises.

"Radio Who."

"Who?"

"Who!" I practically yell.

"Who who?" Like an owl speaking.

Come on, the light is on, we see that, another familiar voice joins.

"So? I'll turn it off..."

Wait. My eyes flash wide open. I leap up and gallop to the door.

It's the girls! They stand there like two cast-off autumn leaves, swept by the wind to my doorstep. Agnieszka holds a white embroidered shirt, and Carmina has Shrimp under her arm. His snotty beak is never "swept," but you get the picture.

I run down the steps. "Damn. Where have you been these last three days?"

In despair, Shrimp quacks.

Carmina scratches her nose. "We texted you, but you've probably left your phone in hell."

"Daddy is missing." Agnieszka's lips are trembling as she speaks. She hugs the shirt tighter.

"We don't know if he's dead or alive," Carmina quickly picks up. "We thought you might say if he... If he went through The Slit."

"Oh." I turn to the goose, and he looks like his face is going to snap in half, he's grinning so hard. "He hasn't gone through mine, that's for sure. But there are many other Baba Yagas who could give him a pass."

Two pairs of eyes fix me with a glare just like my torch-skulls do, burning from within. I can almost sense their cheeks tingling. "Are there more Slits?" Carmina frowns in confusion.

"The Slit is just one, but the gates are many." I look around at the stony faces. "Didn't I tell you that? I'm afraid I can't know if…"

Allow me! Shrimp wriggles with his feet, gaggling, and Carma puts him on the ground. *My detective skills allow me to trace anyone. I'm a good snoop with an eagle eye.*

I gaze at him silently for a moment, with my eyes narrowed. "You don't look like an eagle."

"What is he saying?" Agnieszka steps in, pressing me with her glare.

No. Shrimp quacks haughtily. *But I'm a bird. And that swarm of birds in the woods talk my language. They are all dead, so they can provide me with enough evidence.*

"Oh, right… Good point." I turn to the girls. "He's gonna Sherlock out your missing dad. It will take time."

Minutes! Shrimp cries, swanking away with his beak stuck high in the air.

Agnieszka plops onto the doorstep and gazes hard into the bleak misty woods that have swallowed the goose, as if they could part at any moment and spit her father out. She holds her face in her palms and bites at her lower lip, probably to keep her heart from jumping out of her chest, because it knocks so furiously, even I can hear it.

We flank her, and Huttuh sheds light onto us from many fish-shaped lanterns swimming lazily in the air, like paper fireflies.

"It's him! It's him!" Agnieszka pops up every time a branch snaps or owls hoot from afar. We pull her back down by the hands. The night woods are full of noises and forms. In the dark, you can see things you can't even start to imagine in the light of day.

I try telling her this, but she gives me a brief, absent glance and with an improvised shrug turns back to the woods. She doesn't stir a jot when I pull a corner of the shirt from her lap. It turns out to be a traditional Ukrainian shirt with symbols of old gods coded in the ornament. The fabric stings me like fire.

I jerk back my hand, suck on my fingers, and watch the fog sink into the woods, softly and subtly. Behind the veil of midnight mist,

there is a moving shadow. It gradually takes the shape of a tall lad with an odd, browless face and drilling little eyes under crazy hair. He strides up in jumpy moves, swinging his arms, almost flying. Black pipe pants stick to his legs, and a white doctor's coat with some lab stuff in the chest pocket makes his shoulders look so fairly tiny. There are a neat dotted tie and a mint shirt underneath, which nevertheless can't dispel the aura of a mad scientist. Or make him look any more normal than he has always been: a Doctor What, someone between a human and a bird.

"Dr Aniol has gone through The Slit, I'm afraid." He speaks in a fairy voice, neither male nor female. "Almost instantly. And since it's been three days already, he's probably at the Second Gates now."

I nod despondently, but the girls keep goggling at him in bewilderment.

"Who the hell are you?" Agnieszka finally bursts, fizzling like a buzzing bee.

He turns his face to her and spreads his arms, grinning. "Fork and knife?"

"Shiver me timbers!" Carmina exclaims, and I feel like I need to offer a proper introduction.

So I imitate a cough, point fingers at them, like I think people do, and say, "It's Shrimp, girls. Shrimp, the girls. Well, actually his name is What, but nobody calls him that."

"Men never get what is What." Shrimp flings his arm. "Anyway, he's dead. Dr Aniol has crossed the threshold. Many saw him do it. I'm sorry, Agnieszka."

"No!" She rises and shouts in his face. "You lie! Like everyone lies! You *want* him to die!" Before anyone can break the spell of her yell that has frozen our hearts, she falls back on the steps, presses the *vyshyvanka* against her face, and sobs. "You all... w-want him to die, no-nobody hopes for my daddy... Nobody hopes," she keeps mumbling between the wild blubbers, and her shoulders shudder in unison.

Carmina moves closer to her on the steps, but she pulls away. "Don't touch me! Don't you say I must accept it, I will NOT! Daddy can't die like this. He *mustn't* die like this!"

Shrimp and I exchange glances. There is genuine concern in his deep frown, and mine probably mirrors it exactly. I think about this man, a doctor, killed while saving others, and can't help thinking there is something badly wrong with it. Of course, everything in life obeys the rule of cause and effect. Meaning if anything happens, it is meant to happen. All people die, one way or another. But what way exactly suddenly matters to me.

Once I asked Mother Death if people can change their fate or if it is fixed in the stars long before they are born. Instead of an answer, she gave me two stories. "You know, today, phones mean so much to people," she started. "At any time, something makes them take their phones out of their pockets and start calling, texting, playing, surfing the Internet. They check this and that, even do business there and make money."

I shrugged. "Yes. So?"

"Now, imagine you walk past a skyscraper, with window cleaners attached to the fiftieth floor. Then that phone in your pocket beeps, or it spurs you to text someone immediately, or check if someone liked your last post on Facebook, something like that. You stop and take it out, at the exact moment when the bucket of water hits you right on the head. Call it fate, or your will. It could be either!"

I sort of got it, but Mother moved swiftly to the second story. "Imagine you walk past a skyscraper with window cleaners attached to the fiftieth floor," she said. I decided she was making fun of me. She just smiled and continued undeterred, "Then that phone in your pocket beeps, or it spurs you to text someone immediately, or check if someone liked your last post on Facebook." She paused for a moment to let me see it coming. "You stop and take it out, at the exact moment when the bucket of water hits the ground one tiny bit from your head. If not for that phone, you'd be dead. Is it fate? Or your free will? It could be neither."

"But…" I stuttered, and a wave of confusion swelled up in my chest. "But what then? If not fate or will, what determines if you live or die?"

"Well, my darling"—she put one hand on top of the other on her belly—"I think it depends on how impeccably you check your phone."

How impeccably I check… How impeccably I do my job maybe? Nobody hopes for Dr Aniol, Nesha says. Well, shit. I raise my eyes at the girls and say quite heroically, "I can bring him back."

Nobody pays any attention because Agnieszka has sobbed herself into a mega nervy spaz like she's gonna cry herself inside out, and that shirt in her hands has already got a damn good wash. Carmina is shaking her to stop her from "falling apart," and Shrimp plugs himself into his iPod (he has an iPod?) and is one second away from tuning into some podcast. I speak up, "I'll bring him back!"

Everyone turns to me, shocked. One earbud freezes in Shrimp's hand. Even Huttuh gasps with all her windows wide open.

"Are you out of your mind?" Shrimp swings his entire body at me, just like he did when he was a goose.

"Yes, I know it's against the rules, and Mother Death will probably kill me, but since I'm sort of dead already, she won't, so ha!"

"Ha?" Shrimp arches his nonexistent eyebrow. "You know the Rules of Mother Nature. It's impossible!"

"Look, it's not about the rules," I try to explain my first-ever major revelation. "It's not even about Nature. That the strongest win is also the rule of Nature, but look at Russia. It could crush this little country in hours, but hey, it's been over a month, and they are still standing!"

The sobbing stops. I've got their full attention now. "What... do you mean?" Carmina asks.

"I mean there is something else that makes history. The rules work alright, but there was a time when someone made this rule first. We follow the rules AND we make them."

"I'm not getting this." Shrimp shakes his head.

"Never mind." I wave. "I've decided to get your father back, Nesha."

Agnieszka stares at me, bemused, still in her sitting embryo pose. "You will get him back?" Her voice sounds like she's talking in her sleep.

"Yes. But... I can't do it alone. Not when he's already at the Gates of No Return. Only the living or the scouts have enough power to push him back from there... If only I had Aidan with me..."

"I'll do it!" Carmina springs to her feet. "Only the living or scouts? I fit. I'm in."

I was afraid she would. "No, it's too dangerous, Carmina, the same as dying. You might get stuck there for good. I might ask an owl, a crow or... anyway, I can find a scout."

But she's already pulled her jeans up and tucked her rainbow sweater in. "Finding a scout takes time," she says. "And Shrimp says he's already crossing some Second Gates."

"... of No Return," I repeat, stressing every word.

It has no effect on Carmina. "I know it's dangerous. Same as for our soldiers. They go to hell daily, knowing they might never return. And I am a good soldier. Don't tell me I'm just a fourteen-year-old girl."

I turn to Shrimp for support, but he gives me a what-can-I-say? little hand wave, which means you can't stop that girl once she gets something into her head. Agnieszka is my last hope, but her pallor almost matches her *vyshyvanka*, which means she might meet her father sooner than she expects.

"You'll do it for me?" she says to Carmina. "I thought you hated me for bossing you about your minefield room."

Carmina throws her head back with laughter, I'd say a bit on the crazy side. "Holy cow, why would I hate anyone for teaching me discipline? My room has never been tidier. And I'm not doing it for anyone. I just do what I think is right. So. Let's take a train into eternity. Or whatever you call Hell in your world?"

My world. Like it belongs to me. "I don't call it anything. *You* do. I'll ask Huttuh to open The Slit." I pass coldly and point at the *vyshyvanka* shirt. "Can I borrow this?"

Agnieszka gazes blandly at her shirt, then nods. "Sure. Why?"

"Well, if it burns my fingers, it can come in rather handy." I lower my sleeve and take it carefully clenched in my hoodie-covered hand. "Will you look after Neshka, What?"

Shrimp salutes me, "My pleasure, ma'am," and turns to Agnieszka, beaming. "I can turn back into poultry if that's too much for you." He swishes his hands up and down his crazy scientist's torso, asking how much exactly is too much. Agnieszka's musing gaze clings to his funky outfit, and I can't really say what scares her more: the goose's hissing or that damn lab coat.

"No, it's fine...," she finally offers in a small, distracted voice, caught between heartache for her father and stark confusion about that goose. Next, she lifts her chin to say "Mind you, I'm not dating boys anymore" and makes Shrimp blink a bit in the goose way.

Eh? He's not even... human.

I roll my eyes. *Ugh, these people! And their stupid mating dances.*

I stride back into Huttuh to gather my torches. The walls are vibrating crazily at me, like the muscles inside a giant living animal. My hut is just as anxious. "It's okay." I pat her on the furnace. "We can do it. Isn't it exciting? To bring someone out, not in."

She's still tense. I notice a flicker of a rainbow in the mirror and say, "Carmina will be fine, too. I'll take care of her. Promise." I pause at the door and say, "Do you remember us flying? It's the same as taking off for the first time. Always a bit jittery before you actually do it."

JUST DO IT

From: Carmina Burana   3 April 2022, 23:43

To: Severin Saint   Booguy

Papa,

Just a quick note that I love you. No matter what happens, this stays indestructible. Remember that Ukraine stands on your shoulders, just like I stood on your feet when I was four and you taught me to dance. We all have a future because our Cossack men and women sacrifice their present. I believe in you. And Ukraine. Believe in me, too, Pa. Cos I am taking that leap…

Slava Ukraini!

31

MARA

The best way out is always through, spins in my head as I take Carmina by the hand and watch the beacon circle start to burn. The one who said that must have been through hell.

The Slit opens. Carmina, tense and stiff, looks into it with eyes reflecting eternity, and I can see the tips of her ginger curls trembling. I try to comfort her.

"It's like being born again." I am so Mother Teresa today, I might just as well be a saint. "All you need is to remember what you are doing. Besides, the war is much scarier."

Carmina's hand in my grip is cold, but hard and dry. "I'm not scared," she snaps icily.

We step into the bright light, and the pulsing abyss swallows us. It's a fall, but not down; it's everywhere at once, like being pulled in with the gravity of a supermassive black hole.

A dazzling radiance envelops my body, tearing it apart. It feels like I get disintegrated into a myriad of tiny, shining-from-within pieces. The shirt tucked behind my belt is slightly heating up. Thankfully, I have the beacon in one hand, glowing brighter with every beat of my heart, and the cold fingers of a damn brave girl clasped in the other. They keep me focused. Otherwise, I'd probably let the

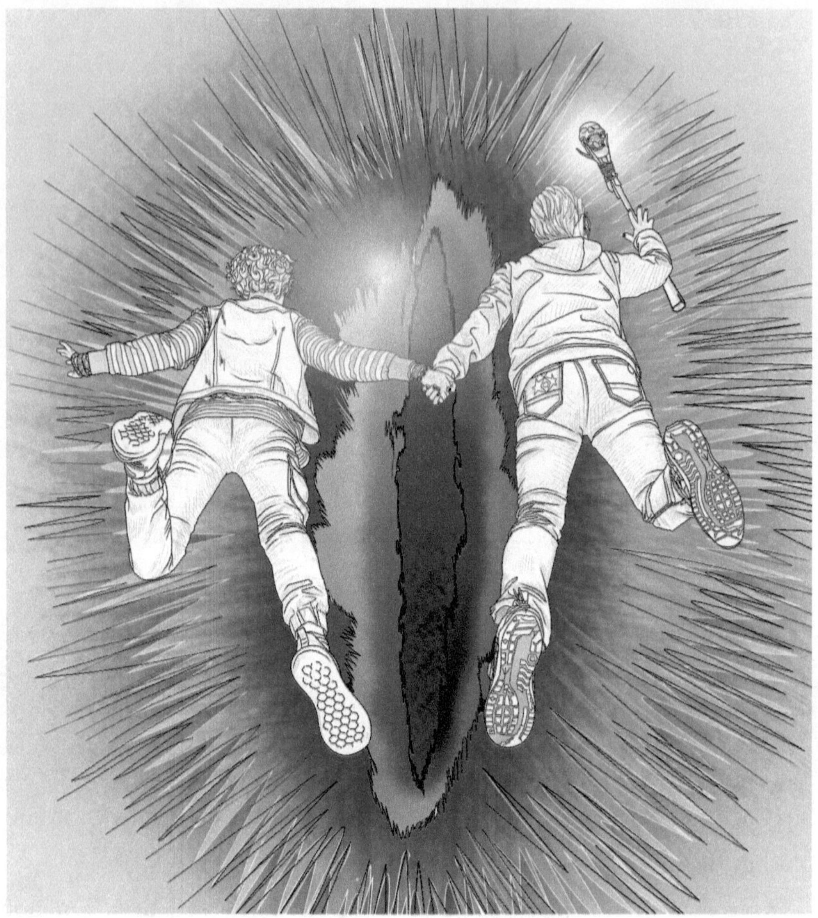

light spread me all around the universe, like particles from an atomic bomb.

Remember what you are doing, I remind myself and squeeze Carmina's hand harder.

The epic free fall ends like they all do—with a jolly good crash. It seems like a jolly good crash at least, which, in fact, is only light meeting darkness. I can't talk just yet, so I pull on my pal's hand in the hope that she's still in one piece and scramble through the jelly net of nothingness into the dim blackness of more nothingness.

My beacon is suddenly dead. Carmina's hand gets heavier in mine.

She almost drops on all fours, and I pant in exasperation, shaking the stick wildly.

Come on, bony face, it's no time for your tricks, shine, SHINE, you little bugger!

Finally, a tiny gleam sparkles inside, and the skull's sockets flare up.

I quicken my pace across the valley of confusion, dragging Carmina behind. I turn to look at her. In the darkness, her hair and sweater glow in a captivating golden shine. She wobbles on her trembling bony legs with her arm up in the air for balance, which is a good sign.

"What's… this place?" she gasps heavily.

"Don't talk!" I hush. "It will drain your energy. Just move your feet. Follow me."

As we emerge from the total gloom, nothing at all turns into everything at once. We walk into all the unimaginable splendour of millions of worlds clashed together: the crossroads of all possible paths a mind can follow while flashing through life. It's not just a place to get to, it's all the places you can get to at the same time.

All I see is not what it is, because whoever comes here sees their own hell. I can only give my side of it: an enormous, fascinating tower-like building growing from the depth of the earth high into the sky (maybe it's the other way around, you can never tell up from down here). It's so intricate and elaborate, there is no way to get it all at once because its ever-unfolding architectural genius is forever in flux. Each time I think like I've seen it all, there appears a new, exquisite flight of stairs, upside-down balconies, moving statues, or another domed tower, and more and more into infinity. I wonder what other Yagas find here. Even Carmina may see just… light or places from her memory. That's the magic of beyond.

I remember how dangerous it is to stare (one can easily get sucked

in and lost till all their energy is gone), so I force myself to simply scan the horizon. The rich landscape in the background is a merging of many, each of which is a breathing being. Hills breathe, woods breathe, air paradoxically breathes, too, changing constantly. I spot an ocean leaking a granite mountain, but then it's a land with a thriving city on it. Then a whirlpool of stars, transforming, moving constantly in its fleeting existence.

Shiny lights—residents of the in-between worlds—swarm around in waves, rushing away from the running shadow cast by a titan walking across the valley. Entire metropolises on gigantic islands fly by. Grandiose whale-like creatures manoeuvre in the clouds, carrying smaller creatures on their backs and inside of them. And beyond it all, there lies a cosmos of colourful galaxies and shooting stars. The planets drift quietly in blinking, pulsing infinity. I gawk at them stupidly and darn, almost forget the important thing! Carmina.

"Don't stare at anything," I yell at her over my shoulder. "Don't let anything drag you in."

"I don't see anything." Carmina follows me with her eyes down and hands groping at the passing wall. "Is death always like this? All blackness and quiet? Like a damp underground cave… in the old video games. You know, with hardly any graphics."

"It's not… wait, you don't see anything? Nothing at all?" I turn to face her and walk backwards across a majestic elven-like bridge over a deafening waterfall.

Carmina blinks around her. "Well, I see you and your torch."

"Oh. Ohhhh… Hmm. Interesting. That probably means you're not dying just yet." I let it settle in my mind, then swing around and speed up. "Well, it's a pity you can't see my home, but don't worry, just keep up. We're almost there."

It's going quite well so far. Nobody has noticed an intruder, and I finally have a companion on my stroll into infinity. A blind one, but nevertheless! Screw cats, I'll have a human scout! I relish this idea while climbing the killer-high stairs of the ancient so-called monastery, the last bastion at the frontier to the land of eternal decay. It's a pyramid with an eye on top. Why everyone here calls it a monastery is a question.

Then a squeal stabs me in the back like a dagger. I spin, sliding a few steps down on my butt, and see Carmina rolling along the ground and kicking. A swarm of fluttering crampfish fliers attack her gleaming shine and make me tumble all the way down. I run back, battle-crying my most feral "Agggrrrr!" At least I think it's battle-crying, not just… crying.

Bloody inorganics! There is little I can do to shoo them away once they've got to the human's shine. My torch is as killing as a cow's tail is to the dung flies. So I snatch Agnieszka's *vyshyvanka* from my belt and flap it at them fiercely, with my skin steaming off my hand.

It works just fine, though: they skitter off like a flock of startled birds. But damn, it burns!

I drop the shirt and shake my hand, shrieking Michael Jackson-ish. Carmina doesn't move. She lies on the ground, crouched into a boiled shrimp pose, pressing her crossed arms tight to her belly. Well, good girl. Surprisingly, she knows exactly what to do to protect her life force.

"You okay?" I ask, still jiggling that hand of mine.

"Are they gone?" she mumbles into her knees.

"Yeah, sorry about that. Those were fliers. They eat energy. I thought my presence would be enough, but you've got quite a light."

She perks up, but her eyes are out of focus. "What light?"

"*Your* light, what else? They eat people's light," I explain with notes of irritation and blow at my palm. "Get up. And put this on." I point at the *vyshyvanka* on the ground with my torch.

"Agnieszka's magic shirt?" She scowls incredulously and brushes dust off her jeans. "But it's for Dr Aniol. It should, like, help him."

I glance at my burnt hand (crap, only Dead Water will mend that). "He's dead already. A bit too late for magic shirts."

Carmina glances at my hand, too, and makes a face at my burns. "Will you live?"

I huff indignantly. "Hope not. Put that thing on. It will protect you from the inorganics." I catch her baffled glance and clarify, "The flying monsters and everyone who lives here."

She grumbles as she pulls the shirt over her head, on top of her rainbow sweater and vest. "Well, I'd never... You sure about this? It's just... a shirt."

"Not just a shirt. There were times when people were powerful enough to come and wander through here." I point around with my chin. "They invented armour like these shirts, belts and all sorts of artefacts called *molfas* to protect themselves, so yeah, if you ask if this will work, it will."

"Cool!"

We ascend to the top with no more adventurous battles, not counting our exhaustion from fighting that hell of stairs.

"Remind me next time that there're no elevators in Hell, and I might never agree to visit the dead again." Carmina pants, brushing sweat off her forehead with her sleeve and literally crawling now because the higher the stairs go, the steeper they are.

"Why, it's good kung fu practice." I flinch at the sound of "never" cos words have power here and I already saw her as my new kitty. Ahem. I mean, *friend*. "Last flight!" I cheer us up.

"Oh, good. Now a nice roller coaster ride down?"

"Um... how do I put it?" I climb on top of the final step and help Carmina by offering her the end of my torch (hell, I'm gonna touch that shirt again). "There is no down. You only go up this pyramid, by any of its sides."

Because as long as you reach the Eye, floating above the spacious platform, you inevitably face the Current of Time, which is just a river. Don't imagine anything too over-dramatic; leave that to the fantasy writers. River, full stop. Some call it the river of oblivion, but really, it doesn't cause oblivion. On the contrary. The flow of its ceaseless running waves can get you anywhere, at any point in time and space, in the endless stream of your life or any life.

However, once you step into it, your current world is carried away like a pebble in fast waters. You can never, for the love of God, get back to your life as you know it. Not because it's gone. It's still there, somewhere, carried past unnoticed in the relentless flux of time.

Only one creature can fish it out and bring you back. The ferryguy.

Their name is so small and freakish—H, just H—that I call them Captain, cos of the boat. They might be "he," "she," or both or neither by the sound of it. I've never actually asked, and I can never tell by the look of their crazy canopy clothes covering their too many legs, heads, or whatever is under there. Anyway, this is the only way I know to reach the Land of No Return on the opposite bank. And that's what I tell them,

"Hi, Cap. Take us across the river, please. And bring us back."

They straighten up to their full, formidable height, and point at Carmina behind me with a tentacle-like finger emerging from under the canopy. "That is not dead."

"Yes, thanks, Cap. Get your paddles, we're in a bit of a hurry." I flap my hand at the set of paddles leaning on the crates on the wooden pier.

"H don't take the living," they say in the stubborn manner of a brainless golem.

"Yes, I know. But you *must*." My sudden anger fizzles out through a crack in my patience.

"H must only take the dead." And Cap H doesn't even know what anger is.

I roll my eyes. "*I* am dead. And she's my… plus one."

Silence inside the canopy.

"Ahem." Carmina pushes me aside, steps forward, and holds out something gleaming in her hand. "Here, Pan-i H, will this be enough to get us there and back?"

She has a few coins in her palm.

H gets captivated by the glitter of hryvnias. I can almost see their many eyes behind the fencer's helm-like net covering their face. In a moment longer than necessary, they stretch their made-on-the-spot hand, mimicking a human's, and, carefully, take the money. "H don't take the living," they repeat, "but Mara can take my boat for a while." Well, that's at least something.

"Great." I grab the paddles and step onboard.

"Can you see the river?" I ask Carmina, settled in front of me, as we untie the boat and I push it off the pier with a paddle.

She smirks with a corner of her mouth. "Yep. And the dude in the palatine. Such a charmer!"

"Where did you learn that trick with the money?"

"From Greek mythology. Dead souls give two coins to the blind ferryman to cross Styx, which divides Earth from the Underworld." She bends over the side of the boat and peeks into the water. "Is this Styx?"

"Perhaps. I call it the Current of Time. It looks like a boring river, but it's actually an ever-circling spiral." My burnt hand aches a little as I fit the left paddle into the socket and push.

Carmina bobs, and the boat lists slightly with her weight on one side. "Cool!"

"Can you stop trying to drown?" I ask, rowing and looking back at the Shores of No Return. "There are no life vests onboard, nothing with 'life' as a prefix, in fact."

She doesn't seem to care in the least but swings her arm overboard and brushes at the streaming waves below. Then she looks at her fingers, dazed. "How come it's fluid but not, like... wet?"

"Because it's not water. It's ... gravity itself. Like time."

My explanation makes it even worse. "What time?" she asks.

I sigh. "Five bloody o'clock. Get away from there, okay?"

"Can I drink it?" Carmina continues breezily. She's leaning even further over the side of the boat, practically kissing the waves.

Just so you know, it's the most dangerous thing, The Slit in The Slit, the fabric that connects all dots in the universe and keeps planets in their orbits, and Carma decides to put it on her tongue. I'd write a long post on Facebook to complain about human curiosity, but I'll probably be blown to pieces before then.

"Absolutely not! I said it's ALIVE." I try as hard as I can.

Carmina giggles, flashing me a don't-be-silly little face. "The water? Really?"

"It's not water, dammit!" I drop the paddle. Because a long shadow sweeps under the boat, like a fret through the mind. "Shit."

Carmina catches it, too. "Look, there's something underwater!"

"Don't look!" I yell, but she loses her balance, whoops, and topples overboard. I jerk up, cursing under my breath, and fall flat on the bench to grab her, sinking, by the scruff. Which I manage just in time before the current sucks her away. With my palms burning insanely, I pull her up till she safely clasps the boat. "You stupid, stupid, stupid... fool! You'll get us *vanished*, you understand?" I shout with tears of pain in my eyes.

She can't talk for a moment, and her breath goes erratic, but her grip is iron. "So s-sorry... I just..." She tries to pull herself up, clawing into the wooden side, but it's too much for her insect limbs. Darkened flow curds and thickens, and the river's torrent condenses into resin. She looks up, hopeless. "Mara... I can't get out," she says between gasps. Carmina tries again, growling, and drops back into the river.

I pull my sleeves down and try to jerk her up by the clothes, but she weighs an absolute ton. "Fuck!" I cry and then again, "Fuck! Fuck! Fuckkk," slapping the bench hard.

"I... don't... understand." Carmina scratches at the boat's wood. Her eyes are huge, and her freckles stand out like blots on paper. "I'm so heavy and... weak. What's happening?"

"Nothing is happening. You're being pulled in by your shadow," I say. "You must let it go."

"What... let *what* go?" Her arms tremble, and her knuckles go white. I bend over and try to grip her belt, but the boat goes crazy, and I rush to the other side for balance. I almost cry now in fear I'll lose another friend of mine.

"Everything!" I say, exasperated. "What you hate, what you want, what you fear. Do it."

For a tiny fraction of a second, I expect her to give me another "what?" face, but she suddenly yells, "No! I won't stop hating Ruzis, never, or stop fighting them. Letting go means to accept it, to agree that they will take over, to agree to yield to this rotten, sick man's world, and to do nothing about it!"

Her muscles slacken with her cries, and she almost slips down into the river. I pounce and grip her hands, pressing my knees against the boat's bottom for a level. "It doesn't mean anything, you fool."

"No, you don't understand," she hisses, with a biting glare in her darkening eyes. "This is what I live for. I want to make a difference. I want to make things right!"

"You're gonna die now!" I sort of both cry and laugh. "Forget Ruzis and men's world and all that. It's not *their* life at stake now, it's yours! You'll just drown here. What difference will it make?"

She pants instead of answering and looks past me blindly. Her head is so low in the river that the waves reach her lips already, and my hands hurt from lifting her growing weight. She could slip off at any second. "Let it go," I whisper. "Just let this stone drop out of your pocket."

"So they won't… kill us?" she asks with her lips trembling. "Ruzis. If I let them be?"

"I don't know," I sigh out the truth. "But it's not your concern."

"What is the point then? Tell me. You know stuff about stuff, so tell me. We live and fight… for our lives… but the fighting is killing us. What the fuck, Mara? I don't understand…"

Okay, I need to think rocket quick, or else I'll lose her for good. "It's not about what you do, Carmina," I say in a different, pitchy voice, and she darts her eyes up at me, baffled. "It's *how* you do it."

"Gran? You? What are…"

"Hush now. Hold on, dear." I put a little more into my grip, now panting not only from tension but also from my age. My hands are spotted and wrinkled, but strong. "Listen, child. I'm proud of you fighting your battles, but I don't approve of *how* you fight them. You see the difference?"

"N-no." She gulps a little of the flow and spits it out.

I try to keep my voice even, but it dives and lifts like a bird playing in the wind. "It's like archery, dear. You aim your arrow and intend it to hit the target." It gets her attention. "Your angst, rage, and hatred pull the bow to the limit, but your angst, rage, and hatred also hold the arrow locked. You see, to let it go where you *intend* it to go, you need to *let* it go. Let it fall where it falls. You have no power over a flying arrow. You already put your all into the pull. Relax now. It will find the target on its own."

She still gazes at me with a vacant look, and her eyes are huge and glassy. I can see my reflection in her pupils, an old woman with big electric-blue eyes and a funny, wrinkled face. My hair is short and white, and I think I can sense the halo of a witch around my head.

A moment longer than life passes between us. The intensity of the silence is so hard, I can actually sit on it and drum, drum-di-dum. Then, slowly, I feel the weight on my arms lighten. The shadow in the river sinks, and Carma pops up on the waves like a block of Styrofoam.

"Whoa, whoa… Haha. Strange water indeed!" she exclaims, rocking on top of it. "Now I can walk on it like Jesus did!"

"Or get back onboard," I suggest and lean over to her jeans' belt to give her a friendly tug.

Charmingly enough, at this very moment, she farts into the river, so bloody monstrous, it bubbles up in a bomb of killing wind that nearly chokes me. One second, I almost drop overboard, the other, I cry, "Saint Heavens, what do you eat!"

"Your bean soup, what else? Are you still Mara or Granny? Jeez, this is creepy." Carmina slugs back into the boat giggling, and I briefly consider hurling her back into the river. She plops on the bottom, brushing her hair back. "Whew, the underworld is fun."

We're so gonna die here.

•

Once we moor at the opposite shore, the atmosphere changes drastically. It's an eternal black desert of hills and holes, with odd-looking stalagmites fading into the mountains on the horizon as far as you can see. The eerie part of it is that the burnt-like ground is a living being, with pores on the rock-hard skin that ooze moisture and puff off steam. The only inanimate things here are horrendous, majestic arches scattered around the island like doors to nowhere.

Snake-ish creatures wriggle about like black lightning, and used-to-be people slowly drift up to the long, knotted stalactites so high above, it looks like they grow into a sky dome. That is where The Eagle, the beginning and the end of all, stands.

If Dr Aniol has lifted, he's forever scattered into innumerable pieces flying all over the universe, because his core will be set loose. Still, I hope we won't have to ascend the local Everest to see if that's so. There are plenty of them crowded at the gates.

I point at one of the arches on the hill and ask, "Can you see the gates?"

Carmina squints. "You mean the Japanese-looking kinda shrine's arcs surrounded by giant floating eggs?"

"Yes, exactly!" I snap my fingers victoriously. Bathing has restored her sight in full.

"I also see snakes. Is this a Snake Island?"

"Forget snakes; they can't hurt anyone in *vyshyvanka*. Now look here, jokes aside, this is deadly important now." I push her slightly forward. "Those eggs are ex-people. I can't touch them. They'll rush away from me like a cloud of flies. But your light appeals to them immeasurably, okay? They miss this light, and so they will stick to it."

"Oh." Carmina beams at first, then drops her mouth open. "Like vampires?"

"No, they don't suck anything, just get drawn to you like a flower to the sun…" I gasp, feeling the pressure of slipping time. "Anyway, your mission is to find Agnieszka's father and hook him."

"What?" She frowns at me.

"Not hook like *hook*, just pin him down, fix, trap, and pull him away from the gates. And I mean physically." I feel the surge of exasperation blocking my throat. Any moment now, it may be too late. "I'll do the rest. Just bring him back to the river."

Carmina looks back, with her freckles almost screaming at me. "They are just eggs," she exclaims. "How do I find him? They all look like eggs to me."

Now I lose my rag entirely. "How should I know? You know him better than I do!"

"Right." She spins on her heels and climbs up the hill, cat-jumping from rock to rock. Her body moves gracefully between the stalagmites, and her bright carrot curls bob in the air. That hair alone shines like a candle in the dark.

When she reaches the top, she flusters the mob of bleak egg-ish shapes. They toddle towards Carmina and surround her like tired travellers gathering around a bonfire. She jostles among them, and her hair beams here and there through the crowd. Then I see her pounce at one egg, clawing into its ethereal shell, and tear down the hill, yelling madly. I dart up as fast as I can (faster than light), brandishing my torch and feeling so much like an ancient warrior, it hurts. Well, it hurts the eggs more, cos they all rush off to the gates and leave the shiny girl alone.

"I got him! I got Doc!" Carmina pants as she drags the egg of living energy three times her size down the shore slope. I can't help snickering under my breath: she looks like a scarab pulling a giant dung ball. "Piece of cake. I only had to pretend I needed a doctor. I cried 'Is there any doctor? A child is dying,' that sort of stuff," she blabbers in between her short wheezes. "And this one sort of gleamed inside. He also looks like he could buy fifty dolls for Nesha and stay, like, sane."

"He *is* Martin Aniol, can you lower your voice a bit? It's a valley of the dead, after all. Now, back to the boat… no, stop!" I block her way with my beacon and root to the ground. My blood turns instantly into ice as my eyes meet a familiar figure on the pier. Involuntarily, I scan the horizon and see the blurry, ugly shapes of Hounds of Hell across the river, a pack of hungry dogs sniffing the air for prey. "Drat! That's what I feared the most. This is the end. Game over."

"What?" Carmina turns the egg in her arms slightly aside and peeks at the man on the pier. "Blow me down, it's Aidan!" she exclaims, and I sense cold creeping up my spine.

"It's not Aidan. It's Mother," I hiss through my clenched teeth and stride bravely ahead. Death has no shape, so it takes any. And damn, she knew exactly what shape to take to hurt me the most. Aidan's.

Carmina follows behind me, gasping, "Aidan is your mother, too?"

"No, dammit." I slowly boil. "She's turned into my cat. Death came to me as my cat."

"Why would death turn into your cat?" Gosh, one day she'll get in trouble with her big mouth. But there is no time to explain that I missed that fluffy moron, and that emotion alone brought Death into his shape.

"Hi, Mom." I try a breezy tone as I step onto the pier. Carmina stands on my right, with Dr Aniol still in his dying trance.

"Hi, Mom?" Aidan puts his arms akimbo. "Is that what you say when ruining the Order?"

"Ah, that." I glance briefly at the egg. "I'm not ruining anything. You told me there is no fate or inviolable rules. People can get back from the afterlife; they often do, and you know that."

Aidan's eyes, fixed on me, are pitch black with no pupils, irises, or whites. His hair moves slowly in the aura of invisible power as if underwater. And his voice is metal when he says, "It is not for you to decide, Mara."

I take a tiny breath (maybe my last) and point at Carmina behind my shoulder. "Mom. This is my friend who risked her life for it. If we don't get Martin back, my other friend will fall apart, as will many others. Many people will die because this man is a doctor, and it's war in Ukraine."

"I know." He bristles. "And it's none of your concern either, to save people. I thought you liked your job of bringing them across The Slit."

"I still do." My voice rises along with the heat in my chest. "But now there's more to that. I've finally realized why I do this. Why this is important."

"And why is that?" Aidan asks, matching my tone.

"Well… Before the war, I saw only mindless bio trash, slogging through life with no purpose, and in vain. People only put their shit together when they crossed The Slit with me. Until Death knocked at their doors, they didn't see or didn't want to see what they were really doing here on Earth. But I was wrong about them. People *can* see, *can* feel, *can* understand more… when they are aware. When they see me every day, not just on their last day. Like all the Ukrainians I met at the train station. Like my friends. They are maybe shocked but also awake and aware."

I take another tiny breath. Mother looks like she's been carved from stone, so I continue.

"What I'm saying is… I think I lost the track already. Anyway, Mom, my job is not to rid the planet of people or rid people of their lives, but to challenge them. Cos death is more about life than life is. And I want them to KNOW it while they are still able to do something about it." My voice trails away now, suddenly drained of energy, met by total silence from Death's side. "So. I'm taking Doctor Aniol back."

Mother in Aidan's shape lifts a brow at me. "Even if I set my Hounds on him?"

"Even if you drop the skies on him." I know I shouldn't have said that, but you can't take your words back in here.

A pause stuck in my chest like a bullet.

"Well." Mother drops her arms down. "That's the spirit." She walks up in her smooth, sliding gait that makes Aidan look even gayer and takes my hands in her palms. One brush of her cold fingers heals the burns right before my eyes.

"You finally see it my way." Mother turns to Carmina, who stumbles back, hiccupping, but she only takes the egg from her and softly compresses it back into a human.

"Don't worry." Mother smiles at my friend with the corner of Aidan's curvy lips. "I don't touch the brave. Not in that shirt, anyway."

•

Whew, that was close. Never before was Mother a bullet to dodge, but look at us: we didn't just ~~steal~~ retrieve a soul from hell, we also returned it with honours! Cos finding our faces "a little peaky," Mother lifts us right back to life on the back of her *magic* gale.

In short: we ride the wind. It looks like we're flying a giant serpent with a horrid dragon head, long catfish whiskers, and a forever-wiggling zigzag of a tail, but sadly only I can see it. Carma thinks she's getting swept through the air by an invisible wind flow. Still, her head spins like a bobbin, gawking at the flying whales, the misty ups and downs of fantasy landscapes below, the tower, crystal woods, forever-changing oceans… She calls it a dream, and, in a way, it is.

Dr Aniol doesn't call it anything, though, and sees nothing beyond his thoughts. He stares in the mid-distance and rubs his fingers nervously. What could trouble him still? I wonder and tap his knee with my finger. "Are you okay?"

He glances over me distractedly. "Hard to tell, Sugar Poppet." He thinks I'm his daughter; that's a good sign. "I can't miss the call."

"What call, Daddy?" I ask, slightly surprised that he's not aware of what is going on.

He murmurs, "Ambulance, or army? Or locals. Someone can get injured; they always do. I heard the blast. A big one… Paramedics must have called me many times. I just… couldn't pick up, I guess. Or was it the call from Masha… I think my phone beeped. Was it you?" he digs into his empty pockets in search of his phone and darts his eyes at me.

I don't know what to say. "It doesn't matter now, does it? You're going home."

"Am I? Well." He rubs his hands harder, pressing his lips tight. "I suppose I should... I promised. It's just... there is this feeling that I missed something important. Some call? Just can't remember. But I must do something, Bunny, before it's too late. Save people..."

"You saved enough already," I offer in a small voice.

"You know, doctors don't count those we saved, but those we lost." He lowers his eyes at his hands, pressing them together. "There was this girl. She was maybe... five? People brought her wrapped in a blood-soaked jacket and laid her on my table. I could see right away she was doomed. It was useless to waste medication, but you never think about that in those moments. Her parents cried in the corridor, and we still had the air alert. I gave her the shot and then... she opened her eyes. Looked right at me, and asked, 'Am I going to die?' Like she knew more than I ever will. I said, 'No, no, you're not. You'll be just fine. You'll go back to your mommy and daddy, eat cakes, and play with your friends.' But she died. Almost instantly. It was just... I still see her face, Poppet. And think... I don't want to miss another call from a child like her."

Now I get why he's reached the Second Gates without even knowing that he died. He must have followed his patients.

"No calls, Dad." I shake my head. "You should rest now." And he nods.

The wind carries us right into The Slit, shakes us off its back like a dog shakes off fleas. We don't just cross the gates, we break through them at full speed, and it feels like tearing through thick layers of cobwebs like when you get pushed out of the dark through a tiny little hole, or... anyway, we did it! We scramble out into the dim light of the Huttuh lanterns still glowing in the air.

Just as we left them, Agnieszka, with her arms crossed on her chest, and Shrimp, with his mouth open mid-sentence, turn to greet us with surprised faces.

"What's the matter? You forgot the keys to hell or something?" Nesha stares in confusion. We've only been away a moment, as it turns out.

But then she sees her father and gasps.

"DON'T!" Shrimp and I pounce and grab her before she flings her arms around his gauzy body. "Don't touch him just now!"

Dr Aniol doesn't seem to see her or anything with his still, peaceful eyes. He sails through the air wistfully and silently with his feet not even reaching the ground.

"What happened to him? Is he blind?" Agnieszka asks.

"He's fine. Or will be in a few hours? You'll see," I promise her.

She knits her brows and turns to Carmina, who stands behind all dusty and crumpled. "Dear God!" she yells. "What have you done to my *vyshyvanka!*"

32

AGNIESZKA

4 April 2022, Day 40

Perfect. Life's perfect. *Perfectamentous!* Spring is finally in full swing, bright and glorious, screaming for action and all the nice, sweet, and beautiful things. I thought it was never going to come. I thought war, cold, and despair would be with us forever. But the rains have stopped, and the sun pours pure diamonds on the puddles in the road. I threw my smelly coat in the wash basket (I never want to see it again!) and ran outside in jeans and a sweater, breathing in the fresh and fragrant smell of… victory? Yes. It smelled like victory. YAY!

Eventually, we reached Daddy. He's alive!!!!!! Some angelic souls evacuated him along with the others to Dnipro. He was in hospital all this time. Unconscious. But he's fine now. We've just called him on Telegram, and he said he did get hurt in that blast but that was just "a scratch." This "scratch" is all across his scalp. Also, there is a nasty cut on his cheekbone that gives him a bit of a Viking look. His face seemed so oddly thin, I almost thought the girls dragged the wrong man from Hell, but then he smiled very Daddy-like, and I knew it was my father alright. Mommy saw hardly any of it behind her tears, though. Because her false eyelashes stuck together.

Anyway, the Buranas will collect Daddy from Dnipro when he's, like, okay to move. Captain Saint will be there, too, on a short leave. Together, they'll catch an evacuation train to Chornoguy. Carmina is so crazy happy to have her pa back for a while, she's running all around the house shrieking like a Native American on the warpath. I'm writing this hiding in Pan Burana's spooky workshop in case she wants to rip my scalp off.

This very Friday. This Friday is not never. Can't wait! Seems like Christmas: no matter how close you get, it's always ages away!

I grew so restless that I couldn't sit still even for a moment and create anything sensible and of value. Which is a pity, because I wanted to give Mara something sensible and of value to thank her for bringing Daddy back. Then I remembered Mara borrowing my *vyshyvanka* and asked Shrimp and Carma if she'd like one for herself.

Carmina laughed like she'd left her brain back in hell. And Shrimp (in his human form) said, "If you want to give something as important, you only give life for life."

"All right then." I brushed the coffee crumbs I was using for my new soap piece off my lap and looked at my friends. "I will need your help, Gran Bozhena's wicker basket… and the gods' will."

And probably a superpower to handle the situation, because never, not in a million years, can anyone put Tofu in a basket.

"Are you sure it's a good idea?" Carmina asked me as I placed a bedspread over her head to disguise her burning-ginger colours.

"Of course!" I pushed her down onto the floor beside the basket. "Just imagine how lonely she is now after Aidan left her for some… boy. Besides, Tofu always hated me."

"He hates everyone," Carmina grumbled, moving under the quilt.

"Exactly! Just like Mara. They are made for each other. Now, stay still, or he'll never fall for the bait." I put a handful of salmon cat sticks in the basket and then plopped on the bed with my Jane Austen book opened at a random page. "Remember, you need to be very quiet, and then very quick," I said with my finger twisting my hair.

Shrimp the goose dashed into the room gah-gah-gah-ing, beating his wings and very persuasively announcing that *Mortal Kombat* had just begun. Right on the dot, Tofu rushed in, scratching at the floorboards and slipping on the carpets. He saw the goose and immediately pressed his body to the floor, ears back, pinning him with his hunter's look and wagging his bum. But Shrimp folded his wings and waddled breezily to the basket. He picked up a salmon stick with his beak, and all Tofu's wildness—puff!—was gone. He raised his head, sniffing, and padded closer, sniffing again. He wanted to slap the snack out of the goose's beak, but then he realised there were even more in the basket and, paw by paw, he wriggled his way inside.

Got you. How does salmon change your life, huh?

"Now!" I fake-whispered. Carmina flashed up and slammed the basket shut. Shrimp spit the cat stick out and coughed with disgust.

We fixed the lid with a gift ribbon and carried it to the woods. Well, mostly Carmina carried it because Dr What (Shrimp) was sick from the cat food, and I was sick of that cat.

Mara met us in her black pyjamas (she will pick another colour when she finds something darker), with a sleepy face and a grumble. "Who's missing this time? I'm not dragging every other dad out of that pit, mind you."

"Okay," I agreed cheerfully. "We're not here for that. I just wanted to give you a present."

Squinting, Mara examined me with a long, suspicious look, then glanced at the basket in Carmina's hands. "I hope it's full of lemonade bottles."

"It's not full of anything pleasant, I'm afraid," Shrimp noted, and I shoved him in the rib.

Mara huffed and twisted her lips in a lopsided smile. "Come in, I like ugly presents."

It was hard to say if she liked this particular one. When we stepped inside and shook Tofu out of the basket, Mara stayed composed and indifferent, gazing drearily at the shaggy-looking, fluffy ball of pure, three-coloured evil. But Huttuh seemed to freeze in terror and rolled up all the curtains on the windows. A picture suddenly fell from its hook and the flowers in the pots shut their petals. Then Tofu came to his senses and clawed into the carpet, hissing at us with his eyes glaring.

That facial expression only said one thing:

I WILL SHIT ON EVERYTHING YOU LIKE!

"Behave yourself! This is your new home!" I demanded and clapped my hands (making the sound he couldn't stand). Tofu darted all around the room for no apparent reason, and Huttuh yanked every rug, pot, and chair out of his way. "It's just stress," I excused my beast with an awkward giggle. "He'll like it here."

"He will?" Mara blurted.

"Well, he may poo in your shoes to show his manliness, but I'm sure you'll be great friends."

"Right," Mara said kind of drily, scratching her eyebrow like she'd already got a headache. "Just to make it all clear. You're giving me your cat. Just like that?"

"Yes." I nod. "So you won't be alone. And we'll have a reason to come and visit you."

"You don't need a *reason* to visit me." Mara chuckled as she walked to the kitchen, stepping over Tofu, which started his mortal battle with a carpet. "But thanks… I guess," she said, glancing his way.

"Can we have lemonade now?" Shrimp spread his arms. "I didn't get dragged all the way here to chat about cats. We need to discuss where to find enough yellow and blue fabric before the great fathers' arrival."

Final

MARA

Again, why did having a cat seem like a good idea? I can't remember now. I'm in my armchair near the fireplace, trying to focus on Mayan gods' feasts, NOT on Tofu scampering about the house with my mop clasped in his teeth and Huttuh closing all the doors on him. He hauls it into the kitchen, and there comes a crazy clatter of pots and plates. Then something slams down from the top shelf and, finally, silence reigns. I smile with relief and turn the page. A moment of peace…

A nasty screech causes me to flinch, and I peek behind the armchair. A cookie box with a long, fluffy tail slides across the floor, bumping into the table legs. The cookies and candies from that box lie scattered all over the floor.

"Seriously?" I slam the book shut and stagger to my feet to clean up the mess. Again.

I wonder if Huttuh will ever accept a new tenant. After Tofu broke her flowerpot, she went hysterical and hunted him through an endless labyrinth of rooms created on the run. She nearly turned into a nuthouse until she began to find it rather fun. Then new games popped up every day. One of them was to make boxes of all kinds. Tofu adores fitting his chubby self into small spaces. Huttuh challenged him with smaller and smaller ones until one day, she gave him a jar as big as a matchbox, and he thrust his paw into it, triumphantly.

Tofu's hilarious, as long as he's fighting his fights somewhere else.

The only not-funny thing about him is that, unlike Aidan, he doesn't use a lavatory. So, every time he needs one, I let him out into the woods, and every time, I sort of hope he won't find his way back. I've already practised the oops-I'm-so-sorry face I'd give Neshka while delivering the sad news, along with comforting phrases about how free and happy he must be now in the woods, following his "call of the wild." But then comes angry scratching at my door, and he meows to *let him bloody in this instant*. I let him bloody in, and he climbs on top of me, no matter what I may be doing, purring and demanding pats, and I forget why I ever really hated him.

Anyway, I've sort of gone off the topic. I sweep my candies back into the box and give Tofu a tinned-sardine so he'll be quiet at least while chewing. There is still time before we catch Friday's train, but I've already spotted three figures through the window carrying a huge Ukrainian flag. Nesha has sewed it from all the available blue and yellow fabric we found in the market. It looks like a knight's pike, two times longer than Shrimp himself, balancing on his narrow (even for a human) shoulder.

"Hey, knock-knock, open up!" Carmina calls for me, leaning her face toward the window, but I give her a password-first look.

She gives me back a you're-just-like-my-mom one and drones, "Huttuh Bohattah, for all good... stand with your face to my face and your *butt* to the wood."

I roll my eyes but still let Huttuh open the door. We take just-made wicker chairs onto the just-made porch, ready to refresh ourselves with lemonade (and the "super healthy" bread drink—kvass—for me) under the delicate April sun.

"How is Tofu?" Agnieszka asks eagerly with a brush of her fingers through her hair.

"Fine…" I say, but she keeps looking at me, waiting. "He's sleeping. I hope."

Carmina clears her throat. "Nesha's dying to ask if he turned into a magic boy already."

"Yes. Well?" Agnieszka's eyes lighten up. "Is he as fat and unmannerly?"

"Well…" I search all the dusty corners of my brainpan for any way to say that's not how it works, but then Shrimp saves me.

"A fat and unmannerly cat is still better than a fat and unmannerly man. Are you sure you don't want him back?"

Agnieszka waves her hand, laughing. "No-o! He's Mara's problem now."

"Well, if that's so"—I put my empty glass down on the floor—"I also have a gift for you."

Agnieszka turns her deep-blue eyes at me, bemused.

"Witches never stay in debt to people," I explain. "If they take a gift, they return it, so… my hut and I decided to give you this."

I clap my hands. Nothing happens. I clap again, and everyone looks around, expecting a miracle, but Huttuh is probably too busy saving her pots from Tofu, cos nothing but sparrows' chirrups answer me. I have to kick back at the wall with my heel to get her attention. Huttuh jolts, and then something small and soft drops right onto Agnieszka's lap.

"Oh!" she cries, spilling a bit of lemonade. "My goodness! It's… a doll."

"*Motanka*," I correct her. Because it only looks like a dummy of a girl in a long, puffy dress with her shoulders wrapped in a patterned shawl. In fact, she's a scout from the outer world, wrapped in soft organic fabric, red threads and grains, with a big red cross embroidered

across her face. I briefly think about telling Agnieszka that, but she's so excited about having A DOLL, I just don't have the heart for it. So I say, "It's a special doll. A magic one. It's a *blessing*."

"She's so cute! But um… why is there a cross on her face?"

"To ward off all evil."

Then Carmina scratches her head and remembers something her granny told her about *motankas*. "It's an old Ukrainian tradition. Yeah, they hexed dolls like that for power and protection. And these dolls, they sort of… knew things."

"What things?" Agnieszka's smile widens.

"Things about life." Carmina shrugs. "Dunno really. You'd better ask Gran, but she did say they kinda served their *panis* as guides and guardian angels."

"What do you mean?"

"She means the doll can talk!" Shrimp cries, swinging around to face me and pointing at his nose. "And these people call *me* 'stupid goose.' They don't even know about *motankas*."

"Shut up. They do when they want to." I clasp my hands and press them against my belly. "You put her in your pocket, Nesh, carry her all about with you, feed her, talk to her, and listen carefully. If you get on, she'll give answers to all your questions and will protect you from all the bad things. Just like, you know… like your *vyshyvanka*."

"Oh… wow!" Agnieszka lifts her brows high and admires the *motanka* resting in her palms. "If she knows everything…" She stutters and fixes her gaze on the red cross on her face, then lifts her eyes to us. "Does she know if we'll win this war? If Ukraine will stand and keep its freedom?"

"Why don't you ask her?" Shrimp suggests.

Agnieszka puts the glass down, focuses on the *motanka* for a long three seconds of silence, then screams, leaping off her seat.

"What?" we all scream back.

She shakes her hands in the air like she burnt herself and cries, "She said something! She said! She…"

"What did she say?" Carmina picks up the *motanka* from the floor.

"Like…" Neshka grips at her hair and twists it anxiously. "*Yes? Like… Yes!*"

"Pfft! And that scared you?" Shrimp brushes invisible crumbs off his lab coat.

"Cool!" Carmina beams and looks at the doll. "And what about me? Is there a gift for me?"

I frown in surprise. "Why would you want one? You have all you need."

"I do?" Carmina frowns back at me.

"Goodness, Carma, you jumped into the abyss and propelled yourself through hell for a soul you don't even know that much.

What else do you need to prove that you have…"

"A SUPERPOWER?" she exclaims, with her smile stretched from ear to ear like a crazy cartoon face. "I have a superpower, yeehaw!"

Well, I have different words for it—courage, power will, stamina, Cossack's drive, stuff like that—but what does it matter when Carma bounces to her feet and goes whooping and chanting SUPER-POWER, SUPERPOWER, SUPERPOWER, and the others join her, doing funny rag-doll moves? Even Huttuh bobs on her chicken legs and makes us all dance about the porch like drunkards. My friends are mad, blimey. But in a nice way.

That's what I tell Arman when he video-calls us to ask about Agnieszka's dad and Cap Saint being back and stuff but mostly yelling about why the hell I didn't tell him about Aidan (which I kinda did; he didn't listen). "I nearly kicked the bucket when I found that out."

"Nah. He's fine." Aidan shoves his smiling face into the camera, hanging over Arman's shoulders like… a cat. "Just being a little dragon queen."

"I'm not a…" Arman protests but stops with a sigh and runs a hand through his golden hair. "Do you realize that my life is never gonna be the same now?" He snaps his face up to the camera.

"Never boring, you mean?" I ask, and Aidan giggles.

"Send us pics, will ya?" He turns towards the camera. "And say hello to Shrimp. I miss that son of a goose."

I take, like, a hundred pics of my friends like a total Instagram addict. Shrimp gives me a passport pose, Carma pulls a clown face, and Neshka keeps her half smile frozen into a mask of a doll. The moment I lower my phone, she grins tenfold more charmingly and asks me if I miss my cat.

"Not as much as I am angry with myself."

"Why are you angry?" Carmina can't help butting in.

I shrug to relieve the tension, and my lips twist in a sad smile. "I kept him by myself against his will and then hated him for being a hopeless romantic. I couldn't see that I liked him for being him but wanted him to be someone else just to make him stay. It was stupid. But it doesn't matter now." I drape my arms around their shoulders and stroke their silky hair like cats' fur. "Y'know, ladies, you'd make fine kitties."

They laugh. Like I'm joking. *Am I?*

Finally, we reach the hill near the station, the best place to wave to the passing trains. We can't stop talking and giggling about silly things. Agnieszka is so nervous that she trips on every pebble on the road and says she's drunk from too much spring in the air. And Carmina says she'd better not bite the dust just now cos she's not going back to hell for someone who died from breathing spring.

When we reach the top and a breathtaking panorama of the valleys slowly dressing in blossoms opens, we freeze in awe. It looks so beautiful, it hurts to take our eyes off it. Then Shrimp points in the distance and cries, "I see it coming! Over there!"

A long iron snake, painted in national colours, meanders through the hills and greenish patches of fields, like a toy from this far. The girls catch sight of it and start to scream and jump.

Carmina hands the flag over to me. "You do it."

"No, it's not my dad there," I protest.

"Doesn't matter. We want *you* to do it." Agnieszka squeezes my shoulder, then clasps her burning face in her hands and bounces on her feet. "Aww, is it really happening? I feel like I'm going to explode."

"It's just another evacuation train, jeez," Carmina tuts.

But when it sweeps closer, and the hum gets deafening, she goes just as freaked out and bellows, "*SLAVA UKRAINI!*" punching the air with her fists. Her favourite saying. I bet if I wake her up in the middle of the night, she'll yelp "Slava Ukraini!" instead of "What do you want?" On the other hand, what else is there to say?

We join her, waving our hands and bobbing up and down on our rubber legs. I lift the flag and swish it high above our heads, feeling like my lungs are torn apart from joy. The wind catches its dance in the air like a giant, happy butterfly.

Then—oh, get this!—the train drops speed to almost a crawl and hoots crazily. One by one, windows slide open, and we see dozens and dozens of arms poking out to wave at us. They all yell something

insane at us, and we go wild screaming back. It is a total mess of sounds. Can't say if any of us give a damn what exactly to shout, as long as that flag flutters behind our backs like a beacon on the stormy seas.

But what I really want to say to all the living, is this: before death taps you on the shoulder, fight! *Against all odds, fight, and remember what you are fighting for.*

Acknowledgements

This story is alive and kicking thanks to so many people (and circumstances) that if I put them all in one place, I'll need a separate continent to keep everyone comfortable.

But first and foremost, I would like to thank the story itself for saving my sanity. The idea of *Until Death Taps You on the Shoulder* came to me shortly after the breakout of the full-scale Russian invasion as haphazard diary entries, flash fiction, and letters to my recently deceased father. In the shelters, bathrooms, and cold corridors, I hid from the missiles flying past my house. In the dark, in fear and despondency because of the absent electricity, water, and any connection but one radio wave, I listened to the wailing of the air sirens and splitting blasts, ringing my windows, shaking my insides, and pondered about death.

There was nowhere to run, nowhere to hide from this daily nightmare and desperation. I scrolled through the never-ending wall of heart-stopping news, stamped with blood, screams, and agony of my people, and thought about the ways, any ways, I could go to keep calm and help us win. Writing and drawing were all I knew, so I wrote and drew whenever I got the chance. The story you're holding in your hands is my battle cry for life and freedom.

I had to let it flow through me and onto the page, or else it would simply crush me. So it's partly autobiographical. Almost all the events you've come across here (or you will when you read it, if you're just like me and start reading books from the back) happened to me and people I know or know about. I collected these horrors as proof of the Russians' crimes against humanity. This stone was too hard to carry on my shoulders, so, naturally, when it grew too big and heavy, I gave my voice to my characters. And the novel was born.

Gladly, I wasn't alone in this abyss. I cannot express enough gratitude to my brave and lavishly talented brister, Wistful Castle, my one-and-forever life companion and the co-creator of the world of Etgoma. There may be just one name on the cover, but know that behind every word, there stand two crazy a-gender asexuals. From the sunny summers of our childhood games, through confusing adolescence and disappointments of adulthood, we followed our Dream together. And this is how it comes to life. You once told me that nobody would want a book by some unknown Ukrainian, writing in their second language about some unknown Ukrainians. Well, look at us now. We did it, bri!

I must also express my deepest appreciation to my mother, whose powerful survival instinct shaped my life, and my elder brother, whose devotion and care kept us all afloat. Vitia, thank you for all the parcels with supplies you sent us. They made this war a little less formidable.

Until Death Taps You on the Shoulder would have forever collected virtual dust in my laptop storage if not for my good friends from Scotland, Gordon and Katherine Lawrie, whose support and guidance inspired me to grow despite everything against me. Gordon, my first English-speaking reader and editor, thank you for your unbending belief in my humble talent, for the safety of *Friday Flash Fiction,* where you published my first awkward attempts to write. I may have never been your student, but you and Katherine are the best teachers I've ever had.

I would also like to extend my sincere thanks to all the writers and readers of *Friday Flash Fiction* and the Scottish PEN who always found kind words of encouragement and appreciation. Friends, I will never find enough words to say how much your compassion means to me. Thank you for standing with Ukraine and taking the time to read my war sketches. Thanks to people like you, we keep fighting with a tad brighter sparkle in our eyes. You are awesome!

Of course, any story is just a raw text first. It will only become a book when it goes through hell and high water of polishing. It takes time, hard work, and a pinch of magic to turn the text I wrote into a book you read, and I'm extremely lucky to board this fantastic ship, Riverfolk, with a wonderful crew who spared no effort to let this story speak to all willing to listen.

Guys, your very first letter toppled my world upside down, because I suddenly saw people behind the words, and Riverfolk felt immediately like home. Thank you, Weaver and Zaq, for your trust in me and helpful advice whenever I need it. Thank you, Freya and Alexa, my guardian angels, for your kindness, expertise, and your shiny personalities. You cast light on everything we discuss, taking my fears away with just one cute emoji. Thank you, Tamsin and Maxine, my magic fairies, for your ability to see through the walls of text and make it flow like music. You lifted my novel to a higher level, and I will always remember it.

And thank you, gifted Sad Knight, for the terrific book cover. You captured the precise mood of my story and made me see my girls from a different perspective, like in the display window of a bookshop I always stopped by to gape at.

Also, my amazing pen pals, my friends from across the globe, Paz, Amy, Justin, and Claudio, thank you for your profound, funny, thoughtful letters. Like magic flying carpets, they have the power to take my mind off the ugly trivia of reality and remind me every time that there is still fun and beauty outside the war.

My people, my brave and strong Ukrainians, my president, the warriors, the volunteers, patriots, everyone fighting this battle, I'm deeply indebted to you all. Dead and alive, you keep inspiring me, shaking me out of a strange coma of cosmic chagrin and lack of purpose. You brought back my will to fight, to love what I am and what I do, and keep going, until it's too late, until death taps me on the shoulder and asks if that was all I was living for. *This book is about you.*

But no less than that, I thank Putin and all Russian invaders who, without knowing it, shook us off the social paralysis, dispelled their vicious mirages, and tempered our spirit. You came here to kill, torture, rape, loot, and defile everything you touch. You thought our souls were free to take, you thought you had the right to dehumanise people just because you lost your own face a long time ago. You covered our sun with black clouds of explosions and dust from our wretched homes. But we are Cossacks, we can fight in the dark with our bare hands if needed. And when the sun rises again, like it always does, demons will go back to their pit.

The war is still going, in fact, escalating, but I have faith in our victory. I have faith in our future. Everyone who comes to bury us deep underground as a nation doesn't see that we are not the victims. *We are seeds.* Слава Україні!

Finally, I thank my dear Aishy, who taught me patience, discipline, and humanity better than all Ukrainians and Russians together, even though she's a cat who hates cuddling and leaves bloody bite marks on my arms and legs for trying. (Aishy, ヽ(*°▽°ƒ*)ﾉ I forgive you.)

But above all, I am immeasurably, irrevocably grateful to *you*, my reader, whoever you are, whenever you are, I thank you for being with me and my girls. I've written this story for you, not to scare you, not to shock you, not to trigger your sense of justice or pity, but to share my little sparkle on the world we all live in. No matter what, let's turn our faces to the light and let the shadows fall behind us. May your skies forever stay peaceful.

Sincerely, Etgoma.

June 2025

Follow us:

riverfolkbooks.com

Facebook /riverfolkp

Bluesky /riverfolkbooks.bsky.social

Instagram /riverfolkp

If you want to discuss our books with other readers and maybe even the author, join our discord server using the link on our website.